The Heart of Stone Adventures

Fool's Proof

Power's Play

Enjoy

Praise for **Fool's Proof**

The inevitable comparisons to Terry Pratchett are accurate.
—Andrew Shanahan, author of Before And After

*A wonderful read for fans of the fantasy-comedy genre
in the spirit of Monty Python.*
—Sydney Rappis, Reedsy Discovery

A cleverly plotted, twisty novel with a gratifying conclusion.
—The BookLife Prize

*Replete with satisfyingly unpredictable twists and turns....
those who appreciate humor and satirical inspection
are in for a treat!*
—Diane Donovan, Midwest Book Review

A book and a writer to look out for.
— Jim Webster, author of the Tallis Steelyard series

*I absolutely loved it. If this is Eva Sandor's first venture
into this genre, then I personally can't wait for the next one.*
–John Derek, Netgalley

POWER'S PLAY

Eva Sandor

 HUSZAR BOOKS

ISBN 978-1-7350679-3-3 (Paperback)
978-1-7350679-4-0 (eBook)
Library of Congress Control Number: 2021907348

Cover illustration and book design by Eva Sandor
Linen texture courtesy of kuesı - www.freepik.com

Printed in the United States of America
First printing 2021

Published by Huszar Books
Visit us at www.huszarbooks.com

to my husband.

...

that is all.

AS THEY ARE GENERALLY *the larger, stronger and more quarrelsome sex, one is not surprised to find the ranks of miscreants populated more with wenches than with wights.*

However, another reason for the discrepancy may be that, despite the low station of a habitual miscreant's son, he has an option denied to miscreants' daughters: society still recognizes his prerogative to acquire learning, just as though he were a gentleman. Thus he may improve his lot. Studies show that for each 100 words such an individual learns to read, his chance of being detained by a peacekeeping officer in any given year is reduced by a half per cent [see appendix L].

This author himself must admit to exactly such origins. The written word (and to a lesser extent, the use of the abacus) were keys that allowed the rowdy brat of a common cut-bundle moll to unlock the grim jail of his boyhood.

—The Foundations of Metropolitan Peacekeeping.
Edited by Gino V. Doak, Grand Constable
of Law and Order in the City of Coastwall.

AIM HIGHER *than money, further than glory, well past the face in the mirror.*

—Theophyllis de Heihome [known as Parafu],
Exhortations.

CHAPTER 1

I T WAS THE MONTH OF THE Peaches, and the end of a long, hot day.

Corvinalias Elsternom e Rokonoma the Fourth, Count of Upper Cloudyblue, wished he could cover his ears, for after a week of travel he was thoroughly tired of listening to his Great-Uncle Jey. But the old Duke would not be silenced; Corvinalias could only sag against the gunwale of the rowing barge as it carved its way up the grayish-green, bluish-brown River Whellen and hear Uncle Jey repeat his story about a long-ago trip to blah blah blah. The young Count huffed out a sigh, smoothed the edges of his neat black cape and yawned. He scratched his beak with the edge of his wing.

Uncle Jey was clearly under the impression that no one else in the world had ever had adventures. Or at least any worth talking about. Sure, his tales about being one of the first people to ride a Uman ship across the Midland Sea had been fascinating— when Corvinalias first heard them as a hatchling. But since then he'd had adventures of his own, ones he was fairly certain would hush Uncle Jey's mouth, if only it could take a break and give his ears a turn.

First of all, Corvinalias had chosen a Uman pet (that part was no adventure; Umans were very popular pets) and followed it from the Isle of Gold to the mainland, sticking with it through a series of mishaps which would have made a fine tale all by themselves. But it was after he shed the pet that the real adventures began: Corvinalias had befriended a pair of wild Umans, male and female, and had journeyed with them out of the Midland Sea altogether. He'd spent months with them on a strange and beautiful boat, seeing things that no civilized being had ever yet seen. Although the stupid albatross hired to bring back the notes he'd scratched lost them all, Corvinalias had been confident that upon his return to the royal Isle, he could refine his memoirs in the telling.

It had begun well: his Elsternom relatives had thrown him a round of soirées and the Rokonomas had made him a member of the Scientific Institute. But somehow no one seemed all that interested in the wonders of Cloud Whales, or the destructive majesty of rotatory cyclones, or the shortsighted economic models that plagued Umans in the Herb Islands. Instead they continued to cling to old bores like Uncle Jey or Cousin Chack, pretending to be fascinated, because powerful old relatives— however tiresome— doled out desirable favors.

Corvinalias wanted no favors. He only wanted what was coming to him: branches E23 and NE1, Whorl Nine, of Lower Cloudyblue. By popular custom those were part of his county; surely Uncle Jey would re-scratch his will to make it official.

The old Duke was in the middle of a sentence when Corvinalias nudged him. "Hoy," he said. "Sorry to interrupt, but do you see *that*? Up the river, there?"

Uncle Jey blinked dismissively at a minute speck on the horizon, washed ruddy by the sunset. Old he might be, but he was a magpie, and magpies could see all kinds of things other people couldn't. "What, Vinny? A clump of Uman-beings. A town. What about it?"

"This one's special. Try and guess why."

Uncle Jey couldn't resist a challenge. He puffed out his white vest and fluttered from the barge's gunwale to the roof of its cabin, catching one fingernail in some decorative trim and nearly falling to the deck, down where pair after pair of Uman oarmaids swayed. He scrambled back up, strode to the inlay of a nautilus in the center of the roof, and squinted at the town.

Corvinalias joined him. He could hear the Uman family bustling about inside the cabin: their servants preparing the evening meal, their baby crowing about something. It hadn't been easy, staying out of reach of that baby. True, he could have chosen to ride in the other barge, the one

"Why, of course I see it *now*, Vinny. So this was your pet? The one you used to show off to us? But he had a hat then. A hat with..." and here Uncle Jey shivered in delight. "...thirteen jingly silver shinies."

"The hat's gone. Now he's got a badge. See it? Hanging from his neck on a chain?"

"Oh! It's so wonderfully shiny! Come, Vinnie. I wish to steal it."

Instinctively, without considering respect for age or title, Corvinalias snatched at Uncle Jey's wrist to prevent him from leaping out of the tree and down into the square. But his fingers closed on nothing; the old Duke had moved surprisingly fast and was falling toward the inn like a black-and-white leaf, wings flaring, ready to reach out and grab the badge of office that extolled Malfred Murd as His Honor, the Esquire of Good Market.

CHAPTER 2

FRED STOOD ON THE VERANDA BETWEEN its pots of red crushflowers, greeting passers-by from under a signboard which, instead of a picture of a strapping wench leaning against a wheel, now featured lettering: SEAT OF MALFRED MURD, ESQUIRE. He knew perfectly well that few of the gentlemen and none of the ladies in his town could read it, but the sign wasn't for them. It was for him, and he admired it passionately.

Strictly speaking, the Coachmaid's Rest was no longer an inn. True, it had a taproom from which it served refreshment to the public, but it did so at the pleasure of its master, holder of the smallest fief in the Whellen Country; technically the barmaid was not a hireling but did fealty to Fred, as did the two cooks, the three porters, the blacksmith, and the groom who tended the stable's single mule.

None of these women were in particular in awe of him. Their fealty consisted mostly in doing what they'd always done— keeping the furniture polished and the sideboard full and the mule clean and fit— and with the exception of their calling this new gentleman "Mesir" and "Your Honor" the place might just as well have still been a coach stop, run by one of the typically prosperous commoners under the rule of Dame Elsebet de Whellen. Those few citizens who bothered to think about their relationship to Malfred Murd had heard that Dame Elsebet appointed him their new Esquire as a mark of favor, but no one cared about the exact nature of this favor, because Dame Elsebet was beloved and could do as she pleased.

She'd ruled the Whellen Country for fifty-one years and in just two more days, the King would finally come and see its wonders.

Fred pushed his hands casually into the pockets tailored in the side seams of his shirt after the very newest fashion. He leaned back onto the heels of his soft, expensive new boots and forward onto the toes. With each motion, he savored the lovely weight of his chain of office, a ceremonious series of links wrought from marbled steel just like the steel of Dame Elsebet's crown. It glittered, it gleamed. Bestowing a smile upon passers-by, Fred withdrew one manicured hand from its pocket and buffed the chain with his sleeve.

Its foremost links were a pair of hooks holding the corners of a colorfully enameled, highly polished badge representing the Great Seal of the Municipality of Good Market and engraved with the enchanting words TO MALFRED - BY ORDER OF E. de W. - ETERNAL GRATITUDE.

Fred was looking right down at the badge when a big magpie with knobby, scaly-looking talons swooped down and snatched it.

"Hoy!"

The magpie paid him no mind at all, but only muttered something in the musty dialect no longer used on the Isle of Gold. Before Fred could bring out his other hand and grab the bird, it was gone— and so was the badge. The empty chain slithered off his neck and clattered to the boards of the veranda.

"Seeping crusty pus buckets!" roared Fred. "Get back here, you boilsore! Scab over it, give me my deep-damned badge!"

In the limestone square before the Coachmaid's Rest, a woman whirled to face him, covering her son's ears. She seemed ten feet tall. Fred raised a few shy fingers in greeting.

"I— ah— evening to you. Just a bit agitated, here…"

"My son is a good boy! He doesn't need to hear that kind of language! I should complain to the Esquire!"

Fred bowed, with what he thought was commendable humility. "I *am* your Esquire."

"Well then, you're an embarrassment," snapped the woman, using her big hands to redirect her son's gaping face. She bent down to the boy's ear. "Come along, Wilmot. I'll buy you an extra picturebox show if you forget about this."

"What's pus?" peeped the child.

Fred didn't see the mother turn back and give him a final glare: he was already on the move. The magpie had crossed the street and flown over a fence; Fred rushed after it and hurdled the boards. He saw the glint of his badge disappear over the copper gutter of a building; Fred threw a handspring on the approach before scaling the wall, just because there was room for it— no one can shed a lifetime of acrobatic training in only a year. From one rooftop to the next he leaped, gaining on the bird, now almost certain that this had something to do with the magpie Corvinalias, who'd followed him to this very country when all the... the events had happened.

The bird ahead of him looked like an older, fatter, slower Corvinalias. Dropping down from the rooftops onto a pallet of empty flour sacks with a graceful flip that he wished someone could have seen, Fred gave a final sprint and vaulted over a hedge with one arm raised high. His fingertips just brushed the shiny badge— the magpie gave a grunt of alarm— but on the other side of the hedge Fred's momentum was abruptly arrested. He landed in a pile of gravel, knocking away the canvas with which three workmaids were trying to cover it for the evening. Chips of stone showered down the tops of his boots and covered the seat of his breeches with dust.

"Aw blisters," one of the workers groaned.

The second one stabbed her shovel into the pile, far too close to Fred's breeches, and said over her shoulder to the third: "Lookit. Them gods brung ya someone after all. Some beefy clod fopped up in fancy duds, whataya think?"

The third one considered him as she stowed her sledgehammer in a cart. "All right, but I'm not spittin out my chaw for him. Any brat *I* sprout hasta be on account of a learned gentleman." Then all of them laughed and laughed, though Fred salved his ego by noticing that the third one actually did spit away her quid of maidenroot.

With a last despairing glance at the sky overhead, he bid his badge goodbye. He stood up and winced at the gravel in his boots. The side of the pile collapsed and took him with it for a few inches; he stepped painfully away and dusted his behind, putting as much decisiveness into these actions as he could. The cardinal rule of improvisational theater is: whatever happens, go with it.

"I see you've been working hard, goodwives. Only a few more hours and you can enjoy the Copperday-night entertainments."

Their blank looks— and the Trade Road Company emblem embroidered on their tunics— told him they were unaware of the Whellen Country's twice-weekly holidays. With exaggerated suavity Fred pulled off one boot, shook it out, replaced it and repeated with the other; his training as an entertainer finally began to pay off as the wenches, despite themselves, tuned into his motions.

"No idea what I mean? What if I told you that in Good Market, by order of His Honor Malfred Murd and that of his liege Dame Elsebet de Whellen, every citizen and imported laborer— imported, that's you, goodwives— is entitled to two full days of restful entertainment, each and every week? That's right, come along and follow me. Your gravel and rails will be fine just where they are. No thieves here—" Fred bit his tongue, thinking of what he'd say to that magpie when he caught it— "no indeed, no crime or uncouth activity of any kind here in my town. Yes, goodwives, I do say *my* town because you're in the presence of none other than the Esquire himself. I am in fact he. And now we've reached my town's main square, where I'd like to show you around the coinpuppets and the pictureboxes and the music barrels and the—"

Fred froze. If he had been a hound or a highcat, a strip of fur along his back would have stood on end.

There, just across the square, prancing back and forth in front of a showman's booth, he spied the ugly mug and heard the braying voice of someone he knew and loathed.

"Hoy, hoy, goodwives an' fellows! Get 'em here, get 'em now! First time in Good Market— Magic poems, that's right, I said magic poems an' they're fresh right off my pen for just a cheap little, thin little, lone little brass penny! *Can*-tripps, goodwives and fellows, is what these are— powerful, magical poetry spells called *can*-tripps what each could make a dream come true. One benny penny, to buy one tonight! Listen while I tell ya what they do!"

The second wench, the gravel-shoveler, turned to the others. "Wouldja lookit that? Ever seen anyone move so fast? I think the ess-squire's about to drill a fresh hole in that bumpy-faced wight selling the poems. This oughta be good. It's always a laugh watching men try ta fight."

CHAPTER 3

F RED'S LOATHING FOR THE BUMPY FELLOW was a long time in the making. Before he became an Esquire, Fred had been a forgotten brat, a novice monk, the royal Fool, and eventually a vagabond— stripped of his Guild license and his position at court, bundled into a boat and shunted off to the mainland. Months of misery had followed. He'd been run out of town after town by low-rent streetcorner Fools whose only claim to superiority lay in the papers pinned to their shoulders, until finally he'd found himself in the Whellen Country, and there he'd spent his very last penny on a drink: a specific kind, chosen as his final taste of the posh life he'd been banished from.

But Fred couldn't even enjoy that simple deep-damned wallow in misery, because the Bumpy Fellow had latched onto him.

On and on that greasy oik with the bumpy face, the rancid breath, the dirty wig and the highly inflated opinion of himself had pestered him, hounding Fred to buy him a drink, insisting that anyone who'd been in the employ of the King must be rich indeed. It was no good telling him otherwise, no good barking at him to be off, no good trying to walk away; what had followed was perhaps inevitable, but still Fred seethed with resentment toward the Bumpy Fellow and now, in the square of Good Market, he wanted nothing more from life than to step straight up to that greasy, bumpy, rancid, dirty, self-inflated raw boil of a wight peddling his lousy poems from a ramshackle booth— and Fred had no doubt whatever that the poems were bad, quite apart from not magic— step straight up to him and, brandishing his badge of office, bid the crowd to keep their money and instead watch a terrific, completely free show entitled "His Honor Malfred Murd, Annoyed, Boots This Blister Out of Town". But without his badge... it pained Fred to admit this to himself, but without it, people might not know who he was.

It also pained him to admit that, while The Bumpy Fellow was no Fools' Guild-level entertainer, he did have a certain vulgar flair. The crowd, probably bored with the high-quality entertainments of the Whellen Country, was captivated by this interloper brandishing a comically oversized quill pen and inkhorn.

"Watch me, wights an' w— good citizens! Watch as I int-scribe a *can*-tripp right spang here on crisp linen paper, in good black, dark black, per-ma-nit ink! There it is! And now I fold it magical like— I bind the spell right in, good citizens! Lookit that fold, it's a mag-pie bird, a lucky mag-pie that swald that poem right into its wil tum-tum!"

The crowd cooed as if the fingerprint-smeared paper bird were the cutest thing they'd ever seen. The whole town was fascinated: cable car operators slowed down to stare. Proprietors of music barrels stopped cranking. Even brats who had been pressing their eyes to the peekholes of a picturebox show left it and ran to watch the Bumpy Fellow, who waved the magic poem over his head, exhorting the crowd to line up and buy, because these lil be-yoo-tees is guaranteed to make at least one of your dreams come true.

"What if it's a bad dream?" piped some wag. Everyone laughed, and the Bumpy Fellow laughed along too because of course that was a joke. But when the woman who'd covered her son's ears against Fred's cursing boomed "I only purchase reputable goods! How can I be sure this poem is working?" the fellow turned to answer her so fast his wig nearly fell off.

"An exident question, ma-dammie, a fine one indeed. The prog-er-ess of your dream is visible in the can-tripp, good citizens, which word by magical word gets underlined, and outerlined, and ee-loominated, and ee-laberated, as your dream makes headway. But no peeking! No unfolding, good citizens! Or else the can-tripp just ups and disappears." The Bumpy Fellow suddenly looked so sad he might die. "In fact, I am willing to give up a dream of mine just to prove it." And with a great show of sorrowful duty, he took the clean, angular pale cream magpie he'd been showing off and opened it up. No poem. The people around him moaned in consternation, others began babbling to one another about how cheap a penny really was for the hope of a dream, and in a moment they were lined up and the Bumpy Fellow plying his pen.

Watching this, Fred had one of his feelings. The ones where something was fake and he just... *knew*.

The ink. It was disappearing ink.

How did he know? Well, obviously because magic— conjurers' magic— was fake; Fred had put on a few shows himself. Real magic— the seemingly unexplainable working of spellbound things such as firewyrm spit— was being studied by Prophessors to learn what made it go, and if this wight had ever so much as sniffed the air of a University, Fred would eat his tailored silk shirt. No, something had tipped him off. In a moment he realized it was the bird itself.

The Bumpy Fellow had definitely blotted inky fingerprints all over it, but by the time he unfolded it they had faded clean away— just like the poem inside, which Fred's feeling told him was also fake; there was no way this dolt could have learned how to write in a year. Suddenly Fred recalled him bragging about his friendship with a crooked scribe. Aha, so the fellow's license was fake, too! That was serious; as a vagabond Fred had taken his chances busking with no papers at all, rather than risk angering his Guild with something so dire. Oh, if only an inspector from the Poets were here...

One could be. Fakes a problem? Fake a solution.

Fred jogged across the square and forced himself to the front of the line.

"Hoy. Let me in, could you? I'm in a rush. Oh? Well, same to you." Then, to the Bumpy Fellow: "Can you customize the poem?"

"Aye, good citiz— what are you looking at?"

"Nothing." Fred made it just obvious enough that he was trying to read the Bumpy Fellow's license.

It worked. The fellow was visibly unsettled: an ugly sight, as it made him bare his teeth in an ingratiating simper. "And what would Mesir like added to his poem?"

"Well, it's for my brother. Who's a Poets' Guild inspector." That jab connected, so Fred went harder. "A Level One inspector, not a Level Two like me. Can you make it out to him? His name is Xaviez Quatsfedignel Jort. That's spelled—"

"Sorry, Mesir. Can't add names."

"Huh. Then maybe you could just throw together a few lines off the cuff. You know, 'roses are pink, lilies are white' kind of thing?" Fred pressed two fingers against his pulse. "It'll only take you exactly a minute. You can start... now."

The Bumpy Fellow broke into a sweat, which was most unpleasant to smell, and pushed Fred to one side, loudly proclaiming: "Line for custom orders— that's a different line, all right?— forms *here*. I'll get to you after the standard ones."

Almost every customer stepped over into the new line. Now the Bumpy Fellow was frantic. When Fred reached into the booth, took a sheet of paper and examined it, murmuring "Is this PG-101 compliant?" the wight lost his composure altogether.

"Know what? Show's over!"

He slammed the awning of the booth shut, scattering quills in every direction. His outsized horn of ink spilled onto the paving stones and he trod in it. In moments he was gone, leaving only some poetical detritus and a line of inky footprints running in great strides toward the automated ferry that ran across the river and out of the Whellen Country.

The customers were unhappy to have lost him. They turned their rage upon Fred, thoroughly unaware that he was of the nobility, one of their betters. He was down on the limestone square, about to get acquainted with the new fashion in boots, when one of the brats in the crowd squealed with amazement. The puddle of ink, and the footprints, were disappearing!

In a moment the tenor of the crowd changed dramatically. Baying like hounds— because suddenly a penny was damned good money to be cheated out of— they took off chasing their new quarry. Soon the square was quite peaceful indeed; even the three imported workmaids had gone.

Fred let his head out from under his arms. He untucked his knees from against his chest. He sat up, watched the inkblots fade from his clothes, and considered the state of his fiefdom.

True, there had been a bit of unseemliness. Yes, he would need to ask Dame Elsebet for a new badge.

But he'd triumphed. He'd enforced the law, ridding Good Market of a noisome criminal— and none too soon. Enrick, Margadet and baby Nedward would be here the day after tomorrow.

For a moment the square was full of deep, purple summer twilight. Then with a barely audible hiss, the wyrmlight lamps up on their posts flared to life and bathed everything in a buttery glow.

After that bravura performance, thought Fred, I deserve a drink. No, not just a drink. I deserve a public celebration.

CHAPTER 4

THE ISLANDS OF THE PEACEFUL OCEAN, where Corvinalias had journeyed with a woman named Ata Maroo, numbered in the many thousands— some as large as kingdoms and some small as dust, just like the major stars and the minor ones in the Sky River. The comparison was apt, for the people of the Ocean Empire said the world and the sky were reflections of one another: every island had a corresponding star, every wave a cloud. Or at least, some of the people said that, for the Ocean Empire was a vast place and nobody there ever really agreed on anything.

First of all was this name, "The Ocean Empire". No Empress, or Emperor for that matter, had ruled for ten thousand years; some said there never had been one at all. But it sounded grand, so people said it— except for the ones who didn't.

Next was navigation. There were those who asserted that charts were a necessity, while others called them a crutch; some navigated by stars and others by swells; some felt that the best way to reach a place was to thread safely from island to island, while others called such routes "ant crawls" and instead struck boldly out for the wide, bright, glittering horizon.

Ata Maroo had been a bold one, but without really meaning to be. Twenty-one years previously, she had struck out for the horizon only because she was fleeing from her husband. She'd left the Ocean Empire in the dead of night, with just two Cloud Whales in harness; one had pulled while the other rested, and to speed their progress Ata Maroo had thrown her dowry treasures over the side of her boat one by one until at last she had nothing to call her own but a spyglass, her sarong and the ivory ring she'd once slipped over her mate's brutish finger. Ata Maroo had torn that ring from the hand he struck her with, the last time she ever saw him. She would be damned if he kept it— her grandmother had carved it from the tusk of a great gray seal.

Her flight had taken her through the devilish maze of the Herb Islands, around the hidden shoals and frightening deep basins in the Warm Straits, across the brandy-black Midland Sea and all the way to the great estuary of the Denna— Old Mama River, Carrier of the World. There Ata Maroo had bid the whale team goodbye and, stepping upon the land of a country so foreign to her it may as well have been the moon, spent the next twenty years changing herself from a poor runaway stranger into the owner of the world's largest overland shipping business.

Many a story would have ended there, with Ata Maroo as the renowned Ox-Train Queen. But this was no bedtime tale. Reality had caught up with her in the form of a steady stream of letters, sent at great expense by her sorrowing relatives, year after year until at last shame and fear had given way to duty. Abruptly the Ox-Train Queen sold all of her holdings and turned back home.

Now she had her whales again, along with their four fine calves. She had a magnificent catamaran with a skillful crew. At the best bank in the Kingdom, she had a private vault whose door scarcely could shut for all the money notes within. And oh: her husband had mysteriously died. She had a new one.

Ata Maroo stood on the deck of the catamaran, swaying with it as it rode easily over the blue quilt of the Peaceful Ocean. Ahead of the vessel, her team puffed their breath and clicked their spiral tusks and traded the harnesses off with one another. From behind her, the sunset blazed full upon a big conical island that had just broken the horizon, an island with a puff streaming from its snowy top like the breath of the whales: this was where Ata Maroo's parents lived.

"Alvie, *ipo*, come look this view," she sang out in the language of the Westlanders. *Ipo* was not a Westlander word. It was a Peaceful Ocean word.

The Peaceful Ocean had many languages, almost as many as it had islands, but they really were all just different pronunciations. Over ten thousand years the language had become very detailed in some places but strangely worn in others, and sometimes Ata Maroo frowned at the idea that there should be at least a dozen different words for relatives on the mother's side but only this one, *ipo*, to use for a cute baby seal or a good friend or a tall shy lovable man who gave you heart flutters and incidentally looked just like God.

Alvert stepped out of the cabin, rubbing the back of his head. His hair had grown back, for he was no longer a servant, and the pale strip of skin across the back of his neck had grown tan, for the strap of a foot messenger's bag no longer covered it. "A volcano?" he asked, striding up to wrap his long wiry arms around Ata Maroo.

"Alvie, *ipo*. You surprise me! How you so quick to know what Mount Grumble is? Maybe you teach *me* something, ah." She turned back and embraced him, pressing her lips against his face wherever they might fall.

This face of his was a marvel. On at least half the islands of the Ocean Empire stood gigantic sculptures that looked exactly like Alvert's long, sad, big-nosed face. In people's homes, there was usually a small one beside the fireplace. Some very pious people even carried tiny ones in their purses, so as always to be in the presence of The God Who Listens, should they need to tell Him something.

"Ow," whispered Alvert. Four of Ata Maroo's teeth had been filed to sharp points, like the fangs of a beautiful black-and-gold cat. He loved that about her and had no wish to complain— he were the right luckiest wight on all the Earth and as far as he were concerned his wife could chip his whole face right off, bite by tiny bite— "ow" had just slipped out, like. To cover his faux pas he squeezed her tighter and she squeezed him back and a moment later they were inside the cabin again and the crew made themselves very, very loud and busy.

The crew were Westlander mariners, but Ata Maroo had taught them everything they needed to know; they were as pleased with this strange huge double-hulled ship as they had been with their own barky. They straightened their sarongs and knotted up their pigtails. They deployed some particularly handsome sails. They blew a horn that made sounds cloud whales could understand, directing the team to line up neatly and display their black-and-white faces as they approached the volcanic island's jurisdiction. After this year-long journey, with its many unavoidable digressions and long, frequent, frustrating delays, they were more than eager to glide into port in proper fashion—everything correctly trimmed and neatly stowed and highly polished. A comfortable new life in the islands awaited them.

Soon they were in the thick of traffic. Fishers and harpoon hunters and traders of goods crowded the sea lanes, driving whales or under sail or paddling long canoes. The puff of cloud over the tip of the volcano dispersed and re-formed, drifting gently away to leeward as if the towering cone were blowing a string of smoke rings. Larger and ever larger it loomed before the catamaran, its black stone sides blanketed pink and gold.

But where were the captain and her mate?

The crowd in the harbor began staring at the catamaran. Many of them appeared quite amazed. The crew smiled brightly and trimmed their sails with delicate pride. A great, open way lay parted before them.

The local people began to shout. They stood up in their boats. They did some animated, arm-waving dance.

Suddenly the two oldest Cloud Whales turned in their harnesses and, with a bedlam of howls and squeaks and crackles, rushed back toward the catamaran and pressed their foreheads against its outriggers. Lines tangled, lashings groaned, the masts lurched and toppled forward. The whales had remembered this place too late and Ata Maroo, the returning Headmother of the Hundred Clans, the most important diplomat in the Ocean Empire, hurried out of her cabin tying her sarong just in time for her ship to strike and ground itself full upon the hidden rocks named for her ancestors.

CHAPTER 5

ON COPPERDAY EVENING, DAME ELSEBET DE Whellen came inside from her last ride of the day and sat down on her wool-stuffed bed in a state of particularly satisfying exhaustion. She had been training her favorite freckled gray gelding in the ways of the hunt: how to follow a pack of hounds and highcats as they sniffed and stared and sought out one of the wild monsters of the Whellen Country.

It was true that there weren't as many of these as there once had been. As a little girl Dame Elsebet had spent many a happy hour astride her pony, charging into the woods after fennemums and bringing back delightful, sometimes surprisingly long, chains of their heads and claws; there had been firewyrms aplenty in those days, and ample reason to squirm into caves after them; further north the blueneedle trees had abounded in bat-serpents with their fascinating motion, and the teenaged Dame Elsebet had even gone all the way into the mountains of Yondstone with her Grandma Annelyn, there to spear a ramphaleon, and catch her one and only glimpse of a nullicorn.

Nowadays the hunt was a mere ritual. Most of the time there was no monster at all, only a false trail of norrange peels, but horses didn't need to know that. Horses needed to learn courage— like the courage of a mother, whose duty according to the old proverb was to stand fast and defend— and display intelligence, like that of a father, who the proverb said ought to reach out and discover. Dame Elsebet was seventy-one years old and had neither parent anymore; but she did have Whellengood Hall, and her wonderful country, and its dear, ingenious, deeply beloved people. There was no longer any danger of these being taken away; for that, she was grateful to Fred.

"Remind me to send a tailor to Good Market with a bolt of the diagonal stripe," she said to the maid who insisted on helping her remove her boots. "Malfred does so love to be well dressed."

The youngest of her maids came bouncing in with a jar of liniment crystals. "The diagonal stripe is so last week, Medame! There's a new pattern now— interlocking diamonds and magpies, in honor of the royal visit. Mesir Jo says it's the most complicated pattern he ever set up." When she uttered the engineer's name, the maid's face became dreamy. "Oh Medame don't you think Mesir Jo is *such* a smart gentleman? Don't you just love watching him think? And he wrote my name!" She stared at something scribbled on the back of her hand. "At least, he said this was my name. Oh, Medame, do you think it was a hint? Could this be the start of a wedding bracelet? Oh Jo Jo Jo Jo..." and she bounced out, before returning to say: "Oh yes. Your bath is ready."

Dame Elsebet was just sinking into the soapy clouds when...

"Medame."

It was not her youngest maid. It was her oldest one, the one who only ever brought serious news. Dame Elsebet stopped with her hairnet still in hand. Long coils of white hair drooped into the water. "Yes?"

"A royal herald has arrived. He is waiting in the grand salon. He asked for some sandwiches, some pastries, a glass of tea and a shot of sherry Lorosso."

Dame Elsebet was already reaching for a towel. "You brought them, of course." It wasn't a question.

"All except the sherry. For some reason there is none left in the cellar at all."

"Oh! How could I forget: I sent it to Good Market last week. Malfred likes it. Oh, dear! There's a bottle in my cabinet, there. Bring it immediately and I'll—"

"Oh, but surely, Medame, you're not going to see the gentleman with your hair all uncoiffed, your face unperfected, dressed in that..."

Dame Elsebet had already wriggled into the kind of waxed canvas overcloak that might be worn by a prosperous cattleman, which in fact it was— her brother had left it behind on his last visit to Whellengood. "I am, and hush! I will not keep the gentleman waiting for one second longer than need be, out of mere vanity. Bring me some pantaloons and some shoes, whichever are closest at hand." And somehow she managed to put these on even as she strode out the door of her suite, a door made of glass and steel.

Dame Elsebet hurried to the grand salon down corridors whose sheer translucent walls and ceilings soared high, full of deeply colored twilight. She passed pillars of polished metal alternating with pillars of honed limestone; room after room fitted with simple, generously scaled, comfortable furniture; doors thrown open onto dark, fragrant gardens, chandeliers hung thick with wyrmlight globes. Just as she reached the grand salon with its stately domes of bronze and cut glass, the globes flared to life with the sunset and the royal herald, waiting in solitary splendor, startled on his chaise and nearly dropped his plate of pastries.

The plump, pale-bearded gentleman's head rotated on the platter of his ruff collar and he looked straight through Dame Elsebet. She stepped forward, holding out her hands in greeting.

"I welcome you to these my lands. Come, enjoy, and take what you will."

These were ritual words to a superior, absolutely proper and polite, as taught to every noble lady by her mother before her. The proper answer, with its double handclasp, came:

"Many thanks to you, loyal vassal. I trust I find you well."

Something about the gentleman's tone didn't sound that thankful or trusting to Dame Elsebet, but she brushed it off as understandable; this entire business was irregular in the extreme. Her instinct, upon hearing that the Royal Family would pay a visit to her country, had been to organize the kind of splendid Triumphal Entry accorded to monarchs through the ages. But Malfred had warned her to do no such thing. *This* King, he'd taken great pains to inform her, was not like any of the others.

"He hates that stuff," Fred had insisted. "It spooks him. If you threw him a parade or blew a trumpet at him he'd probably lose his mind." And here Fred had winced, aware that using such an expression was a faux pas, given Dame Elsebet's history. Of course she forgave him, and the point was made: there would be no pomp, no pageantry whatsoever. The King and his family would arrive discreetly, in a comfortable rowing barge hired from The Nautilus, at the bell of nine on Goldenday morning.

"I'll get right to the point," rumbled the herald, brushing crumbs from his beard with both hands. "My name is Janush Baekenfahd, and— hoy, you strike me as familiar. Well, I'm pleasantly surprised at these pastries. Now if only there'd been— oh! I see you *do* have Lorosso after all. The bottle, please, while I tell you why I'm here. There! A perfect pour. Smells good— ahhh. I have come, Your High Honor, to inform you that the Royals are already in your country. The craft was swifter than expected, or the current wasn't so strong, or else that sail did the trick, because we're moored up just a few towns downstream. King Enrick, Queen Margadet, Prince Nedward and their retinue will now be arriving on Solderday." He set his sherry glass down on a side table next to its unused companion. "That's tomorrow," he added, sounding as if he really thought Dame Elsebet didn't know the days of the week. She forced a smile.

"I met you last year at my cousins' home, Mesir Bagafat. Oh dear, let me try again. Ba-ken-fodd. There. You'll be happy to hear that I'm perfectly prepared to receive their Majesties at any time, in exactly the warm and homelike style recommended by my vassal Mesir Murd."

At Fred's name, the arm with which Janush Baekenfahd leaned on the side table buckled and he did in fact fall off his chaise. Dame Elsebet pretended she hadn't noticed.

"Malfred Murd? He lives here now?"

"No, Mesir Baekenfahd. Mesir Murd dwells in his fief, the town of Good Market."

Now Baekenfahd was biting into another pastry; at the word "fief" he choked on it. Dame Elsebet prepared for the unpleasant necessity of squeezing him, but it passed.

"He does," —cough— "does he? Well, well. So Fred's gone and landed in clover. Well, they do say 'every Fool finds his motley's missing patch'. I'll send him a note." Baekenfahd stood up, dusted crumbs to the limestone floor and poured himself one last whet of sherry Lorosso before concluding his mission with "I will see myself out, Your High Honor. I believe it was this way."

And then, striding boldly down the brilliantly lit glass corridor, he walked into a glass wall and fell on his generous seat.

———

BUT SOLDERDAY CAME, AND THE bell rang nine, and no one arrived; Dame Elsebet stood at Whellengood's front gates, as tense and jumpy as a hound held back from a scent. So Their Majesties were late. It was their prerogative. But where was Malfred?

To her own surprise, Dame Elsebet found herself remembering parts of her earlier acquaintance with Fred in which he had been less than trustworthy. She was appalled at herself, but things once thought could not be unthought. She began to doubt his advice. She began to ransack her mind for some unique way she could welcome the Royals herself, Fred or no Fred. At last she hit upon it: the power carriage.

The latest iteration of the power carriage was a wondrous mechanism that would showcase the very best of the Whellen Country: its productivity, its ingenuity, its openness to new thinking. She would conclude by giving it to the King and Queen as a gift, to emphasize her fealty to the House of Castramars. Because that frightful misunderstanding about the war— that was settled now, wasn't it? The King wished the de Whellens to keep their title forevermore... didn't he?

Dame Elsebet, the two archers who followed her as guards, her chief knight Lady Verocita and her major-domo Nicolo climbed into the graceful, brass-fitted power carriage. An engineer released it from the capstan that wound it up; Dame Elsebet loosened the grip of her glove upon its handbrake; and off they flew down the crushed-limestone path toward the boat landing.

The morning was hot, but the breeze of the carriage's motion was exhilarating. It ran faster than a galloping horse, with no more than a gentle ticking over and above the crunch of its delicate painted wheels. It was an improvement over those models that required horses as supplementary power: this one would make it to the dock and back on a single charge of its clockwork heart. Although certainly she wouldn't drive it so very fast with the Royals. She planned to bring them back Whellengood Hall at a much more sedate pace, so as to enjoy the most delightful approach to its gleaming, reflective, crystalline modernity.

"Malfred said not to do this," shouted Dame Elsebet to Nicolo as they rolled over hills and through groves, "but I think he might have been pulling my leg! About the King, I mean!"

"Mesir Murd has a gift for deception, Medame," Nicolo shouted back, holding his geometrically perfect wig onto his head with one hand, and his spectacles on his short, sharp nose with the other. "Personally, I'm keeping an eye on him."

As the power carriage drew up to the dock, Dame Elsebet was horrified to see the grassy riverbank filled not with the milling bodies of newly arrived visitors, but with a set of pavilions. They'd clearly been there for hours. Her heart began to pound.

Oh, gods. Oh, Ye Gods in their brightest heavens. She'd snubbed the Royals on their first visit to the Whellen Country in three generations! They had encamped far away, shunning her! Suddenly the power carriage seemed like a frivolous toy. What, what, *what* could she give to them, to let them know how sorry she was? Think, think. And it had to be something she had on her person, at that very moment. She scrabbled inside her sleeves: nothing there but a bronze fan and a handkerchief. There was nothing else for it. She knew what she had to do.

With one of the deep, deep breaths she'd learned could quell even the most horrific emotions, Dame Elsebet climbed down out of the power carriage and approached the largest, handsomest pavilion.

"I beg leave to enter," she announced in a voice as steady and proper as she could make it. The red and yellow stripes of the pavilion, the white lozenge with the device of a magpie upon it, rippled slowly in the hot breeze. A drop of sweat trickled from her brow.

"Come in please come in," sounded a man's voice from within. Dame Elsebet lifted the edge of the curtain and slipped into the shadows.

CHAPTER 6

B Y THE TIME THE TOWN BELL at Good Market chimed— three sets of triplets, bright and delicate— the air was already oppressive and the cicadas in an uproar. The pots of red crushflowers that decorated the balcony of Fred's comfortable upstairs suite were releasing great clouds of their famous fragrance, for they'd been tipped over and stomped to shreds.

Fred's big, deep, wide feather bed was off its frame and jammed in his doorway for some reason, rolled up like a slice of flatbread around the third imported laborer wench but failing to muffle her snores. The first and second wenches lay on the floor in the corridor, surrounded by pens, musical instruments, and the remnants of an abacus; from the railings of the staircase dangled a few long-tasseled hats.

The taproom reeked of spirits. The staff of the Coachmaid's Rest were among the fallen, and fallen lowest of all was Fred— this literally, because he was to be found not inside the inn at all but out on the veranda, with one arm and one leg dangling into the deserted street. A pewter drinking can still hung from one of his fingers, but at the sound of the bell the fingers twitched, the can clanked to the cobbles and Fred moaned.

What, oh what, had he done? He'd only put out a cask of Sherry Lorosso and invited some of the people who'd come back from chasing off the Bumpy Fellow to join him in a free drink. Slowly memories returned: a second cask, a third. The squareful of Copperday night vendors and celebrants flooding the inn, including a dulcimer-drummer, a tubehorn player and a knee-fiddler. A troupe of street Fools (properly licensed, complete Fools) had begun a folly in the taproom and Fred hadn't been able to resist joining them, and from there it was all a blur until the part where some wenches he seemed to remember had chased some engineers up the stairs, trod all over his crushflowers and kicked him out of his own room.

The place looked like a cyclone had blown through. Thank all three heavens nobody remembered he was the Esquire. At times a forgettable face could be an asset.

He heard a bit of gravel crunching: someone was standing beside him. Gingerly he opened one eye and his mood improved.

He saw legs— feminine ones, deeply tanned, nearly bare, as lean and muscular as the legs of a bullfrog. His aching head was difficult to turn, but as he looked over the rest of her, Fred was glad he'd made the effort. She was just his kind of woman: not the typical tall, hardy beauty but a specialty item, small and slight and slim, just like... *her*. Yes, right down to the— Fred frowned. This woman wore short knitted pantaloons, cleated goatskin shoes and a canvas bag around her neck.

"About time ya woke up," said the foot messenger, unslinging her bag and reaching inside. "I been here since bell of two. I gotta say, yer some kind a acrobatic fella. Ya juggle, ya sing, ya tell po-ams and jokes and ya do every damn thing a fella can do, except hold still a deep-damned minute to take *this*." She bent down, unfolded Fred's shaky fingers and pressed a note card into them. "It's pre-paid. Hope you're the right fella after all— genel-man said ya could read?" The way she cocked her head told him she doubted this highly, but when she saw him unfold the note and begin, she nodded and ran away.

"No! No!" howled Fred. "Oh, my reeking god!"

The note read:

> *The Royal Family will be arriving a day early (bell of 9,*
> *Solderday). Sorry I forgot to tell you until now.*
>
> *P.S.   No, I'm not actually sorry at all*

P.P.S.   I also didn't really forget

P.P.P.S.   & isn't it deliciously ironic how, now that you're a
nobleman, even a pathetic smallholding one, you
can't lower yourself to reply to provocation from
a commoner? Even an important one, like me?
Ha ha! Finally got you back, you boil! This is for
putting cheese in my boots, wearing my collar as
a tutu and all the times you called me "Johnny
Baconfat". I don't care how funny the King used
to think it was when you were brats.

Love and kisses, Janush Baekenfahd.

Fred stood up. He fell down. He stood up more slowly and staggered into the Coachmaid's Rest, calling for his groom to go catch the mule, for one of his porters to get herself up and make like a valet, and the other one to mix him a revitalizer. Fred raised a holy fracas from the moment he downed the spicy glassful of secret ingredients until his carriage— a sporty open runabout drawn by a swift-looking piebald jenny— was flying up the Trade Road at a flat-out racing trot.

CHAPTER 7

$\mathbf{T}$HE FABRIC OF THE ROYAL PAVILION was heavy. It was very dark inside, but Dame Elsebet supposed that didn't matter. The Queen, she knew, was blind.

Fred had told her all about Margadet de Vonn, but he hadn't said much regarding Enrick of Castramars. She only knew that the King was Fred's age— thirty-four— and that he had some unusual preferences. Now, in the darkness, she could only guess what he might look like. She dared not raise her eyes from the ground, for she was about to offer the Greeting of Deepest Supplication.

"I welcome you to these, my lands," she began: ordinary words, the very ones she'd spoken to the herald. But The Greeting of Deepest Supplication hinged not upon words, but gestures. Heartbreaking gestures, rarely seen any longer, except on the stage— though Grandma Annelyn had made them, on that terrible day when she begged the man who then was King to overlook the uprising she hadn't meant to cause, to spare her life, her family, her country...

Dame Elsebet sank first to her knees and then lower still, pressing her forehead into the grass, and continued, "Come, enjoy, and take what you will." Her hands trembled as she raised them to the collar of her robe and folded it away, exposing the back of her neck, clearing the way for a blade...

Too late, Dame Elsebet realized this wasn't deferential at all. Far from it: it was presumptuous. Without warning or context, she'd just swanned into the royal pavilion and begun a frightfully self-serving display. Oh, gods. Her blood ran cold. Would the King now reply "Arise, our servant, and have no fear", signifying that all was forgiven? Or...

"I didn't hear what she said. It was too quiet I didn't hear what she said."

"She said hello, sweetheart." The Queen's Vonn Country accent was smooth as honey.

"Oh yes yes hello lady."

Dame Elsebet's eyes, staring into the shadowy grass, opened wide. Was he mocking her? Carefully she turned her head, so that she might at least die having seen him...

The pavilion curtain flew open to blinding sunlight.

"Enrick! Margadet! Sorry I'm late, but— what's going on here?"

It was Fred. He tucked the curtain up out of the way and stepped inside. "Why's Her High Honor down on the ground?"

"The ground?" gasped the Queen. "Enrick! You didn't tell me she was *kneeling!* Oh, please don't say she put her forehead on the—"

"No, no, of course she didn't," interrupted Fred, hurriedly helping Dame Elsebet to her feet. "Enrick, allow me to present the Domina of Whellengood."

The King was a medium-sized gentleman of graceful build, with hair and brows and natty little pointed beard all of the same deep, glossy black. Much of his clothing was also black— but then again, almost as much of it was white. The strong contrast of his barred linen cloak, the stripes forming his silken sleeves, the zigzag piecing of his featherweight khashme collar— all were like nothing Dame Elsebet had ever seen.

Taking the King's lapel, Fred gave an admiring whistle. "You're looking sharp as all hells. Did old tailor Angio finally learn some taste?"

"I have new garb Fred Margadet taught me the word garb it means clothes this new garb helps Margadet see me. Margadet can see me in my new garb if the sun is bright enough and I am moving look." The

King stood in the opening of the curtain and waved his arms. The Queen's doll eyes darted toward him in reflex and remained there while she spoke to Dame Elsebet.

"Your High Honor must think my husband looks ridiculous. Perhaps it wasn't one of my best ideas."

"Oh, no, Your Majesty! To the contrary. It is stunning and original. You know who would love this new... garb? My cousin, Irona de Brewel." Suddenly Dame Elsebet was sorry she'd mentioned the de Brewels, but relief that the Gesture of Deepest Supplication had not been recognized made her babble. "Irona dotes upon anything artistic. Or theatrical. Some of her dresses are very much like theater backdrops. Her daughter is an artist—"

"That's right, she sketched my portrait," interjected Fred, and did a back flip.

This habit of his still startled Dame Elsebet, but the King seemed used to it.

"Fred hold still I command you." Without a breath he continued in a speech that it was Fred's turn to seem used to. "I command you because I am King now since four years ago it feels good to be King but if it gets too tricky I ask Margadet to help me she is really smart Fred she is really smart some people say don't ask her anything they say she's a woman so she only knows to fight and work and have a baby but Margadet is really smart so I tell them I don't care and I ask her..."

"Dear, please! That is too much praise, really!"

He reached out and took both his wife's hands. "But I love you Margadet."

The Queen wore no gloves and at the sight of the motifs inked into her skin, still sharp and beautiful at only a few years old, Dame Elsebet's chest filled with a terrible, painful happiness. Young love! Fifty-one years ago she'd lost her husband, her father, and leave of her senses all at the same horrific moment. But life went on and each new generation found beauty in it; wounds healed— even deep ones such as madness, and whatever it was that had happened long ago between de Whellen and Castramars. Absently Dame Elsebet rubbed the back of her glove. Her own wedding bracelets were so faded they looked almost like smoke. Yet, perhaps, she *would* have someone touch them up, and once again let the world see them.

"Shall we go on to Whellengood Hall?" she asked, buoyant with hope, and stepped out through the pavilion's tucked-up curtain. She pointed toward the power carriage. "I have a wonderful surprise for—"

The heavy curtain fell between her and the Royals, knocking the King and Queen back into the darkness. Fred had pulled it down. Dame Elsebet turned to him, indignant, and opened her mouth to protest, but to her astonishment he put his fingers over her lips.

"Take that thing away. Hurry. I mean it. Trust me."

His insistent tone struck Dame Elsebet as a bit odd. She recalled what Nicolo had said about Malfred Murd being a trickster, and her own earlier thoughts on the matter. Indeed, in the single year she'd known Fred, the pendulum of his behavior had swung widely across the moral spectrum. He'd taken her for a ride, he'd left her in the lurch— but he'd also pulled her from the brink. Which Malfred was advising her now? *Trust me,* he'd said. Could she? Should she?

Dame Elsebet decided. Frantically she gestured for Lady Verocita, Nicolo and the archers to take the power carriage away; they were still scrambling over one another to choose a driver when the King opened the curtain again— oh no, surely he'd see the machine—

But he didn't, because just as he was turning to look, a childish squeal rang out. Abruptly a baby rushed across the interior of the pavilion at a rapid toddle, grasping something black and white as though it were a ball.

"Caught that bird," the child announced, thrusting his new treasure to arm's length and waving it about. "Bird frumtha boat. Looky, Da-da, Listen, Ama. Bird sing!"

"Make him let go, make him let go-o-o," warbled Corvinalias. The baby squealed again and shook him harder. Fred swooped in.

"Nedward, no. No. He's alive, not a toy. That's right, let him fly away. Bye, bird."

"Bird looks like Da-da."

Fred handed the little Prince up to his mother. "Yes, he does. You know what? When we get to Dame Elsebet's I'll sing you a song about that bird. He's named Corvinalias."

"Corvinalias Elsternom e Rokonoma the Fourth," Dame Elsebet surprised him by remembering. "He was with us last year."

Before she could say any more about last year, Fred cut her off and began talking volubly about a whole bunch of nothing, very entertaining nothing. And then somehow, the whole crew of them were on the move, Royals and retinue together, strolling.

On the soft grass beside the road, Fred flipped his legs in the air and began marching about in a handstand.

"Enrick. Listen." He pointed with one of his feet. "That-a-way is Dame Elsebet's palace. It's made of glass. Don't be afraid when you see it, all right? And I have a palace, too. Tomorrow we can go see it, in my town."

The King laughed, a series of whooping bursts. "I just thought of a poem Fred you have a palace and a town I bet it is an upside-down town oh Fred that is a poem I said a poem."

Fred flipped back and walked right side up. Dame Elsebet found herself guiding Queen Margadet as if it were the most natural thing in the world. Little Prince Nedward toddled along in front of them and the courtiers, including the frowning Baekenfahd, followed behind. The King jabbered to Fred in a manner that grew less and less disquieting the further they went; Dame Elsebet soon felt herself becoming used to his ways.

The retinue made it all the way through the front gates, where Nedward was the first to see Whellengood Hall.

He pointed up the drive. "Looky, Da-da! Listen, Ama! Shiny!"

The King stopped in his tracks and stared. "Fred what is that gem there it is big much too big."

"That's Whellengood Hall, Enrick. I told you about it. It's only made of—"

An unhappy note now crept into the King's tone. "It is too big for a gem that gem is too big." He began to stamp his feet. "It can't be as big as that either it's wrong or else my eyes are wrong something is wrong with my eyes!"

"Your eyes are fine, all right? Stop it. Calm down. It's a building. And it's glass, that's all. Metal and glass, like— like a mirror. In a few minutes we'll go inside."

"No! NO!"

Before Fred could say any more, The King fell to his knees on the gravel.

"We can't go into a mirror!" he shouted. Behind him, his feet began a frenzied drumming. "We can't do that you are lying to me no one can go into a mirror *stop lying!*"

The baby wailed. The Queen's face registered horror. For a split second the King wavered between giving in to his fit or pulling himself out of it; then he threw himself face down, clawed the driveway for a few moments and froze, his hands clenched like the paws of a bat-serpent hiding in a tree, but his feet still pattering madly.

The Queen pushed baby Nedward into Dame Elsebet's arms and rushed toward the King with impressive agility. But Fred caught her by the hands and swung her away.

"Don't touch him, Margadet. That'll make it worse."

"*You* tell me what I shouldn't do? I'm his wife!"

"And I'm his— his—" again and again, Fred blocked her way. "Damn it deep, no, I tell you! When he's like this, all you can do is—"

"Stop holding me back! I *will* console my husband!"

Fred lost his head.

"Oh? You *will*? Go to it, then, Your Majesty! I'll just bid farewell! Hoy, Enrick, listen up! It's good old, dumb old, nobody Fred your laughing stock! The brat your Da found you for a deep-damned pet, remember me? Spent twenty years at your elbow, Ricky, but who the triple-whipping hell cares about that, am I right? Margie's the new thing now, she'll take it from here. So bye bye! Try the venison! Pay the barmaid! You've been great, and I— "

"*Malfred!*"

Fred turned to face Dame Elsebet, startled. He'd clearly forgotten she was there.

"That is quite enough." Though she'd never had a child, still her voice was fierce and motherly. Something about it even made Prince Nedward stop crying in fascination.

"One does not shout at a frightened horse. One does not push oneself between husband and wife." Much to her own surprise, she discovered within herself a fount of indignation. "One does not come as a vassal, to the home of one's liege, and berate another guest! That's a fine trick to play! My duty is to provide Their Majesties a place of comfort and refuge, and you, sir, disturb my plans. As your hostess *and* your ruler, I insist that you go."

Fred stopped moving.

"Go?"

As a girl, Dame Elsebet had once found an oblong gray lump of silk in the garden. It was soft and squeezable, so squeeze it she had, only to gasp in anguish as all the colors of the rainbow began seeping through the silk and she realized she'd crushed the cocoon of a soulcomet, the most beautiful moth in the world. Malfred Murd was far from being as beautiful as that, but she felt she had crushed him just the same. He fell silent, grew small. Dame Elsebet wanted to cry out *wait, I didn't mean it*— but that would imply she sided against the Queen. A terrible pain clamped her temples. Baby Nedward stared at her. She had an inspiration.

"Yes, Malfred, I insist that you go— on a vacation. For a few weeks, at least. You may take my power barge. Nicolo will write you a letter of credit for whatever supplies you require. "

Still Fred looked quite deflated. "Where are you sending me?"

From behind them the Queen raised her voice. "Both of you, I must apologize. I—"

Dame Elsebet spoke quickly: "Brewel Hall."

And something about that was perfect. Oh, thank Ye Gods, it seemed to heal poor wounded Malfred.

Fred replied to the Queen: "You know what, Margadet, don't apologize. I was out of line. It's time for me to move on, and time for you and Enrick to sink or swim together. I think you'll be all right. As for me, I'll..."

And here he shrugged, drawing a swath of resignation all over his blank slate of a face.

He had to be careful: he'd lose the moral high ground if he let on that he was happy to go. But he was. Oh, how he was. Fred left Whellengood Hall at a slow, defeated pace, but inside he was glowing. Because Brewel Hall— or, to be more specific, Kestrella de Brewel's art studio there— was exactly where he went in his wildest dreams.

CHAPTER 8

THE BROAD BROWN DENNA— OLD MAMA river, Carrier of the World— flowed toward the Midland Sea in ever-increasing width and majesty as it entered the Whellen Country's southern neighbor, the Brewel Country. Through that land it wove and wandered, forming sloughs and marshes and oxbows of enormous size, until at last it became a great surging estuary where powerful tides drew almost the whole of the Kingdom's shipping in and out like the breath of some vast, biddable beast. Indeed the emblem of its masters, the de Brewel family, was a seahorse wearing a draft collar emblazoned with the words "Ours To Command".

The de Brewels lived in a massive palace of ivory-glazed terra-cotta on the eastern bank of the Denna. On the opposite bank lay their capital city, Coastwall, which had accumulated over the centuries and was generally as cosmopolitan and staggeringly wealthy as the de Brewels themselves.

But where there is money, there is crime. And in such measure as Coastwall had splendor, it also had mazes of crumbling sandstone tenements bracing themselves away from one another with arches like the arms of exhausted fighters, warehouses with windows tarred to deny the sun, scabby slum quarters and down-at-heel rumbuckets. Those parts of the city belonged to someone named Granny Almantree.

Granny had been the doyenne of Coastwall's crooks for many, many dozens of long and ruthless years. She no longer actively committed any sharping, or snaffling, or den-kenning; she bent no more shins, packed no more casks with flumbers' flesh, nor made any more slack talkers kick up Dizzy Dan at the end of a three-stranded lullaby. Others now did those things for her. All over the city, thousands of frolly fingers and weepers what never shut kept Granny Almantree at the ridge of the game.

So powerful was she that, one frosty night the previous winter, some of Granny's crooks had pulled off the most staggering, the most audacious, the benniest bump ever attempted in the history of thieving. They had cracked a shuckle— that is to say, breached a private vault— at DeCoastwel Bank, a place slightly more secure than the hands of the Great God Almighty. From it they'd filched a cubic yard of golden garnish: the cached money of the Ox-Train Queen.

Granny was triumphant. If crime were a contest, she'd have won it. But crime was as vast and changeable as the Midland Sea itself, and in Coastwall the tide showed signs of turning, threatening to float her victories away.

Granny Almantree's empire was founded upon her connections as a fence. She sold stolen items to a clientele that spread all the way out to the Warm Ocean: jewels, art, devious weapons, artifacts with which to perform subtle blackmailery; even once a pair of highcats that bore stripes instead of spots, and were trained to hunt man: these last she kept in the care of her least-favorite flunky until they somehow escaped, never to be seen again. It had been decades since any real competitor had dared to threaten Granny's place.

But now there was Hamel Fliss.

Outwardly, Granny evinced nothing. But in her heart, which was buried deep within a figure resembling a cold boiled potato, Granny was enraged. Hamel "Hamflesh" Fliss was a man, and worse: a learned man.

His gang of crooks could read and write. Somehow this helped them steal, and cheat, and go round behind Granny, in ways she'd never even thought of. She'd been slow to catch on, and had lost a few rounds to Fliss already; and though those rounds had been for small stakes, Fliss had now managed to nip something really big betwixt his pincers: The Tacular Specs.

The Tacular Specs were an old pair of sun goggles. Granny had never seen them, nor met anyone who had, but they were famous because they weren't just any old weepershades, oh no. They were spellbound.

Spellbound objects were worth fortunes, huge and gleaming fortunes. They did strange and potentially useful things. The Twin Cans, for example: what was said into one, could be heard from the other. The de Brewels had owned those Cans for centuries, until— and whenever she thought of this part, Granny would sway to her feet, ask one of her flunkies for a knife, and calm herself by hurling it into the bullseye of some handy target— the de Brewels had lost the Twin Cans to some early thieving by Fliss himself, and he'd come to Granny for help fencing them. If only she'd had the Tacular seeping Specs then, to show her the future! She'd have known to slip Hamflesh Fliss a special drink or, failing that, tap his back with a little steel finger.

Granny was determined to stay on top as long as ever she breathed. Fliss must be crushed, like a blood-filled flea: not only that he might plague her no longer, but as a warning to any upstart gang who might be floating about in Coastwall's corners.

Granny had a plan for the destruction of Hamflesh Fliss. In it, she was no longer selling, but buying. She would start shopping for a spy.

CHAPTER 9

"**O**H, COME NOW, VINNY. SURELY you don't think any Uman really *needs* a shiny, what? Shinies are only toys to them. Half the time they trade them away for something else. It's here today, gone tonight with Umans— short attention span, don't you know."

Uncle Jey had Fred's badge of office propped up against the trunk of the blackbud tree he and Corvinalias had perched in when they first looked down at the Coachmaid's Rest. The place was a shocking mess now— some kind of storm seemed to have hit it— and in this it matched Corvinalias's mood, not to mention his ribcage.

That's what I get, he thought, for trying to help anyone. He'd gone to meet Fred at the Uman royals' pavilion, waiting for the right time to tell him Uncle Jey had the badge, and then what had happened? Baby Uman got him.

In the cradle of a swaying twig, Corvinalias toppled on one side and groaned. Uncle Jey flipped the badge flat side out and regarded himself in the surface engraved with Fred's name. "This shiny is so magnificent it's going in my collection. No. Better. It's going to the Museum of the Scientific Institute!"

"Come on, let me give it back to my Uman. Please. You don't really care about the Institute," said Corvinalias. "You said" —and here he mimicked Uncle Jey to perfection, the way only a magpie can mimic— " 'the Rokonomas and their hangers-on may pat their own backs and call themselves scholars until the swallows come home, but we all know their Museum is nothing but a vanity project, or more likely a tax dodge, what? Science, my cloaca.' "

Uncle Jey stopped preening himself and turned around. "Oh, but this will be different. I'm going to donate those two branches in Whorl

Nine to the Institute, and have them rename the Museum for me, its great patron. Ha! Let the Rokonomas try and say no to *that* —E23 alone produces over thirty baskets of nuts a year. Imagine what fun I'll have, demanding they attend my lectures! That'll frizz their whiskers, what?"

Corvinalias hopped painfully upright.

"But Uncle Jey! Those should be part of *Upper* Cloudyblue. Everyone who lives there thinks they already do— the serfs give me a lizard every New Year. They'd be good to leave to my—"

"Tsk, tsk, my boy. If you were about to say 'hatchlings', well, you're putting the eggs before the nest, aren't you? It's time you settled down. Perhaps I *will* leave you those branches, if you'd only marry Rooki."

At this, Corvinalias was aghast. Rookappella Elsternom-Elsternom was the worst shrew on the whole Isle— and that included literal shrews. Her own parents admitted they'd heard her shouting from inside the egg, days before she'd hatched. Plus she hated travel, even more than she hated every other thing in the whole wide world.

"*Rooki?* Are you kidding me? She'd *never* go on adventures!"

"Well, but what are adventures for, Vinny? For making a name, what? Once you've got the glory, you settle down and tell your stories. It's what I do."

Stories. Ugh, stories! At the thought of marrying Rooki and becoming another Uncle Jey, Corvinalias wanted to regurgitate.

You know what? He didn't want those branches anymore; the serfs could send their lizard to the new museum. Hatchlings could wait— maybe forever. And then, with a feeling like a profound bass chord from the bottom of his soul, Corvinalias realized he didn't even want to go back to Upper Cloudyblue. Not anymore. That life wasn't him at all.

The whales had changed him; the cyclones had changed him. The sting of ashes hurled from the heart of a volcano, the sweet hot breath of Herb Island spice plantations, the vast quilt of the ocean, the longwolf's eerie cry: these had made him someone new, who didn't need to tell any stories. The adventures would be his alone, to keep in himself. And someday when he was older than Uncle Jey, if he lay down on a floating lily, in a river under a cathedral tree, and never woke up again— that would be all right. The adventures would start over with someone new.

The old Duke of Lower Cloudyblue was blathering on: about Rooki, the branches, the museum, something, nothing. Corvinalias paid him no more attention. Instead he looked up through the boat-shaped leaves of the blackbud tree.

High above him, something passed behind a cloud. Two things. He focused sharply and saw a pair of adventurers: long necks stretching before them, long legs streaming behind, great wings gathering and releasing armfuls of sky.

"Uncle Jey."

"...so really I...mmm? What, my boy?"

"Are you *sure* I can't make you give back Fred's badge?"

"Certainly not. Your Uman will find something else to amuse itself with."

Corvinalias sighed. "That's what I thought. You know where the boat is, don't you?"

"Of course I do, Vinny. So as I was..."

"Goodbye, Uncle Jey."

The Duke looked up through the leaves and saw the black-and-white shape of his grand-nephew vanishing into the distance. "That's rather abrupt, what?" he cried. "I was in the middle of a story."

CHAPTER 10

D URING THE NIGHT ATA MAROO'S SHIP had become even more
woefully grounded. Despite her best attempts not to let anyone
know who she was, by morning the rumor had got out and soon
everyone knew. What seemed like an army of freight canoes came out
to unload her ship until it was light enough to float clear of the rocks;
she sat in one of these canoes now, along with a silently confused Alvert
and her father, Re Ata Pako.

"Rooey, *ipo*, hold one corner of this, please. It wants to keep rolling up."
The old gentleman holding a big chart of the harbor gave his daughter
a smile that was all apology. "This isn't one of mine. I'd never keep this
type of chart rolled in such a way— you see what it leads to. Just when
you most need it to behave, it won't."

Ata Maroo kissed her father's forehead, right where there was a big lock
of pure white hair among the gray. "Papa. Never say you aren't poetic—
that was a metaphor. For me. I know *I'm* the one who misbehaves when
she's most needed. And I know you've needed me back here at home.
Oh, Papa, this journey was ghastly. Storms! Wrecks! Rebuild the boat!
Change course! Live with these people, or those people, until I could get
us away! And there wasn't a single day of it, Papa, that wasn't 'darkened
by the rain of my tears', as the poem says. I know what a wretched
ungrateful child I've been. I know twenty lost years are going to be hard
to make up. I mean, I do so... so deeply, so immeasurably... apologize for
running off and leaving you and Mother here. To— to deal with—" She
shuddered at the memory of her first husband.

And then, to Alvert, in the Westlander language: "Alvie, *ipo*, you hold
map for my Da, ah? Hold corner, here and here, like so. You arms
long enough."

Re Ata Pako smiled at Alvert, who hadn't had much smiling in his life until he met Ata Maroo. Alvert gave his father-in-law a timid but sincere return of the courtesy.

"Your young man really *does* look like The One Who Listens. Are you sure he isn't from the Ocean Empire?"

"Papa! Don't be ridiculous. Alvie's from a land with hardly a stream wider than my arm. In his homeland the mountains are so high, Mount Grumble would be just a pebble. The snow there sometimes sweeps down fiercely enough to wipe away entire towns."

"Oh, dear me," said Re Ata Pako, imagining all the maps that would need to be revised after such a disaster.

He shook the image from his head and, taking a red pointer from the waxed pigskin purse on his hip, indicated something on the chart Alvert held. "You would've been all right if it were only a bit later in the month— your number One and Two whales didn't remember the enhanced amplitude of spring tides, and of course Three through Six couldn't know Ata Rocks at all, as they were calved in other waters. But in future, you'll note that Ata Rocks lack any truly notable visual markers. Perhaps this is due to their composition as..."

Ipo Papa, thought Ata Maroo as his voice blurred into its familiar drone. Even back when she'd dared to read letters from home— back before she'd become so paralyzed with shame that she had turned herself into the Kingdom's biggest shipping tycoon rather than admit to having panicked and fled from home without considering her family— even in writing, Papa had always managed to lull her into a stupor. Compared to him, Alvert's shy and halting descriptions of a hard childhood, hauling message bags beside his appalling Ma, were rip-roaring tales from the mouth of a natural bard. Perhaps it was just as well that her attempts to teach Alvert the language of the Peaceful Ocean had fizzled— if he had to listen to Papa, he might die of boredom.

"...your mother's green feather crown," Re Ata Pako concluded.

At that, Ata Maroo's ears seemed to snap back into place.

"Mother's what?"

"Her crown. She looks forward to the day you'll be ready to take it up. Everyone does."

"But why put it like that?" demanded Ata Maroo, and upon overhearing her tone, Alvert's eyes grew rounder than ever. He still held the chart, patiently stretched wide, though his arms trembled. This annoyed her. She pressed the center of the parchment until it collapsed, and continued to Re Ata Pako:

"Why say 'your mother's green feather crown'? It's not *Mother's* crown. I mean I know she's been filling in for me, and obviously I thank her from the bottom of my unworthy heart— but that crown's meant for the Headmother of the Hundred Clans and everyone in Wahayee knows the big scandal of how the Headmother ran away."

"The little girl who was just about to become Headmother ran away."

"Little girl? Papa, I was twenty years old! I had a husband who tried to kill me!" She didn't say: *who you and Mother picked out.*

Now Alvert was worried. "Maroo?" he asked. "Are you and your Da—"

"Not now, *ipo!*"

"All right, all right, very well, then," sighed Re Ata Pako, taking the chart away and folding it against the gunwale of the canoe. He folded so hard, the tips of his sun-leathered old fingers turned pale. "This is something you'll have to take up with your mother."

"At-last-yes." The word Ata Maroo used was the special "yes" one gives after thinking about something for a long, long time.

Then there was a big silence. The canoe slipped into the cool shadow of one of the clouds over Mount Grumble.

Re Ata Pako had folded the chart into a very neat, flat triangle that kept itself tucked shut. He stuck this in his waxed pigskin purse and nodded to his daughter.

"You know what, *ipo*, I'll go tell your mother to order breakfast made. You remember the eastern creek, don't you? It's a nice canal now, very easy to navigate. See you at home." And with that, the old gentleman slipped over the side of the canoe and swam away, underwater for a good part of it so that his blue and white patterned kilt flashed through the waves like the fin of a crystalfish.

Ata Maroo watched him go and realized he'd left his pointer behind. With a frown she stuck it in her smooth black hair and looked at Alvert.

"Well, ah. That not so very good."

"That word you kept a-sayin'...what's it mean?"

"It word of family-level politeness, mean 'mother'." She forced a smile and took his hand. "Our language a bit complicated."

A school of hardy-looking young women swam toward their canoe. One of them raised her hand and said: "Younger Medame Ata. Your father sent us to paddle your craft. We—"

Then, catching sight of Alvert, she froze. All of them froze. They stared at him, treading water, until Ata Maroo laughed.

"Alvie, *ipo*, remember what I say about you face? Now it time for me to teach you word you will hear a lot. Ready? It mean 'god'."

CHAPTER 11

WHAT IS LIFE? CAN ANYONE EXPLAIN it? And if yes, might I be able to meet this person? For some tea, perhaps?

From the first moment of every day, young Kestrella de Brewel pondered such weighty questions.

She pondered as she brushed her glossy dark hair, bathed and dressed. She pondered during her broadspear practice, which was decidedly more interesting now that she had entered society as an adult, for her trainer had finally sharpened her weapon's blade and it was remarkable how well it now slashed down sheaves of straw, wicker targets, and hanging sides of mutton. But back to the pondering. She pondered as she exercised the buckskin ponies Cousin Elsie had sent her from Whellengood last birthday— the little runabout carriage that came with them had long since been wrecked, alas.

For a few hours at midmorning she ceased pondering in order to take some breakfast with her parents, but then it was back to the grind as she pulled on a smock and followed the helical path down to her art studio in the Spiral Garden.

The Dominelle was in fact a very skillful artist. Her charcoal studies, which included portraits of every visitor who came to Brewel Hall, numbered in the thousands and were neatly stored in deep wooden files very much like the ones her brother Petir's Prophessors used to store valuable old texts. And although a proper lady such as Kestrella or her mother Dame Irona would never have been caught dead trying to read, or do any other such mannish thing, still she consulted her past drawings now and then, just the way Petey consulted his books. They helped her improve. She hoped she'd improved enough, because tomorrow, at Mitsa-Konig University's College of Justice, a very special jury— an art-show jury— would render their verdict: the name of the artist who would paint the mural in their new building.

"Oh, I hope they choose you, Medamselle," said Kestrella's studio assistant, laying a selection of chalk and charcoal on a tray. But on hearing this, Kestrella's amber eyes flashed with pique and her ink-black brows converged toward the center of her broad forehead.

"*No*, Teesha! I never entered that competition, do you hear? We want them to choose *Gustoph Glint.*"

"Oh, yes! Yes! Beg pardon, Medamselle."

Kestrella strode over to an easel, limbered up her arms and chose a piece of charcoal. For about an hour she sketched furiously: the model before her, a sadly muscular and illiterate young wight one of the cooks had found on the streets of Coastwall when she went out marketing, changed poses to the rhythm of a thirty-second sandglass. Or rather, to Teesha's shouts of "Sit. Now stand. Now do something else. Move, fellow, move!"

Kestrella studied the one hundred twenty-three drawings she had made and chose the best one, leaving Teesha to burn the others and pay that day's model a silver bit before sending him back out to rejoin the unwashed masses. So went the practice of art. It was arduous, but life's questions weren't going to ponder themselves.

KESTRELLA'S MOTHER, HER HIGH HONOR Dame Irona de Brewel, Domina of the Brewel Country, was seated on a sea-green upholstered bench in the midmost chamber of her apartment, letting some little servant girls change her gloves as they did every hour, when her daughter burst in upon her.

"Mumsy. I just went back to my room after drawing and Lily is gone. I can't find her anywhere."

"Well, I'm quite sure I have no idea where your pets go. You overfeed them— you give them nothing to do— naturally they grow restless."

Kestrella looked under the bench. "I hope Babou didn't eat her."

"Babou is not under there, Kiki. I turned him loose in the garden: he needs exercise. He's become so lazy it's shameful. You ought to take him with you next time you— Kiki, are you listening? Oh, boils, she's out the door."

But the more Dame Irona thought about it, the more she began to suspect that perhaps something sinister was afoot. Perhaps Lily hadn't escaped; perhaps she'd been stolen! A frisson of excitement traced her spine. She decided that an agitated exclamation and a gesture of fright were in order. She opened her theatrically painted mouth and eyes very wide, clapped her gloves to her cheeks, and said: "Oh! The most frightful thing occurs to me! We may have been burgled! Just like last year! I'm positively faint with worry! Should I call for help? Should I— oh, now, *really*."

The nearest servant girl was offering her one of the thick, decoratively twisted silken cords that hung from the ceiling of every room in the suite. Dame Irona took it and gave it a sharp tug, but spoke peevishly to the child who'd offered it.

"How many times must I tell you? First I exclaim, next I hesitate, and *then* I summon the Grand Constable! Otherwise it kills the drama. Really. You'd think it would be obvious by now."

CHAPTER 12

GOOD OLD BREWEL HALL!

Fred had a decided bounce in his step as he strode from Dame Elsebet's power barge— a handsome craft with a large clockwork engine— onto the golden teak dock of the boathouse at the de Brewels' palace. On the barge he'd dined well, slept well, breakfasted well. He'd bossed the oarmaids around because they really weren't rowing, were they? The machine was doing it. That left them very much free to trim his hair, shave his face, and press his clothes. The oarmaids were obviously unhappy to be serving as valets but could do nothing. Orders were orders, and Dame Elsebet had ordered them to take orders from him.

Brewel Hall's boathouse would have been most impressive to Fred if it weren't old news. It was made of white tiles with art sculpted all over them— merfolk and krakens and stars wrought from lumps of pure gold and suchlike. It was also really big: last year he'd mistaken it for the de Brewels' actual palace. Fred chuckled to himself, remembering his gauche, jejune naïveté.

This time he knew the drill. He waved the glaring oarmaids off to the dorms meant for guests' servants. He sat in the sea-green painted sedan chair. He clipped open the curtains embroidered with the de Brewel seahorse and let himself be whisked along a walkway of crushed oyster shells, through a series of bronze gates adorned with more seahorses, across a courtyard filled with fountains, up a sea-green marble staircase, past a conservatory filled with miniature trees and finally into Brewel Hall proper.

There, with a mild stumble no one noticed, Fred exited the chair at a guest room with a pecky cypress door.

"Leave the bags in there," he told the porters who had followed him with an ostentatious tower of mostly empty trunks. "I'm going to look for"— and here he was about to say *Their High Honors,* but he corrected it to an airy "Felip and Irona."

Fred strolled blithely through the maze of the Hall. Where Whellengood was sleek, and the Royal Palace was ceremonious, the de Brewels' home was simply over the top— and then over whatever lay on top of that. Silk, satin, suede, lace, tapestry, skins, feathers, marble, porphyry, bronze, gilt, crystals, mirrors... had he missed something? Oh yes, murals.

He paused beside a sea-green floor vase to contemplate a wall filled with lost souls, keening into the cold void of an indifferent cosmos. *Gods, is this ever morbid,* he thought— but then his eye fell upon a signature stamp at one corner of the work, nearly hidden behind the vase, and when he saw the letters *K. de B.* Fred gave the mural a second look and decided it was pure genius. He could hardly wait to tell Kestrella so.

In fact, the thought of talking Art with Kestrella filled him with so much excitement that, rather just stand around making a spectacle of himself, Fred used the zigzag feelings bumping about in his abdomen to propel him into a long, highly expressive tumbling pass down the carpeted hallway. His final somersault nearly knocked down an unobtrusive gentleman he remembered from his last visit. A memory popped up: Dame Elsebet had addressed this man as "Rhonso".

"Ah, Rhonso, good fellow. I believe Elsebet sent a dove to let you know I was coming. Now, if you don't mind, I'm on my way to that big garden with the gazebo in it, to see if I can find..."

"The Map Garden is in *this* direction, Mesir. His and Her High Honor are taking bruncheon there. I was just on my way. Allow me."

Rhonso walked with him for some time, then showed him through a set of doors whose glass looked like fish scales. Donn Felip and Dame

Irona were seated at opposite ends of a whitewood table, while servants fanned them with palm fronds against the afternoon heat. Dame Irona spoke up.

"I'm sure you did an excellent job in the studio, good fellow. But before you go, please exercise our cat. And you may keep that costume you're wearing— it does fit you surprisingly well." She stood up to her full, impressive height and, reaching across the table, pressed a golden coin into Fred's hand. "This is for your trouble."

Then she prodded something under the table. There was a growl and a roar. A slim, tawny beast covered with black spots burst forth and leaped at Fred.

The highcat's jaws opened and it lunged for his face— before he could raise his arms, it was licking, licking, licking him with its raspy tongue, leaning its front paws on his shoulders, fanning the air with its great spotted streamer of a tail and purring. Babou leaned till he pushed Fred down to the tiled plaza, then curled up into a big loaf on top of him.

Donn Felip considered them. "Hmm! The cat seems to know him. Fellow! Have you modeled for our daughter before?"

"Yepth," sputtered Fred from around more licks. "She drew me last year." This information did not produce the recognition he expected. "When I was here with your Cousin Elsie." This produced only confusion. "It's me— Brother Malfred."

This, at last, rang some bells. When the de Brewels had last met Fred, he was understood to be a spell-casting mystic, helping Elsebet de Whellen undertake a perilous mission; Dame Irona had wanted a mystic of her own, and Donn Felip had been delighted to find a fellow lover of books.

"Of course! I found you napping in our gazebo!"

"Ah yes, I showed you around our library."

"And I met you, too," came a voice from among the frond-fanning servants. The man who strode around the table to Fred, helped him push Babou away, and pulled him to his feet was a municipal peace officer in a particularly trim and important-looking uniform. "Not sure if I introduced myself, though. Gino V. Doak, Grand Constable of Law and Order in the City of Coastwall."

Fred remembered him: an older gentleman, his brow set in a benign scowl, handsome in a rugged way. His expression, however, was that of an overtaxed entertainer struggling to keep up the facade.

"So, Brother Malfred. You find yourself on another visit here. I'm a frequent visitor, too— what say later we have a drink? You might be able to help me with something."

"I suppose I could join you for a— a-a-a-a," Fred's reply turned into a yelp.

Something was flowing down his back. It wasn't a trickle of sweat. It was distinctly bigger than that. He pawed wildly at it, but couldn't reach. Babou, who had been about to crawl back under the table, took notice.

The thing was going sideways now. It was in Fred's armpit. He yelped some more and began flailing; the thing expanded its motions greatly, into a comprehensive tour of his torso and some distinct attempts at the waistband. Babou was treading his hind legs, preparing to spring. With a wail of panic, Fred sprinted across the garden, slapping at the intruder. Babou leaped at him and missed, rolled, righted himself and took off after this exciting new plaything.

Back and forth they raced, acrobat and highcat, across the Map Garden, which was exactly what it sounded like: a miniature of the Brewel Country. Fred skidded over the blue-and-brown tile of the Denna Estuary, stumbled through shrubs representing the Dark Forest, tripped over a replica of Micalossa's Theater in the suburb of Oldmarsh; Babou finally caught up with him, dragged him down and pinned him when they were once again before the bruncheon table.

"Oh, how truly kind of you," exulted Dame Irona. "Rather than resent my faux pas in mistaking you for a peasant, you took the trouble to give Babou a good workout. How simply— oh! *Oh!* Look at this, now. Look at *this!* Kiki will be delighted."

In a trice she was beside Fred, plucking at his collar. From the corner of his eye he saw her draw forth a long, strongly squirming, multicolored and not inconsiderably sized snake.

Holding it aloft by the tail, Dame Irona looked past Fred. Her face lit up.

"Kiki, dear! Come look! Lily is back, safe and sound."

CHAPTER 13

A LVERT HAD BEEN BORN A DRAGONSSON, in the far north of the Whellen Country, a place called Yondstone. Dragonsson was not a name of any renown.

Yondstone was thin mountain soil and bleatin' goats and vales o' small wild flowers, *linkapaa* what stung when you drank it, leathern britches what squeaked till you broke 'em in. Yondies— as the people there affectionately called themselves, though they resented it when others used the term— kept mostly to themselves. They rarely went down into the lowlands, out into the world. But Alvert's Ma had done it. She'd run away— the standard mode of transportation, for a foot messenger.

Ma hauled a bag back and forth across the laughably easy low country for some bit o' time, stretchin' her lungs by shoutin' at customers who displeased her, which were pretty much all o' them; most of her fellow flyers displeased her, too, although one particularly tall and gaunt male road-pounder pleased Ma long enough to leave her a brat.

Ma raised her son to shut his gape and not ask for no second helpings. Her footprints had led up and down the Trade Road, hin and yon cross country, and Alvert had followed 'em till he grew so tall he stuck out like a busted finger. After that Ma said it cost too much to feed him, so he ran off himself and then, by some miracle o' luck, Ata Maroo the Ox-Train Queen had married him. So now he was an Ata, which *was* a name of renown, indeed.

Dragonsson Ata Alvert raised a hand to shade his eyes and to hold back the wavy straw-colored hair that twisted with the sea breeze toward the shore of his wife's homeland. Here the mountains were green as moss. Here the flowers grew on terraces, in vast blocks of single colors. Black stone aqueducts zigzagged the valleys, running down to a city of fat thatched rooftops and great wooden columns and rippling canvas walls bright with geometric paintings.

One of the paintings was of a cloud whale, like the ones Maroo drove.

Maroo, seated behind Alvert, was saying something to the crew paddling them in. Closer, closer to the city their canoe came, through a busy, noisy harbor, past some dockyards, into a maze of canals where flower vines dangled down black stone levees. Further, till the noise turned to birdsong and the water grew shallow and clear.

Abruptly the building with the whale painted on it loomed before them. Onto its broad balcony stepped a woman who wore a slightly more weathered version of Maroo's face under a glowing, parrot-green halo.

Maroo drew a breath. A small one, but Alvert heard it.

Then the woman clapped her hands and called out. Servants came running to take away the canoe while Alvert and Maroo climbed a great wooden staircase.

That is how Alvert came to be sitting on a black stone floor, cross-legged upon a thick feather cushion, eating ham with toasted bentfruit dumplings, and drinking something sweet, dark and hot. He shut his gape and watched his wife wi' her Ma: watched 'em smile wi' their dark golden cheeks, and chat wi' their coral-red lips, and size one another up like mountain goats, a-meetin' at a pass only wide enough for one of 'em.

CHAPTER 14

Night had come, and with it a cooling breeze that rushed across the great brackish swath of the Denna. Fred actually shivered a little, as he stood with the Grand Constable on the roof of the ivory-glazed boathouse. Mariners' signal flags snapped and flapped all around them; having long resided on an island, Fred could read these perfectly well. PET FOUND SAFE, said one string of flags. MAKE FLAGS REMIND COOK TO GET CAVIAR, said another.

The lens-lamps illuminating these signals cast a glare into Fred's eyes. But after a few moments' adjustment he could see through them to the city beyond: Coastwall was a glittering arc around the harbor, a flight of twinkling spots like flashbugs climbing up the hills, and behind the lights, a great bleak wash of darkness.

The Grand Constable set an empty crystal glass on the parapet, wiped his mustachio and pointed at the dark place. "That's where all the crime happens. Sure we've got a man up in the Lantern, but even with a high-powered spyglass he can hardly see anything on account of the harbor beacon. Oh, what I wouldn't give to be able to get down there into the gutters and—" Here he made a furious set of gestures, as though he were fighting something and beating the red-rimmed boils off it.

"So Irona calls you over here pretty much twenty-five hours a day? Makes you eat honey-bons and tea cakes and look for a lost button? Huh, sounds rough. I'd complain."

"You laugh, Murd, but for me it's like the drip-drop torture. I wrote the book on fighting crime! I mean I really did. You can find it in their library."

Fred took a sip from his own drink and leaned over the parapet. Through the embroidered silk of his latest shirt its sculptured tiles were still warm from the day's sun; the one under his elbow represented a mermaid— a coiling mermaid who was half eel, slim and slinky, like Kestrella. Or Lily. Fred shuddered.

It had been worth it, though. Kestrella had looked down at him and made one of her saucy, suggestive witticisms. She'd been wearing not the tunic and robe and pantaloons of a stolid lady but a gown, that shameless radical new fashion— when news of gowns had first reached the Isle of Gold, one of the Old King's sisters had dismissed them as "on top, nothing over something; down below, something over nothing". What a perfect description, thought Fred, although it hardly captured the way a flare of flame-colored satin had cascaded down from around Kestrella's slender neck, where it was held in place by a single ivory button. And on her feet she'd worn slippers, not boots. She'd stepped on his hand with one of them. He rubbed it now and wished it could happen again.

The Grand Constable was still talking. "Every day something comes up that I'm not allowed to touch. Now the son, Petir, he writes that a thing called the Tacular Specs is missing from a research laboratorium at Mitsa-Konig. A spellbound object! Do you know what could happen if one of those fell into the wrong hands?"

"It could threaten the world as we know it?" yawned Fred. "It could keep two lovers apart?"

He'd meant to make fun of theatricals, but suddenly the idea of lovers being kept apart felt personal, so he shut up and let the Grand Constable continue.

"Again, Murd, you laugh. And maybe I did sound a little bit like *her*. It's because she's got my leash so deep-damned short. But I know exactly what could happen with a valuable thing like a spellbound object— Granny Almantree could get her paws on it and sell it out to the Herb Islands, and poof, there goes another one of the Kingdom's treasures. Just between you and me, I think it's oxwash about the Twin Cans now being in the possession of the Crown. I think Granny sold 'em. Great grimy gods' guts, what I wouldn't do to smash the Almantree gang! The de Brewels have no idea how much it would help their country if they only let me. But once I did, they'd see it. They'd give me whatever reward I wanted. And I know just what I'd ask for: a little deep-damned freedom."

Fred traced the eel mermaid with some of his fingertips. "Whatever you wanted? That's generous."

"Oh, the de Brewels aren't stingy, Murd. They don't even know what money is anymore. It means nothing to them, literally nothing. That's why for rewards, they grant favors. Like last time, I got Dame Irona to redesign my uniform. Needed somewhere to stash my skull-duster." The Grand Constable patted his smart kelp-green jacket and adjusted the belt holding his truncheon.

Fred thought about what *he* wanted. Across the beam of one of the lens-lamps danced a soulcomet, its translucent wings glowing like stained glass, its antennae streaming away in twin spirals like nullicorn beards. It seemed like a sign: maybe he'd ask for a stroll in the garden, on a night like this, with...

"What could I do to help you smash this gang you hate so much?"

The Grand Constable's face, already bizarre and theatrical in the lamplight, made a change extremely seldom seen. His scowling brows unknotted and his thick gray mustachio rose and widened to reveal a smile from which only a few teeth had been knocked out. He shook Fred amiably by one shoulder.

"That's the spirit, Murd! I'm not going to lie: the minute I saw you come up to the bruncheon table today, I had an idea. I wanted you to do something for me. But it had to be voluntary, and here you come volunteering."

Now Fred wasn't sure what he'd got himself into. "Volunteering for what?"

"For a mission. Look at you, Murd. A literate gentleman, from what Donn Felip tells me, but built like a ditch-digger and with a face no one would ever look twice at. Do you know what I could do with a combination like yours?"

Fred wanted to snap *Be a little less insulting?* but he took a deep breath and let it pass. The wight was a commoner, after all. Instead he murmured a noble "No, do tell me."

"I could slip you into Granny's gang and have you write me a whole book, from under her crooked nose, about her every crooked move. Of course she's too cagey to take you in right away. You'd have to build up to it. I could put you in with the Harbor Street Mob... then after they'd knocked you about and put your arse on a street corner..." the Grand Constable rubbed his chin, planning his approach.

Fred coughed a lump out of his throat. "Just to be clear, this mob wouldn't actually, ah, knock me anywhere."

"What, are you scared of a few dents and scratches? Justice is a lady worth suffering for, Murd. She doesn't let cowards take her by the hand."

Take her by the hand. Oh, how Fred wanted Kestrella's hand in his, by the moonlight, in the gazebo. Maybe she'd get bored with a hand and explore further possibilities.

"I'm in," he said. "I can slip into any mob you want. As a matter of fact, just the other day I busted a crook, as I believe the term goes, by pretending to be a—"

But the Grand Constable didn't care about Fred's triumph over the Bumpy Fellow. He was already imagining the favor he'd ask when he showed the de Brewels a jail cell with Granny Almantree in it, finally caged like some loathsome monster from the northern wilds. Granny's head, stuffed and mounted! Well, perhaps figuratively. He'd trade that for three days a week— hells, more— at the Station House in Coastwall, where his officers had probably forgotten he existed. No more lost snakes, lost buttons, imaginary bumps in the night. Only Justice, sweet and true. The Grand Constable sighed, imagining. *I'm on my way back, good lady.* You're the love of my life. Oh, how I've missed you.

CHAPTER 15

RHONSO DIMACHI, THE MAJOR-DOMO WHO ORCHESTRATED the complex workings of Brewel Hall's multiple departments and all the servants who busied themselves therein, was a literate man. Obviously not to the extent that his master was— no one could sit in a library all day like Donn Felip de Brewel— but still Rhonso was capable of maintaining an eloquent correspondence with the major-domos of other noble families: Cousin Elsie's Nicolo, for example. Thus he was always very well informed, a positive fount of current information.

If Rhonso had a fault, thought Donn Felip, it might be his plainhand. The gentleman wrote in such a tearing hurry that the letters were frequently malformed, impossible to decipher. But no matter; he was an indispensable help and knew how to keep everything in Donn Felip's huge, ornate whitewood desk neat and organized.

Let's make this the last one. Any news from abroad? Donn Felip scribbled on a corner of his desk blotter. It was a levee morning. Four times a week, he presided over this event, at which he dispensed a somewhat arbitrary form of justice for those citizens displeased with their local magistrate's decision— always a goodly number, far more than he could concentrate on. Right now the petitioners on the sea-green carpet before his desk were a droopy fellow holding an empty halter and a strongly built, surprisingly beautiful peasant goodwife.

At Donn Felip's shoulder, Rhonso straightened some papers and with a discreet piece of charcoal pencil wrote on the blotter: *Royal fam. arr. safely @ Whelngd.* A few seconds later he wiped this message away, but the impact of it remained. Donn Felip felt as though someone had thrown a beehive at his immaculately barbered head.

The Royals? Visiting Whellengood Hall? How? Why?

"...so I brung the matter here to Yer High Honor, ta getcher take!"

The beautiful peasant woman was glaring at him. She seemed to be awaiting a reply.

"I'm so sorry. Please repeat your plea. You say you purchased a, a, donkey? Or a pony? Or a sheep, was it?"

The wench glared, the wight drooped, Donn Felip caught the words "paid this oik the seepin' money" and "calls it my problem" and "boot to the beanbag, if it's up to me". But after she had finished her second run-through, Donn Felip was alarmed to find that he was still no wiser. He'd been thinking about the relationship his family had with the Crown.

It was an unpleasant one, lacquered over with a coat of civility, whereby the Royal Family agreed to not mention the de Brewels' alleged part in an utterly misunderstood and objectively nonexistent uprising that was completely in the past, if only the de Brewels would kindly allow a representative of the King to choose a gift every year from Brewel Hall's collection of priceless antiquities. Up until now, Donn Felip had consoled himself that, though the Royals saw fit to treat his home as their own private goody jar, at least his family wasn't on such odious terms with the monarch as were the de Whellens. The Royals simply did not acknowledge the existence of the Whellen Country at all. In fact, for the past three generations they had been waiting for their chance to abolish it entirely by refusing to renew the de Whellen title. Then something had happened; the King had relented; and for a time Donn Felip's solace had been that the King was still ignoring Cousin Elsie. But now?

"...on account of the judge is down in Granny's bottom pocket, Yer High Honor!" the peasant wench concluded.

With a start, Donn Felip realized he couldn't ask for another repeat. His eyebrows went up, down, took on a quizzical off-balance slant. In a burst of inspiration he turned to Rhonso and said:

"I am of two minds. What do you recommend?"

"The fellow must refund her money, Mesir. In sales of livestock, the law states unambiguously that..."

What could Cousin Elsie possibly have that the de Brewels did not? Whellengood Hall was an experimental horror, all slick and smooth and angular, with no Treasury full of art and gems and spellbound objects. True, her country had some sort of gadgets, but the Brewel Country had control over the entire estuary of the Denna, and of the brandy-black deeps of the Midland Sea— everything between the Lantern and the Perdoffino Light, which was in Donn Felip's learned opinion quite a deep-damned way.

"Rhonso, let us conclude today's business. I know it's early, but I'm feeling indisposed." A groan went up from the crowd of citizens waiting their turn on the carpet and the peasant wench decided to take justice into her own hands by swatting the droopy fellow with the halter, but Rhonso herded them out in short order and left his master to sit alone.

"What's wrong, Darling?"

Dame Irona had entered, barefoot and wearing a simple morning wrap that required only four little servant girls to carry its train.

"Rhonso said the Royals are in the Whellen Country. Actually visiting it."

Dame Irona's hand flew to cover her mouth; in perfect synchrony, the little servant girls covered theirs.

"But— they would have had to go up the Denna. Or up the Trade Road. And pass us by!" She wrung her hands; so did the little servant girls.

"Why, that is correct, my dear. Ever since you redesigned the garden, your grasp of geography has grown quite surprisingly."

"Pocks on the garden— this is appalling, Felip! To have been *snubbed*! Why on earth would they prefer Cousin Elsie and her, her..."

Rhonso appeared at Donn Felip's elbow with two fresh, cool glasses of tea on a sea-green platter. For some reason, Dame Irona's hairdresser was with him, and as he set down the platter Rhonso said to her, in a quiet but strangely penetrating voice: "My friend Nicolo writes that his mistress, the Domina of Whellengood, takes the advice of her fashionable new protege."

"Oh?" asked the hairdresser, helping Rhonso set out the tea.

"Indeed," replied Rhonso. "She eschews ceremony, instead welcoming her guests into an atmosphere of refreshing authenticity."

"Oh!" exclaimed the hairdresser and, taking Rhonso's arm, departed with him.

Donn Felip and Dame Irona were quiet for a while. They drank the tea. Behind Dame Irona, the little servant girls sipped from imaginary glasses.

At length Donn Felip spoke. "Do you know what, my dear, I just had a thought. I can't imagine what put it into my head, but do you suppose we are just a bit old-fashioned here? I've heard the culture is changing. As it does. Why, even the eminent Doktor Fu wrote about the phenomenon in his—"

"Darling, I'm only a lady and cannot possibly understand Doktor Fu's pheno-mono-minimums. Will you explain?" Dame Irona put her hand on Donn Felip's shoulder; the little servant girls paired up and did the same to one another.

"Well, I think the *new* fashion is to have an atmosphere of refreshing authenticity."

"But are we not authentic?" Dame Irona and the little girls froze in puzzlement.

"I think the term, as it is used, equates to a certain unrefined simplicity, to—" Donn Felip remembered the peasant woman's broad, sensuous back— "to an ardent embrace of the rustic."

Dame Irona clapped her gloves together; from behind her echoed a smaller, sharper-sounding flurry of hands.

"Oh! You mean the poor dear *Poor*, the poor dears!"

Irona de Brewel had enjoyed enough theatricals to know that in fields and tenements dwelled a class of people known as the Poor, and they were audience favorites, the most exciting people of all. The Poor were often in troubled straits, crying out for something or speaking up against something; and after much ado, they never failed to triumph by their wits. If Cousin Elsie made every guest feel as though he or she were living out one of these exhilarating lives, then it stood to reason that they would prefer her hospitality, and wish to keep it somewhat of a delicious secret. After all, if everyone did it, then being Poor would become merely common.

A surge of ambition filled Dame Irona. "Darling. We positively must take part in this authentic new lifestyle. Immediately! Why, if we put our minds to it, we can be more delightfully Poor than anyone!"

"I have the utmost faith in you," said Donn Felip, and in the slant of sunlight through his apartment's tall crystal windows his wife suddenly did look a bit broad and sensuous. "You'll know just how to— to—" he let his voice become gruff— "tell an oik you paid him the seepin' money."

Spots of pink flared into Dame Irona's cheeks.

"Oh, Felip," she said, her eyes growing unusually bright. "That was perfect."

As one of her gloves eased itself under his collar, the other one waved the little servant girls away. "Off with you, little misses. You may go elsewhere until I send for you."

CHAPTER 16

DONN FELIP HELD NO LEVEE THE following day. In fact, he was not seen until after the noon bell, when he and Dame Irona emerged from his apartment for bruncheon, conspicuously tousled and free from ornamentation, as though they might already be taking their first steps toward being Poor.

Under a canvas shade in the garden, flanked by servants and their palm fronds, Kestrella slouched at the bruncheon table. The weight of the world lay upon her: she'd just learned that someone had leaked the true identity of "Gustoph Glint" to the College of Justice mural selection jury; her winning of the commission now seemed hollow. Why, oh why, had she been cursed with all of this money and authority? Artists didn't need any of that. They just needed a nice home, some good food, and plenty of free time to do whatever they felt like doing.

Now and then she jabbed her fork into a plate of swans' eggs and moved them about. She bent under the table to pat Babou, who was purring loudly and chewing on a smoked eel, then sat up to find her parents taking seats opposite her.

Kestrella scowled at them. "You're late. And what *happened* to you?"

Donn Felip and Dame Irona did not reply; the two of them only kicked playfully at one another under the table, chuckling as if they shared some mildly offensive secret.

Kestrella crossed her arms. The gems embroidered on the bodice of her gown flashed just like her eyes.

"Da— is that a costume from one of Mumsy's plays? You look like a, a manual laborer. And Mumsy. Where's your maquillage? I think you two are trying to shock me. Why?"

"Aw, get off our backs," growled Dame Irona, grabbing a piece of shortbread from the bruncheon board. She pushed it lustily into her mouth and chewed hard, the way she imagined someone married to a laborer might, and wiped crumbs from her unpainted face with a hand that bore copious waves and seahorses, but no glove.

"That's right, you— you—" Donn Felip hadn't quite got the swing of it the way Irona had.

" 'Kill-joy'," she whispered to him. "Or else you can say 'party popper'."

Kestrella rolled her eyes. "It's *pepper*, Mumsy. Now tell me what's going on!"

"Very well, young miss. If you must know, your father and I are updating our mode of living into one of refreshing authenticity. Aren't we, Felip?"

"Indeed, we are, dearest. Ah, I mean..." Donn Felip slumped casually in his chair and waved a lazy hand at her. "Hells yessie, li'l Bessie."

Kestrella was thunderstruck. Her arms unfolded. One corner of her rosy mouth turned up.

"And what's more," began Dame Irona. She had taken a bite of redmelon, meaning to spit one of its seeds in a raw, earthy fashion, but instead it just stuck to her chin. "What's more, if we don't become the most authentic people in this whole country, why, I'll— I'll—"

"Be a monkey's brother?" suggested Kestrella, reaching across to pick the seed away.

"Yes, exactly!"

A miracle was happening. The corners of Kestrella's mouth continued to rise. Her fierce eyes began to twinkle. In a moment, her face was transfigured by a sunburst of genuine delight.

"Mumsy! Da! You're really not joking! This is outrageous. It's subversive. It's the most complete assault on entrenched social hierarchy I've ever seen! It's what real artists do! I'm in! What's the plan?"

Unfortunately, Donn Felip and Dame Irona had not thought that far into their project. They could only blink at one another as though expecting something, until Donn Felip said: "Irona. What, exactly, do the Poor *do?* That is, when they're not outwitting the dastardly villains who conspire to keep them down."

"Hmmmm. I seem to recall they work a lot. That is to say, they make things... hush, Kiki, not art. They make boring things. Like..." she scanned the table. "Like bread."

Donn Felip picked up a crumbly, golden piece of shortbread and examined it. A servingmaid had come to refresh their tea and he turned to her, leaning authentically on the table and scratching the back of his neck.

"Say now, lady miss, could you tell me what's in this bread, here?"

"Oooh, spot on, Felip."

The servingmaid, desperately trying to avert her eyes from the spectacle of her disheveled master, replied in something not far from a stammer. "Butter, ah, butter Your High Honor and, and, and flour and sugar and some, some salt."

"Well, much obliged to you, good missie! That's that. Rona. Why don't we start out by baking us up a nice, big loaf of bread? I'll make plans forthwith. I mean— in two shakes of a ram's tail."

"It's *pig,* Da," Kestrella corrected him. "Two shakes of a pigtail. I imagine it refers to a sailor's untrimmed hair."

Dame Irona's expression lit up. "Sailing? Do you think we could—"

"Nah, Ro-ro. Let's just stay with the bread angle. For starters."

"Sure thing, Butterpat."

So far Kestrella had managed to contain herself. But upon the discovery that her parents possessed nicknames, and adorable ones at that, a series of coughing sounds wracked her. She tried to keep her lips pressed together, but she could not; she gave in to laughter and— Ye Gods be praised— found it felt good. So she laughed on, imagining the authentic art she would create when she was finally Poor enough to start enjoying life.

BEFORE INSTITUTING FULL-SCALE AUTHENTICITY AT home, however, the de Brewels decided to rehearse by creating a test environment. Rhonso— under strict orders to "retain the realism"— was sent to purchase property in a district of Coastwall famous for how very Poor it was. The property included a lovely hovel, an outsized outhouse, a drafty barn for draft animals, and a pretty well that did, in fact, work pretty well. The surrounding neighborhood was quickly demolished to create the space for a modest little farm, upon which the de Brewels meant to raise the butter, flour, sugar and salt that were to compose their loaf of bread.

The putative owners of this property, meanwhile, were equally modest: Buddy and Ro-Ro Dabroo, simple bakers who had fled from the Vonn Country after Ro-Ro punched out the dastardly villain who'd slandered her man. Their daughter Ella was an illustrator of medicine-show posters, while their son was off at some wretched school where they served bad tea.

After days of frenzied preparation, the Dabroo family was prepared to move into their new, although yet unfinished, home. Dame Irona's theatrical designers had prepared a vast wardrobe of worn and torn outfits for each of them, as well as a suite of the most delightfully dilapidated furniture: tables with tops made of marble that was gouged

and stained, chairs whose velvet had obviously been brushed in the
wrong direction, and a bed consisting of a wooden frame supporting
a mattress. Kestrella announced that she would sleep sailor-style, in a
piece of cloth hung from the ceiling: how such a thing was possible, her
parents did not know, so they simply threw up their hands, saying well
ain't that just like our Ella.

The great trouble was what to do about the Grand Constable. Kestrella
had pointed out the fact— quite obvious, upon consideration— that
their neighboring Poor would surely recognize him as the proverbial
Man, whose presence was incompatible with the story of Ro-Ro's
being wanted for villain-punching. In fact, upon more consideration
it seemed that the Grand Constable would be something known as a
downer and he should therefore stay away from them. As to the rest of
the de Brewels' houseguests— of which they always seemed to have a
goodly number— surely Rhonso and his underlings could keep them
adequately cared for until Brewel Hall's new, improved lifestyle was
perfected at the farm. Then they'd bring it on home.

"ARE YOU READY, FELIP? I mean, Buddy?" called Ro-Ro. She settled into
her position atop a vast heap of canvas-covered housewares, lashed to a
splintery wagon with scratchy old rope. The wagon was drawn by Ella's
buckskin ponies, who had been transformed into woebegone nags by
the simple expedient of not brushing their tails.

"Hoy, Pappy!" shouted Ella, slapping the ponies' backs with the lines
and wiping maidenroot foam from her chin with the back of one wrist.
"Time to get going!"

Buddy hurried after the wagon and climbed aboard as it rolled. He'd
never done anything so thrilling in his life. Even opening a newly
discovered copy of Grandmaster Bharr's classic *Observations* had not
made his heart beat quite so fast, his breath draw quite so deep, as did

crawling up to the top of the canvas heap for a view of his old home, in all its ivory-tiled splendor, as it disappeared behind him.

CHAPTER 17

IN THE RANCID MAZE OF COASTWALL'S bent warehouses— that is to say, the ones everyone knows, but won't admit, are not really warehouses at all but mere meeting-places for criminals— lay a few that were especial favorites of the Almantree Gang. For secrecy, however, their rotation would change. So by way of example, for a few weeks the heavy-beamed old barn of the Wool Shearers' Guild, with its thick tarred roof and windows boarded up against moths, might be the place to find one of Granny's flunkies; but then suddenly that game would be up, and anyone looking for a flunky there would instead meet a garrote artist, or a worker in fine stiletto needlepoint. Meanwhile, the cognoscenti would be going to the facility of the Tincture Soakers' Union. Thus did Granny keep her competition, small though it was, on their toes.

Granny currently had one of her own flunkies in just such a position: the wight's breeches were hooked up on the wall so he was tip-a-toe just off the ground. He was there to discuss a mission. Which he apparently didn't care to undertake.

Granny scowled. "Why no news from Fliss?"

"Be— be— because I haven't joined his— his— his gang yet. I'm scared, Granny!"

She regarded the long-nosed oaf with disdain. Scared? Well, *that* was as obvious as a curly-tailed dog's bunghole. There must be more to it.

"So yez sayin' Hamflesh weepin' Fliss is scarier than me."

"No! Maybe! You're both— both—"

"Thez no third choice, me mally gentleman. Join Fliss like I esked thee, or else take consequences." And here Granny strolled to a table and began browsing among some things. The wight on the wall couldn't see what they were. She kept talking. "Findin' thee, me mally gentleman: how hard was that fer Granny?"

"Wha— what? What do you mean?"

"I *mean*," growled Granny Almantree, finally deciding upon an object, "dez tha really think thez anywhere in this town— neh, in the whole weepin', seepin', shriveled-up country!— where a wight who don't obey me can hide?"

She held up the object: a dart. Leisurely she took a paintbrush from the table and dabbed something on its point.

"Well?" she demanded.

The man couldn't remember what he was supposed to be agreeing to, or disagreeing with, or whether he should be saying anything at all. He only bleated out a string of ineffectual noises, scrabbling at the wall, at his breeches; he tried to give himself a bounce, so as to dislodge himself from the hook; all to no avail.

"Thez disgraceful," pronounced Granny. "A cryin' brat an' a bad talker. Mebbe the reason yez not joined Fliss is that he won't have thee." She blew on the point of the dart and stepped up to what the man could now see was a line, chalked on the filthy boards of the warehouse floor. Granny's feet were as shapeless as the rest of her, but she appeared quite serious about keeping them in bounds.

"I— I— can! I *can!*" wailed the wight on the hook.

"Can what?"

"Can read."

"Big benny beans! It's neh shakes to Granny if ye can read Donny Fill da Brool's whole pockin' libererry! Question is: can ye join Fliss? Like yer Granny eskt thee?"

"Y- y- y—"

She cocked her arm. "Say it quick or be the bullseye."

"*Yes!*"

Granny grunted in satisfaction and strode toward the man, but somewhere between the line and the wall, a nasty little knife appeared in her lumpy hand. The man let out a high-pitched scream as she reached for him. But he only slumped to the floor in a heap: Granny had split the waist of his breeches. Her laughter was a series of short, croupy bursts, and she stepped on the breeches so they tore still further as the wight tried to scramble away.

"Then it's agreed, me benny bare-tailed rat," she said. "Yez goin' to squeak out a secret or two, bout Mesir Fliss, nex we meet." She lifted her foot. "Pick up an' run. Thez jus disgraceful."

CHAPTER 18

CORVINALIAS HAD BEEN HIGH BEFORE. AT least, he'd thought so.

But now, straining to catch up to the adventurers he'd seen soaring above the clouds, he realized that all his adventures till then had been a question of how *far*. Never in all his life had he truly understood how *tall* the world was.

Up till now, all he clouds he'd ever flown through had been the puffy kind. Sure, everyone knew there were strips of cloudwisp on the ceiling of the sky, but those were like the sun and the moon: outside the world. On the rare occasion that anything was seen flying into cloudwisp, it was generally understood to be an optical illusion, like a mirage. Corvinalias had never even considered trying to reach those clouds, much less follow some mirage people who seemed to be flying above them. But once he got started, he saw no reason to turn back.

Up he'd gone, to a normal height, where the fields and hedges of the Whellen Country underneath him were quilted pieces of various greens and browns; where rivers were bluish-brown streaks fringed with the roofs and pathways of Uman dwellings; and where other winged people, some of them fairly civilized and some mere darting, staring barbarians, crisscrossed his path. But then he'd gone higher.

The air had been cleaner up there, the other people fewer and more polite, the configurations of earth below him more diagrammatic. This was the height from which scholars of Corvinalias's people observed the world for the purpose of scratching maps. Lower Cloudyblue had an excellent collection of maps on the trunk of the northeast sector, just above Whorl Four: some of them had been re-engraved for so long that they were out of date; Uncle Jey and the Rokonomas argued over whether they should be kept that way for future generations. Map height was where Corvinalias had flown on his previous adventures,

gazing and memorizing as his old schoolmaster had taught him—
except, of course, when he returned to Ata Maroo's boat to eat, roost
and preen with her, her mate and their whales. It was a good height. But
now he went higher still.

He passed through a few puffy clouds and the land below him began
to look a little bit hazy. No good for mapping. At the edges of his
vision, something began to waver and glow. Corvinalias realized he
was breathing harder, as if the day were humid and he'd flown a long,
long time. But he hadn't been gone for that long at all, and there was
no sign of impending rain. The air was just not as good here anymore.
That's why nobody flies here, he thought. But then he looked up and
spied the adventurers, unnervingly high above him, moving as easily
as waterbugs on a pond, their white bodies nearly motionless between
pairs of black-tipped wings and their long white necks pointed into
some distant unknown.

Corvinalias concentrated on his breathing. One-two, one-two. His ribs
were still a little sore from the squeezing the baby Uman had given
him, but deep breathing soon massaged the feeling away. He puffed
himself out, clenched himself in, drawing gulps of the clean and now
decidedly chilly air into position, through his lungs, and out. Still the
adventurers soared far above him. Clenching his jaw and ignoring the
roar of the wind in his ears, he adjusted the angle of his wings and went
even higher.

Suddenly the wavering glow he'd noticed at the limits of his vision
snapped like a bubble. The edge of the world leaped into view, clear and
bright, rimmed with pale blue against something darker. The sight of it
almost stopped his heart. He'd heard some Scientific Institute lectures
speculating that the world might be an object and not a space, but that
was only a possibility for scholars to scratch about and argue over— not
a fact hanging there below him, outlined like a pearl, raising the very
real possibility that people could fly off the world entirely and lose it
altogether. Afraid of what he might see, Corvinalias forced himself

to look up again— and there were the adventurers, both of them, flying, living.

One of them turned his— or her— head.

With an unintelligible shout, the adventurer held his— or her— wings half shut. He— or she— fell, fell, quicker than a raindrop, thrown back by the roaring air, fell into position beside Corvinalias and almost knocked him down when he— or she— outstretched those vast snowy black-tipped wings.

"Sorry! Forgive! I no mean hit!"

The adventurer's voice had a penetrating, trumpeting quality like the voice of a goose. His accent was strange but the language was undeniably correct. As Corvinalias struggled to gather enough breath for a reply, he studied the fellow.

His beak was short and dark, jutting from a featherless red face that gave him a monastic look. He blinked pale golden eyes at Corvinalias and shouted, "You good, magpie gent? What you up here why?"

"I want— to— follow you!"

"Why you want this? Magpie never go more far than back there." The adventurer gestured with his long graceful neck, pointing backward at the Heart of Stone down in a valley of the Whellen Country. "You lose mate? Something happen?"

"No. Just— for— adventure."

The adventurer's laugh was a note like one of the pipes Umans danced to. "We bad for you then. Mate and I, not adventure people. We late for summer trip to visit fer-lock. You come with us, fer-lock will laugh at you, call you slow flyer. We are old, you see."

Old? Left behind? Ye Gods, Corvinalias was working hard enough already. If they ever caught up to this flock, their pace would kill him. Maybe he should give this up. Wasn't he already outside the world? Wasn't that already an adventure?

The old fellow beside him flew politely while Corvinalias fought the idea of giving up and, in the end, defeated it.

"I don't— mind. Can I? Come?"

"Yes! Welcome, magpie gent! Listen, there is air river." He pointed up into the wild dark blue. "We go in, flying is easier. You ready? It easier, I promise. Big push now! Up, up. We go!"

CHAPTER 19

FOR A WIGHT WHO'D ALWAYS MADE his living by running, a year at sea is a strange absence from reality, even without all the swimming and fishing and occasional incidents of near-destruction by the wrath of a measureless ocean. But the wait had done Alvert a power of good. Under the care of his new wife, his lank, perpetually harried, ill-fed weatherbeaten aspect had mellowed into a striking sculptural leanness, and what was more: the foot he'd broken had healed.

Sound again, with solid land under him, Alvert ran with great zesty joy.

Of course he slowed down a lot for Maroo. She wasn't much of a runner, having spent half her life riding or driving oxen. She laughed a lot at her own slow going, but still she managed to follow Alvert as day by day they explored New Port Ata, the capital of Wahayee.

"Left, *ipo*, left!" or "Go up hill, ah," she would shout to him as his new pigskin shoes flashed over the black cobbles. They might even stop, while Maroo caught her breath and pointed out places she remembered.

"This another one of our warehouse, ah. And that workshop there make our whale harness. Or maybe it sail loft. One or other. Oh! Look down at harbor, *ipo*. There: Papa and one of his sister bringing in shipment. You see? That not very big one, only two whale pulling raft of six barge. Look like load of sugar loaf, from isle call Nennai. Or maybe sugar cane isle is Wowmi. I forget. But it important place, ah? Two sugar mill, four rum distillery..."

And then, whatever Maroo said, she would often end with "...it all right, *ipo*, you do not need to say or do anything. They only looking."

This was because, whenever Alvert stopped running, passers-by would slow down and stare at him, nodding their heads firmly or perhaps even breaking stride to bow. Just as Maroo had warned him, he often heard the word that meant 'god'. But no one disturbed him about it; the citizens of Wahayee were polite.

After their wanderings of New Port Ata, Alvert and Maroo would return to the big house with the cloud whale on the canvas wall. Alvert liked this painting. It resembled the rugs people used back in Yondstone— except about a hundred times bigger, an' wove from some kind o' jute instead o' goat's wool, wi' a black and white whale, not a brown cow, that had long spiral ivory tusks instead o' horns. It was comforting to find something so exactly like the art of his native land.

At the Ata home, people were always coming and going. Whenever they reached the top of the great wooden staircase and stepped into the deep and breezy shade, they would find Maroo's mother engaged in some intense conversation, and if Alvert slowed down too much on the way to Maroo's rooms, people would ask his mother-in-law to bring him over. Then the people would show him platters of ham, or roast chicken, or fat red slices of the fish known as hot-heart, and also some of the many kinds of fruit— it seemed there were thousands— that grew in these parts. They did this so often that one day, Alvert finally smiled and bowed, and took a chicken leg.

His taking of it threw the man who had offered the platter into an expression of dread. He cried out as though someone had jabbed him with a fishhook. Maroo had to do a lot of talking, and a lot of gesturing toward Alvert's face, before she hurried him away back to her rooms.

"All right, *ipo*," she said, lowering the canvas door behind the servant who had drawn them a scented cool bath. "It time for a talk. Most people in Peaceful Ocean worship god that look like you, ah? You know this already. Like you remember very first thing happen when I meet you."

How could Alvert possibly forget? He had been running through a crowd in the town of Good Market, in a thunderstorm, chasing a magpie that had stolen the message bag he was supposed to be taking to Dame Elsebet de Whellen. In the middle of a blinding blast of lightning, he had run whump into the side of an enormous bull— a bull upon which was riding the Ox-Train Queen, richest shipping operator in the Kingdom, a tall wide magnificent dark golden woman with a sweep of hair blacker than the storm and a grip as strong as the feelings that had flooded through him. She had taken Alvert's hand and pulled him up and told him to come along with her because... she wished to offer him meat and fruit. Aha. It dawned on him then.

"So you actually thought I was—"

Maroo pushed Alvert into the scented cool tub, new silk kilt and pigskin shoes and all, and jumped in along with him. Her sarong floated up all around them in a cloud of brilliant flowers. Between laughs and kisses she said:

"*Ipo*. I not stupid. I knew you were living man. But habit so strong, ah? You. Look. Like. Him." With every word she planted a kiss on his big nose, big chin, big brow. "And people here, we worship by giving offering and telling our problem."

She settled herself into Alvert's extensive lanky embrace. "Two kind of problem in life, ah? Fruit problem and meat problem. With fruit problem, when time is ripe, answer fall into our hand. It true that if we try fixing fruit problem too soon it still bitter, or if we ignore it too long we find everything rotten. But fruit problem usually easier one.

"Meat problem not so easy. With this one, solution will hurt somebody— like for meat, some animal have to die. And maybe it hard to find right animal, maybe we afraid of it, or feel sorry for it...*ai!* This much bigger trouble.

"Worst trouble of all come if we confuse two kind: hunt and slaughter animal, when it really only fruit problem— or wait and wait, never admitting it meat problem, while animal grow and grow too big to kill.

So for prayer, we tell our problem to One Who Listens, ah? We put out offering, and we hear ourself talk, and we think."

This was interesting and Alvert would have thought about it himself, but now Maroo was making waves in a way that rendered thinking quite impossible. He raised his hands from the flowery water, pushed them into the flow of her hair and met her eyes just as a small bell rang at their doorway.

"Ah, boilsores," growled Maroo.

The voice of her mother, Ata Steera, came from behind the canvas door. "*Ipo*, someone important is here. Get yourself ready and meet us in the reception chamber."

"Oh, Mother. Quit calling it a *reception chamber*. You just mean the front room."

"Wherever the Headmother is, that's the reception chamber." Steera's voice sweetened into a singsong. "You can bring your husband."

"I don't think Alvie needs to be gaped at any more today. But fine. I'll be with you soon."

"Make it *very* soon, Maroo. This is someone you should remember, who's come a long way to see you. What a loss of face it would be, if this went wrong."

CHAPTER 20

I N THE SPACE OF A FEW days, Fred transformed himself— as thoroughly as a clump of silk turns into a magnificent, glittering rainbow of the night. Except in his case, the change was for the worse.

Telling the de Brewels that he was off to some faraway grotto for a meditation retreat with other mystics, Brother Malfred sequestered himself with the Grand Constable and learned all the ins and outs of the undercover officer trade.

Together they crafted his new persona. Fred drew on his decades of experience as the Royal Fool and all the upper-level Fools' Guild certifications he had earned— most of them were exactly equivalent to Players' Guild; the only difference was that Players were expected to know about costume, false-face makeup and set design, while Fools specialized in creating personal interactions. He expanded on many of his own characteristics, and listened intently as the Grand Constable taught him a dictionary's worth of criminal slang. Then finally, unhappily, Fred had folded away his wardrobe of fine silk shirts and overcloaks, richly embroidered doeskin breeches and bespoke dress boots of lizard, shagreen, and eel. He allowed the Grand Constable to badly shear his hair, let his cheeks grow coarse and stubbly, and crawled into a ratty old linen smock and moth-holed woolen trews that were just as bad, if not worse, than the ones he'd been wearing when he'd been a vagabond.

Now he was a former miner. Just like last year's Fred, this fellow had been ousted from the Isle of Gold— although in the case of his new persona, it was for thievery rather than sass. This wight had found himself unable to cope with vagabond life, and had tried seeking employment with some of Granny Almantree's worthless, petty rivals. But alas, he'd angered them. He'd earned himself a smarting, dirty handprint on one cheek— applied by the Grand Constable in a manner

Fred found unnecessarily condescending— and a mass of bruises elsewhere: these, Fred ingeniously applied to himself by asking the Grand Constable to fill a ballroom with wooden furniture, then rushing in blindfolded and doing ten minutes' worth of cartwheels in it.

He was ready. His mission began.

On the fateful night, somewhere in the crime-ridden, grime-bitten part of Coastwall, a sedan chair lumbered to a halt. Its tatty curtains writhed with some muffled altercation. Out of the chair flew a bruised, slapped, woebegone man with no remaining means of supporting himself except that which, for a man with self-respect, was lowest of all that's low: selling his intellectuals to any wench with coins. Yes, as a streetcorner singer.

"Uh-hem. H-hem." Fred cleared his throat a bit and stayed in the shadows. The moon was only the merest sliver and in that part of town, street lamps numbered nil. His whole world was the few feet he could see up a grimy lane that stank of trash and stray dogs. But every now and then a glitter passed by, and it was the hilt of some bravo's knife or some trinket she dared to adorn herself with.

"H-hhem. Goodwife, I adore you..."

"Not interested."

"There you are, my love..."

"Pus off, lousebag."

"What a vision you are, oh dearest..."

"Yah, all right. I've got a penny. Make it good." The wench who stepped up to Fred smelled like a ditch full of onions and what little he could see of her seemed to include a broken nose and a mat of hair that had been cut with a sickle.

"Call me 'Honey-bon'. On account I'm—"

"Sweet, yes," Fred agreed. Gods, he could actually taste her reek.

"—called Bon. Did I tell ya ta start, fellow? Shut it till I give ya th picture. Right, call me Honey-bon, sing about my bottom, an say yer name is Rodge. Go."

Fred normally did possess an excellent voice. But now it was rough and strangled as he began: "Sweet, sweet, honey Honey-bon..."

"Get to the part about my bottom."

"...sweetest little can I ever got my hands on..."

"It's big! Big!"

"...bigger than a barrelhead of sweet, sweet wine... O to me, I mean uh, *Rodge*, there's nothin' near as fine..."

Hearing only a grunt of approval, Fred felt confident he was on the right track. He wailed more of this drivel, watching the lumpy silhouette of his customer as she swayed, and told himself he was only playing a character. Somehow he kept himself at it until he could finish with "... heedin' passion's call... givin' it my all... up against a wall with my tall Honey-bon."

There was a pause. For a terrifying moment Fred thought the song might actually inspire her to action. But she only laughed— or perhaps it was a belch— and gave him a companionable swat on the chin before turning to leave.

"Wait! What about the penny?"

The answering belch was already halfway down the street. "Nex time ask for it first, oaf. 'To Rodge, mmmm, Rodge there's nothin' near as fine'…"

As her awful singing faded away, Fred sighed. He swallowed, took a deep breath, shuffled his boots, plucked at the laces of his smock's greasy neckhole. He'd call out again in a minute. Just a minute.

In the darkness someone sidled up to him and sounded a deep, crystal-clear carillon of laughter. Whoever it was didn't stink, either; she only had a smell of wholesome exertion.

"Poor you. Singing to Bon Hullitt. And don't tell me the money's good— I saw what she did there."

"At least I sharpened up my lying skills."

Fred's visitor laughed again. Sure, his falsehood detector was sounding the five-bell alarm, because of course this person couldn't be anything but a crook— but her laughter had a melody that wasn't false at all. He was just wondering if she might be his type when she took his arm and pulled him into the wan moonlight for a look-over.

"Well, win a few lose a few. I liked your voice, though."

She was lean and broad-shouldered, with the kind of face most people would find pretty. At some sound she turned to look sharply up the street; then down. For good measure she also gazed overhead, into the sparsely lit windows of the slums that seemed to hunch over the street. A dog ran by with a squirming rat in its mouth.

"In fact, fellow, I liked your voice so much I'm going to make you a business offer."

Here it comes, thought Fred. She wants to be my manager, take half of what I earn and charge me an astonishingly moderate fee to safeguard the rest. And if I say no I'll be singing through a new gap in my teeth. Oh, well, it could be worse. Honey-Bon might want an encore.

"I need someone to put on a show while I harvest brass."

Put on a show? That sounded easy. The Grand Constable never said he had to sell himself short.

"Well then, Goodwife, you've found your man. With me putting on your show, you could harvest silver. At least."

Her eyes opened wide and one corner of her mouth creased her cheek.

"A confident one. I like it. But I'd rather stay in the modest neighborhoods, just the same. Let's go somewhere and talk." She led Fred by the wrist in a way that was friendly, but quite obviously could make an abrupt change into something painful.

"You're new around here."

"In a way. I've been…"

"Letting the Harbor Street Mob hand-decorate your face and play a kick drum solo on everything below your neck?"

Fred was impressed with the groundwork the Grand Constable had laid. "How'd you guess?"

"I saw you fall out of a chair." She jerked a thumb over her shoulder. "Besides, there's not a lot we don't hear. So what's your real name, Rodge? I only need the first one."

"Fred."

"Short for Malfred, or Frednick?"

"Frednick."

"Well, Fred, you can call me Dok." She laughed again. "Because I might not know how to read a single word, but I've got a Doktor Magistre in fingerwork from the University of never even knew it was missing."

Fred stopped in his tracks, which almost pulled Dok off her balance. He smiled up at her with great delight. "Really? I have that same degree. What year were you?"

In his time with the Royal family, his skills had expanded far beyond the acrobatic stunts that had first attracted the attention of the Old King. Back-flipping, hand-springing, wisecracking thirteen-year-old novice monk Fred had become a certified Fool of all stripes, as much at home performing classical dances and crooning sentimental songs as writing poems and pulling off conjuring tricks— also known as sleight-of-hand maneuvers. Prestidigitation. The frolly fingers. If this goodwife wanted to harvest brass, why...

"By my god, you're good. Show me that move again," said Dok as she pushed another tot of rank mariners' rum across the table to Fred. The tavern she had taken him to was on the waterfront, where Granny's mob had an undeniable presence among the longshoremaids and stevedores.

"What move?" and he showed her both sides of his hands, spread his fingers apart, pulled up his sleeves. "Uh-oh. You left something there."

He pointed at the damp ring the glass of rum had left on the table; in its center lay a brass penny. Dok snatched it up and laughed.

Her laughter is the only nice thing in the whole filthy place, thought Fred. Other than her smile, of course. Most people like her kind of smile.

CHAPTER 21

THE BETTER PARTS OF COASTWALL HAD oil lamps, hanging above the streets and squares from thick wooden posts that seemed to have begun life as ships' masts. These lamps shed their light upon the doings of better people, who patronized better taverns, wore better clothes and— what was of far more interest to Dok and her kind— carried more valuables.

Fred, dressed up in a well-worn jester's cap with a long striped tassel and with a properly folded— but blank— sheet of paper pinned to his shoulder to simulate a Fools' Guild license, was holding an impressively large crowd in thrall. It was near midnight. The ladies and gentlemen in this particular square were well primed with drink from the better taverns, ready for a few laughs at foolery and a few gasps at daring. Fred offered them great heaping helpings of both, pulling off wild stunts on the tables and chairs one tavern-keeper had set out and cracking joke after uproarious joke. He felt himself floating on familiar waves, hearing himself as if from afar, directing his movements the way he imagined Kestrella must direct her paintbrush. This was it, this was the feeling that made it all worthwhile. For a moment he wished Corvinalias were there: the show could have been even funnier with an assistant. But— Fred reminded himself as he whistled a hornpipe, did a mariners' jig and juggled three, then four, then five, pewter drinking cans— right now *he* was the assistant. The crowd had no idea what the real performance was.

Dok, carrying a half-empty can of grog and apologizing for her clumsiness, lurched her way through their midst. Ladies glared as she stepped on their boots, gentlemen pushed her as she backed into them, and by the third time someone had threatened to call a town officer she had reached the front of the crowd and was shouting at Fred.

"Is them cans empty?" she cried. "Can ya cartwheel while ya sing me somethin? Hoy, fella, flip over here an I'll show ya where to stick yer landing!"

The ladies and gentlemen near Dok resented this. They shoved her away. She shoved back. A ball of angry patrons formed around her and, like bees ousting an intruder from their hive, they hustled her to the edge of the crowd; but now the spell was broken and all the fun was gone. In moments Fred's audience thinned, and although a few of them apologized as they left and dropped brass pennies and silver bits into his hand, it looked as though the entertainment hadn't been much of a success.

Looked that way.

Fred knew what really had transpired, and so it was with great eagerness that he slouched into the nearest tavern, as slowly and unhappily as possible. He reached the back of the taproom and caught the barmaid's eye. She kicked the corner of a cabinet and it opened inward, just like Dok told him it would, hidden from view in the darkness. Fred crouched and disappeared through the opening. With a soft thump, the door pulled shut behind him and he stood up in a hidden back room.

"Very neatly done," said Dok, rising from a threadbare upholstered bench.

She looked frowzy and drunken. Her sash was beginning to uncoil, one leg of her pantaloons was hanging outside her boot and her robe was pulled so far askew that its lapel crossed under her armpit and strained tight across her enormous bosom. At this, Fred did a double take.

Dok hooked one hand under her displaced lapel. "Ready to check out my goods?"

She gave a sharp tug. Her linen-covered mounds bulged out at Fred in an alarming rush and as she bounced they rained coins, handkerchiefs, purses, gloves, spectacles, smoke-boxes and even a reading lens. When she was smooth and lean again, Dok fell back on the bench and laughed.

"Ye Gods! If you'd only seen your face!"

"I've— uh, I've just never peeped such a bodey bump of winnings."

Dok laughed some more and picked something from the heap on the floor of the back room: a handsome silver flask. She stuck it into the pocket of her sleeve. "Go on," she said with a chuckle. "Pick yourself a prize from the... ha ha! The 'bodey bump'. I'll count it as your commission."

As Fred kneeled and dug into the pile of pilferage, Dok unwound her sash and removed her robe. The tunic and pantaloons underneath it were nondescript plain linen, but the inside of her sash and the lining of her robe were in colors and patterns as different from the reverse as a trout and a tree. She tied the sash with a new kind of knot, pulled both pantaloon legs out over her boots, repurposed her empty fake bosom as a turban and by the time Fred had chosen his prize— an intricately stitched eelskin wallet— Dok might as well have been a complete stranger. Even her face looked somehow different: colder, more imperious.

"Mind me now, Fool," she began. Then she winked, and the old Dok was with him again. "I mean Fred. Push our loot into that locker over there in the corner, and give this back to me when you're done with it."

She tossed him a little brass key and watched him cache the prizes. Fred considered keeping the coins the crowd had given him, but only briefly: Dok might be pretty but Fred had seen plenty of pretty creatures that had sharp fangs. Kestrella's Lily for example— as he recalled the snake, a chill ran up his spine; but as he recalled its owner, a thrill ran from his heart in quite the other direction. He put the coins in the locker.

"Good." Dok took the key back and tucked it into some unseen pocket. "This tavern is run by a friend. One of many— I've got dens like this all over, guarded by chums that take only a little bit of a cut. Now. Mesir Frednick. Are you ready for *your* debut on the stage of the frolly fingers?"

"Uh, sure. Just one thing. Would you, um, mind... lighting my dip?"

"Oho! Another piece of slang from olden times. Light your dip, eh. Maybe later— for right now, you only need to know you're working for me. Unless you'd rather part ways?" Dok raised one eyebrow.

Fred bent down as if to buckle his boot. But really he just didn't want Dok to see his face turning red— gods, he'd almost botched himself out of this job. The Grand Constable would have been furious. How much more of that fellow's slang was from olden times? But when he stood back up, he was suavity itself.

"Never, oh nursemaid of those sweet little twins, cash and plunder. I'm with you. I just wondered who else we'd have to give a cut of this to."

"Ah, ah. Don't get curious. 'If idle questions were but horns, then we'd have no nullicorns'. Do you need any last-minute instructions?"

Fred did not. He assured Dok that he could handle lifting a few simple prizes from the patrons of the tavern, and do it so neatly that they wouldn't discover they'd been clipped till long after they went home. But when the time came for him to pull his tricks— Great God Almighty, it was harder than he thought it would be.

For one thing, many of the patrons were hard to approach. This tavern was full of bentwood stools and high tables, all crammed into little nooks and snugs and cozy corners. In the iron chandeliers above, candles were thankfully few, but this advantage was canceled by the unhelpful fact that each table had its own individual tallow dip, lighting up the drinkers a bit too much for Fred's comfort. He brushed against a few patrons as they walked back and forth to the bar, but succeeded in getting his fingertips down only one pocket; its owner turned and glared. One gentleman had a pen-case sticking so far out of his sleeve that Fred was able to lift it by the simple expedient of pretending to recognize the man and shaking his hand— but that was the only thing he'd managed to lift, and he was now almost to the front door.

Through a fug of tallow smoke and dissipating rings from patrons' pipes, he noted that Dok was hardly exerting herself at all. She sat at her ease, chatting with the barmaid who'd let them under the counter, now and then throwing back her linen-wrapped head and laughing. Suddenly she sprang to her feet, frantically patting her sleeves, her sides, her bodice. She whirled and pointed straight through the busy taproom at Fred.

"He's getting away!" she shouted. "Out the front door! Thief!"

Fred could jump far higher than most other people, and land on his feet from almost any trajectory. He thanked his god for that. He knew he was leaping from place to place, zagging through the crowd like a hare chased by a pack of highcats, but it all seemed unreal. He felt someone just miss grabbing his collar. Then he was through the door, ramming his way down the street past neatly dressed ladies and gentlemen, then past common wights and wenches, then past streetcorner singers and sailors who were decidedly lost in a fog. He didn't know Coastwall. The streets were a puzzle. The hue and cry behind him had been taken up and more and more pursuers were joining in.

He'd been chased before, of course. When he'd been a vagabond it had happened with dispiriting regularity. But it had been a long time and he was out of practice. His old vagabond self would surely never have been so trusting as to follow the grubby little street brat who rushed up beside him as swiftly as a fellow hare, took his hand and pulled him into the gap behind a loose panel that covered the front of a vacant building. But rookie pickpocket Fred did follow, and in a moment he was in a dim room full of greasy, lumpy mattresses, a few irritated crooks, a tumbledown cookstove and the street brat and Dok.

He lunged at her in a rage.

"Easy, easy, easy!" Dok repeated, trying to calm him, holding his flailing arms down tight to his sides. "By my god, you're strong for a fellow. Fred. *Fred.* Slow down."

"You snake! You, you, turncoat!"

"Hush, shush. I'm sorry. I'm so sorry. It's just— it was too good a chance to miss! Didn't you see it? Half of that tavern was a party from the Secondhand Clothiers' Guild annual meeting. The minute they chased you out the door, they left behind a thousand bits' worth of silk overcloaks. My friend and I had about ten seconds to stuff them all down the hidey hole. Easy, easy, now." Dok's hands slid around to Fred's back and she pulled him to her, lowering her cheek against his head so that, though she kept her voice very soft, he could hear her through his skull. "My fault, shhh, my fault. I'm bringing you into this too fast."

Fred nodded and felt his arms floating up to wrap around Dok. Damn it deep! He squirmed away from her. The brat was staring at him.

"What do *you* want?" he barked. The brat flashed a mouthful of dirty baby teeth and disappeared into the shadows.

Dok spoke up. "Listen, I know what'll make you feel better. Let's have a sip."

She settled onto the least filthy mattress and reached into her sleeve pocket for the handsome silver flask she'd chosen as her prize earlier that evening. But Fred didn't take the bait. He retreated to the soot-blackened opposite wall.

"Three times three hells I will! It's probably poison!"

Dok looked hurt. "All right, I deserved that." She sniffed the flask and tested a sip. "Rum. Not that cheap rot we drank when we were just getting to know each other, Fred— this is prime stuff, good sugar cane from the Ocean Empire. Gods, I should sell this, it's almost full." She put the flask away and patted the mattress beside her.

"Don't be afraid of me. You'd have done the same, wouldn't you? If you'd seen all that money just itching to get lifted? We're not brats, Fred. We know why we're playing this game— don't we? It's for the garnish, me benny wight. Neh?"

One of the crooks huddled near the stove croaked, "I'll drink that rum if yer man don't want it, Dok." The others chimed in with the same request. As she answered them all, kindly but firmly, Fred thought it over.

By his god, she was right. In her place, he would have done the same. No two ways about it. And it really was pretty thrice-damned funny. Imagine all those kings of the rag trade, coming back to find their fancy plumage had flown away!

Fred listened to the crooks jawing to one another and thought some more. The Grand Constable had warned him that he'd never be allowed into Granny's presence until he'd proved himself in the lower strata. Here was as good a place to start as any. And really, the only clean place in that whole hideous sty was beside Dok, so he might as well go sit there.

"Hoy, Frednick," she said, nudging him with her elbow. "You're all right. Once you catch on, I think I can really use you. I hope you stay."

Fred gave a grunt that could have meant anything. He was careful not to look at her too much, but all the same he knew she was smiling in that wry, half-serious way; even her breathing sounded only half serious, as though she were amused by some universal spectacle.

Someone boiled tea on the cookstove. The night was sweltering, but there was no ice and no one wanted to wait until the tea cooled, so they drank it hot. The crooks groused and bragged and sighed whenever a breeze crept through the room's tiny, high window; their talk was an interesting little education, but nothing Fred heard gave him any better idea of whether Dok would, or even could, lead him to Granny.

The night crawled on. The breeze picked up and almost drove the heat away. And then Fred was tired, tired enough to lie down on one side of the only mildly grimy mattress, and let Dok press her back against his as they slept, and have a dream where he couldn't tell if the woman in it was her or Kestrella.

CHAPTER 22

KING ENRICK GRIPPED THE TURNED WOODEN railing with both hands and leaned out over it— further, further, until Dame Elsebet really felt forced to warn him.

"Please take care, Your Majesty!"

She had to shout, because the textile mill was so noisy. Down on the floor below the observation deck, dozens of looms rattled and roared, each with a chain of drilled leather slats stepping to a stately dance above thousands of metal rods and shafts that pranced like an army of trained centipedes. On a beam before each machine, a huge bolt of cloth grew thicker and thicker at an astonishing rate. This cloth was soon to become the latest clothing fashionable in the Whellen Country, where citizens often changed their minds about clothing, or else become picnic pavilions, flour sacks, carrying bags, draperies or bedding or horse blankets, or any of the other myriad woven and knit and felted things that changed hands at markets on the Whellen Country's twice-weekly holidays.

The King did not reply. In fact, he leaned out further still. The knot at the collar of his shirt dangled straight down. Dame Elsebet had just decided she would grab him and pull him back, King or no King, when the Queen shouted too.

"Sweetheart! Come here!"

King Enrick straightened up, turned and went to his wife's side. Dame Elsebet let out the long breath she hadn't realized she was holding in.

"Her High Honor was telling you to stop doing something!" Queen Margadet shouted. "When people say 'take care', that's what they mean! What were you doing?"

"I was watching it go back forth up down back forth up down it moves fast that is for sure whatever it is moves really fast!"

Little Prince Nedward, tight in his mother's arms, reached out toward the factory floor, waving his limbs about in clear imitation of the machine.

"Listen, Ama! Making a big BIG blankie!"

One of the looms stopped. Two workmaids with scissors came to cut the cloth free and Nedward, overcome with triumph at seeing a task completed, giggled and squirmed so wildly that Margadet nearly dropped him. "All done, Ama, all done! Looky, Da-da!"

But Enrick ignored the women shouldering the huge, colorful bolt of cloth and lugging it away. He continued to stare at the now-empty loom.

"Margadet why did it stop I am surprised it would stop it was moving so fast!"

"Nedward says it's finished making the cloth!"

"What cloth all I see is a lot of string there are a lot of machines here we saw a lot of machines today didn't we Margadet this country is very full of machines!"

Dame Elsebet, only a few feet away, couldn't hear what he was saying. But she had the distinct feeling that the King wasn't impressed by his tour of the Whellen Country's industries.

She had taken the Royals to mills where grain moved from hopper to grindstone in a series of mechanized buckets, where ore was stamped by a line of dancing hammers, where iron and charcoal, limestone and mirror-stone burned together in a gigantic egg-shaped furnace until workmaids poured out a fiery white river of steel; she'd taken them to buildings full of lathes and potters' wheels; to a factory where a substance Prophessors had recently developed— a substance that was not glass but could be made to look just like it— was spun into thread finer than the finest silk; and even, finally, to a factory where still more Prophessors combined various secret liquids, whirling them in a huge drum until it wept droplets of the artificial firewyrm saliva that brightened night-time streets all over the Whellen Country.

But to Dame Elsebet's dismay, His Majesty was unmoved.

True, he'd watched some of the machines for a very long time, particularly the ones with obvious moving parts. But he had made no comment at all on the products they turned out, or how the manufacture of them would make the Whellen Country an asset to the Kingdom. A small sad voice at the back of her mind suspected that he might never do so; perhaps that was what happened when one's ancestors displeased the Crown. The damage might be permanent.

But there was a final wonder left in store. Dame Elsebet did her breathing exercises for a few more moments, pressed her marbled steel coronet more firmly into her coiffure, and strode to the Royals' side, shouting over the din of the looms.

"Now it is time, Your Majesties, to learn just what powers all the ingenious works we've visited today! We call it the Heart of Stone! Come, let's get back in the coach— the Heart is very big, so we'll need to go some distance up a mountain in order to..." she glanced at the Queen in dismay. "...to, understand, to..."

Margadet put her hand on Dame Elsebet's shoulder. "To see it. It's all right. You can describe it to me."

The power carriage was a new invention, still far too difficult to handle in mountain country; instead they rode in a machine powered by both a spring engine and horses. Coach, passengers, driver and the two archers guarding them crept higher and higher up a narrow switchback road where the horses had to pull with precise care. Broad shady trees gave way to those with slim white trunks and tiny, shimmering golden leaves and below them spread a valley, touched with gold from the sunset. Finally, at a perilously narrow overlook, Dame Elsebet ordered the driver to rein up and she said to the King:

"I won't suggest exiting the coach. But please, Your Majesty— trade places with me. Sit here by the window and look." To the Queen she said: "We are high above the valley where most of the factories were. Down in the center is the Heart of Stone. It's a monolith, a piece of limestone with a footprint big enough to cover a town." Then, quite without meaning to, Dame Elsebet suddenly inhaled; the King was leaning dangerously far out the window.

The Queen spoke up.

"Sweetheart. Something has frightened Dame Elsebet— is it you? Remember, *take care.* That means stop whatever you're doing."

The King settled back into the coach and announced: "I see a lot of rocks they look like fins sticking up from the ground but which one is the heart and why does a heart have a footprint a heart is not a foot."

Dame Elsebet pointed. "The Heart is the biggest one. The pink one. You may think it's doing nothing. But if you watch it for long enough..." she trailed off and let him watch, waiting for the moment, the brilliant moment, experienced by everyone who beheld the Heart of Stone.

All those who gazed upon its noble salmon-colored expanse, upon the shadows formed by its surface undulations, upon the stunted trees that clung to it, sooner or later would suddenly discover its secret and react. They might cry "ah!", or let out a sigh, or clap their hands together in amazement...

"You are right it is pink and I do think it is doing nothing thank you you are right."

Dame Elsebet felt like she'd stepped in a hole.

"Please, Sire. Watch a little longer." The wait, oh Ye Gods the wait.

The wait drew out until finally the King said: "You are right thank you I do think it is doing nothing thank you you are right."

In desperation Dame Elsebet turned to the Queen. "Your Majesty, please give me your hand again. The Heart does this—" she moved Margadet's smooth young fingers into an upright position, pointing them toward the upholstered ceiling of the coach, and then, holding her hand gently by the wrist, Dame Elsebet made it turn.

Queen Margadet's face, which up till then had been a blank, burst into a smile so warm it made little Prince Nedward squeal for joy.

"So it's a wheel," she whispered. "A wheel the size of a town..."

A breeze from the valley blew the curtains of the coach inward upon the King, who continued looking at the Heart of Stone much as he had looked at the empty loom. Before he could say anything Dame Elsebet seized the moment and continued, to the Queen:

"Yes, Your Majesty, a wheel! A vast wheel, surrounded by a circle of water. And because the stone is narrow when seen edgewise, as it turns it appears to wax and wane, like the moon. Or beat, like a heart. Hence the name. And though I don't pretend to know how they do it— I am only an old woman— my engineers capture power from it. Somehow they take the slow turning of the Heart and they speed it up, send it to all of those factories, turn it into pottery and cloth and steel and wyrmlight and *time*, your Majesty, time for my people to do more and be more than they otherwise could." She realized that she'd been talking faster and faster, with a thrill in her soul like the one she'd felt as a youngster, when the tall grass rustled and the hounds started baying and her pony felt ready to fly. "My country can be useful to you, Your Majesty, valuable! Let us prove ourselves. Let us—"

"Margadet what are you and Her High Honor talking about I think bugs are coming in the window it's getting dark I hope we're done with this now it's getting dark."

"Oh! I do beg pardon." Dame Elsebet reached up and thumped on the ceiling; the booted feet of the archers, in their jump seats on the roof of the coach, withdrew from sight at the top of the window and, with a whistle from the coachmaid, the horses took off back to Whellengood.

As the coach picked its way through the lush dimness of a broadleaf forest and the wyrmlight globes hanging from the ceiling flickered to life, Dame Elsebet opened a basket filled with sandwiches.

"I know dinner will be very late. So I brought this tidbit for Your Majesties. Smoked mutton and ham. For Prince Nedward, may I suggest a few candied plums?"

"Plummmm ew!" winced the royal baby, disgusted by the very word. The Queen laughed and pulled a few paper-wrapped honey-bons from a pocket in her sleeve.

"He is spoiled, I'm afraid. These are the only sweet he likes. I carry them with me constantly. I'm surprised you didn't smell them! I must have a pound of—"

The coachmaid cried out. On the roof, the archers' feet scraped and scrambled and their bowstrings began trading hum after hum.

"Do you see it?"

"Left! Low!"

"Right! Low!"

"Where'd it—"

One of the horses, then all four, screamed. Before Dame Elsebet could say a word, a flurry of clawing sounds resonated through the floor of the coach, as if it were driving through a wheel-high field of thorns, and although her snowy hair was braided and pinned, she felt it stand on end. Into her mind sprang the image of the monster she knew was trying to tear the coach open: a meldragore.

The clawing grew louder, more furious. The King yelped. The baby shrieked. The Queen was silent, but her horror-stricken stare was aimed at the spot where Dame Elsebet would have been, had she not already swung out through the open window. Using the same ladder the archers had used, Dame Elsebet climbed up and joined them, taking the broadspear they had ready for her.

"Down, Medame!" yelled one archer, pressing her mistress out of the way as a branch swept by overhead.

"There it is!" cried the other one, firing her last arrow down at the attacking monster.

Up from beneath the coach emerged its vaguely humanoid head, followed by the long silvery train of its bristling body and four— no, six— no, eight— of its sixteen legs, stout and dark and terminating in claws like butchers' hooks, clinging to the speeding vehicle with caterpillar tenacity; at least a dozen arrows jutted from its back, but of course arrows were less than nothing to a meldragore. Before it could tear into the coach for the honey it craved, Dame Elsebet leaned out toward it, trusting to the grip of the archer who had run out of arrows and was now holding her about the waist, legs hooked into the luggage rack. Dame Elsebet took aim and swung her broadspear with every speck of precision she could muster.

If the meldragore had been only a fraction of a second slower it would have been slashed in two. But somehow it shied away and through an explosion of black and silver hair, the broadspear's long, wide, curved blade embedded itself in the rim of a wheel. Dame Elsebet and the archer holding her were jerked almost completely off the roof; the horses were now under no control at all, running wild as the coachmaid braced her feet against the dashboard, heaving on the lines like a sailor.

Dame Elsebet caught herself against the side of the coach and let the archer pull her back. She twisted the pistoning broadspear free; when she glimpsed a few scarlet drops upon it, she rushed to check the other side of the coach. Fresh gory pawprints led back underneath. The meldragore was still with them and in less than a minute it would attack again, this time thirsting not for honey, but for blood.

"The father reaches out to discover— the mother stands fast to defend." She quoted the old proverb to no one, her hands moving as if in a fiercely accelerated dream, unmounting the broadspear's blade from its long, wool-wrapped staff. Fighting short-handled. She'd done this countless times. Well, with firewyrms.

But the challenge of slaying a firewyrm was cornering the monster in a deep, dark cave, of rushing up close to it before it could open its lightning-bright jaws, spray its incendiary spittle. The firewyrm did not have claws that could tear open the stony nest of the diamond hornet, or loose twisting skin as tough as boiled leather, or venomous spurs on its hindmost legs. The right way to slay a meldragore was to stay far, far away from it. Well, Dame Elsebet told herself as she swung back into the coach and faced the Royals, we don't always have the luxury of doing things the right way.

"Majesties! The seats lift up! Throw out what's in there and climb inside. Now!"

The Queen was not foolish enough to disobey— she was on her feet, swaying with the wild motions of the coach, her fingers seeking out the edge of her seat and lifting it up— but opposite her, the King seemed to be frozen, staring at nothing: someone who did not know them would have supposed him to be the blind one. Queen Margadet's voice was filled with sorrow as she threw blankets and pillows out of the storage space and crawled into it, clutching the baby to her heart. "Enrick can't hear you. I pray you'll save us. But if this is goodbye— then goodbye, Elsebet. My friend."

No sooner had the seat closed upon her than in rushed the meldragore, hissing and growling. Dame Elsebet stood fast, blocking the King, and plied her weapon. In the tight quarters of the coach she fought not short-handled, but with no handle at all; the tang of the blade was harsh and narrow, painful to hold. One slashing claw caught her glove, revealing the startling youthfulness of a hand that had not seen broad sunlight in fifty years. One of the wyrmlight globes fell off the ceiling and it rolled madly about underfoot, illuminating the fight from bizarre angles, painting a thousand fearsome pictures.

The meldragore wanted blood, and blood it got: some of it came from Dame Elsebet but, at long and terrible last, most was the monster's own, shed as it writhed away its final breath upon the tip of a weapon last used on some sheaves of straw in the practice arena back at Whellengood.

Dame Elsebet did not dare look back at the paralyzed King. In a daze she gathered the serpentine, oddly sweet-smelling carcass of the meldragore and heaved it out the window, one armful after another. There was a bump as the carriage ran it over and then only slowing hoofbeats, creaking wheels and a deep, strange well of silence.

CHAPTER 23

A TA MAROO WAS FRESHLY BATHED AND neatly dressed. She had decorated her hair with a bright green silk band, to represent the crown she would soon wear as Headmother, and carefully rehearsed her language.

The speech of the Ocean Empire included a system of politeness levels quite unknown to the Westlanders. Certainly they had such terms as "Your Majesty," "Your High Honor," "Mesir" and "Medame" and all the rest. But the language Ata Maroo had grown up speaking went far beyond this. In her language there were terms for "you" used toward superior and underling, friend and enemy; there were ways of saying "I" which meant the speaker considered herself a host, a guest, a bystander; a relative might do things with one form of a verb, while a friend would do them with another and a stranger would do them with still a third. Thus a speaker of the Peaceful Ocean languages could, if she so chose, say "I welcome you" and have it really mean "Get out of here immediately, unless you'd like to meet one of my cousins who's good with a dart gun".

But of course, Ata Maroo now prepared to go to the other extreme. Someone important wished to confer with her. As she stepped into the reception chamber— and though that did sound a bit silly, she knew her mother was correct in using the term— Ata Maroo silently recited the politest verb forms she knew, reminding herself of words she hadn't used in twenty years.

"Ah! It's Owa Lulu!" Ata Maroo bowed deeply to the sweet-faced old lady sitting on an extra-thick stack of feather cushions. "I'm honored, beyond honored, to see you again, lovely and distinguished friend of my dear mother! It's been so, so long. When did I last see you, Owa Lulu? At my wedding, wasn't it?" And then, since her first marriage was a dangerous topic, Ata Maroo steered gracefully clear of it. "Oh, but so much must have happened to you since then. I'm eager to hear it all."

Owa Lulu bowed back, slowly and politely, to Ata Maroo, then turned and addressed her mother. "Steera. The years have agreed with your daughter— she is beautiful, just like you."

Something was wrong. Ata Maroo heard the sound of it in her mother's voice when she replied, "You're too kind, Lulu. I'd say she's come to resemble Pako, though, wouldn't you? She's missing his white forelock but other than that, she might as well be him with all his endearing... ways." It was how she said *ways*. That was what sent a chill through Ata Maroo.

"Do, do you have any questions for me, dear honored guest?" She dug deep for words to express the greatness of her regard for Owa Lulu.

The round, ancient, kind-faced lady had been chief advisor when the previous Headmother had at last given her final breath to the winds of the Peaceful Ocean. For a hundred days afterward, Owa Lulu had scoured the islands to find the baby girl who had taken the breath back up. Owa Lulu had been holding Ata Steera's hand when the soothsayers, gathered around baby Maroo's cradle, announced that *this* was the child who, exactly twenty-one years from that day, would become the chief diplomat of the Hundred Clans.

The young Ata Maroo had always looked up to acting Headmother Owa Lulu with the utmost reverence. Long years of absence had only deepened the feeling: surely she deserved the highest, brightest verbs there were. Therefore Ata Maroo heaped these on with great abandon, adorning them with the "I" which meant host and the "you" which meant superior; still a cold wind seemed to blow from the corner of the room where her mother stood, adjusting her green feather crown.

At last Owa Lulu had asked enough questions about the life Ata Maroo had led in the Westlands, about her shipping business and her mooing brown land-whales and how she had met her auspicious second husband. She rose to her feet, accepting Ata Maroo's elbow with the dignity of Wowmi nobility, which of course she was. Ata Maroo guided the ancient lady as she toddled down the great wooden staircase and into her canoe, and bowed as her attendants paddled her away. The canoe had only barely disappeared around the turn of the canal, when Ata Steera turned on her daughter— with a heat that Mount Grumble could only dream of matching.

"Why? *Why?* Why did you need to humiliate me, Maroo? In front of Lulu!"

She didn't stop to let Ata Maroo ask what she was talking about, but instead tore a handful of flowers off the nearest tree and wadded them up as her voice descended into a growl of fury.

"I wait an eternity for you to come to your senses, I write so many *ow palak* begging you to come home that I think my wrist might just break in two, I make every effort and then this? As if I didn't teach you any better! How dare you!"

"Dare I what?" Ata Maroo was able to yelp.

"You know very well what!"

"Obviously I don't!"

Ata Steera's eyes flashed like poison darts. "You mean to tell me— and let me remind you you're not a child, Maroo, you're forty-one years old, although it's unreal to hear myself saying that— you mean to tell me you *didn't* deliberately address my oldest friend, and that makes her *your* oldest friend, in such a manner?"

"What such manner? I was as reverent as I could be!"

Ata Steera seized her only very slightly gray hair in both hands and bent double, very gracefully for someone who is sixty. "Ai, ai, ai! She'll drive me insane! Oh One Who Listens, hear me!" and at this she turned pointedly toward a flower bed surrounding an unobtrusive statue of Alvert's head.

A long-buried panic began boiling inside Ata Maroo. She had enjoyed such success in the Westlands that she had nearly forgotten the feeling of making a horrific, incontrovertible, shameful blunder. Oh, gods— wait, no, Ye Gods were a Westlander thing— could she have used the wrong verb form? The wrong *I*? She hadn't spoken her own language to anyone since she was twenty-one, other than reading a few of the many letters her mother had taken the great trouble and expense to send.

"Tell me, Mother. Ebeyee. Ebee." She kneeled in the herbs and grass in front of Ata Steera, trying to grab her flailing hands, using more and more babyish terms to address her. "What did I do? What did I do wrong?"

The fury went out of Ata Steera and now she only looked sad. "Oh, Maroo. You really don't know." She shook her head. "Ah, I blame myself."

"But *ebee!* What, what did I do?"

"Don't you remember, my little Headmother, that people who've known each other a long time don't use those high-and-mighty names and terms and"— here Ata Steera's voice became a caricature of a child's— " 'dear, dear honored guest'? No. Didn't you hear how I spoke to Lulu? Very intimately. Almost as a relative. To put such a distance between yourself and a valued old friend: that's cold-hearted, Maroo! Downright cruel! Poor old Lulu, she can hardly walk anymore, and she came all the way from Wowmi to be treated like a stranger? How in the world could my very own daughter have forgotten a simple and basic thing like that?"

"I— I never—"

"Come, don't tell me you never knew, Maroo. Of course you knew: you've heard adults talking to each other all your life."

In the Peaceful Ocean grows a plant that weeps a slimy sap which, in large doses, can kill a full-grown hog right in its hoofprints. Dart-makers use it for just that. But in smaller doses, this sap causes a form of localized paralysis, so healers use it too: a drop in one eye, and the eye holds still to allow the removal of a splinter; a jab in the hand, and the hand holds still for other surgeries. And while the sap doesn't exactly block pain, it does stop the patient from shouting, which for the healer amounts to the same thing.

Now Ata Maroo felt as if a diluted drop of that sap had fallen right onto her brain. Or maybe onto her tongue. Or maybe onto her heart— wherever might cause her to simply freeze and listen rather than crying out: But Mother, I *haven't* heard adults talking to each other *all* my life in *this* language! The most recent half of my life happened somewhere else, somewhere where they behave differently! It was a natural mistake!

Into her frozen brain came reason. Ignorance was no excuse. If she didn't know her very own language, that was her very own fault. There was much to rebuild. She must do better.

Her fingers wandered to the silk band tied around her hair; suddenly she was ashamed of it and fumbled to undo the knot. She didn't deserve to wear that green, and as for a feather crown— the very idea now seemed as far away as the broad brown Denna.

CHAPTER 24

I F FRED THOUGHT THE CROOKS' DEN had smelled bad before, by dawn it
was worse. The fug of sweat, breath, belches and gas filling the room
was so thick he almost felt it before he smelt it. When he rolled over and
opened one eye he was confronted with a bunch of reeking, wiggling
fleshy nubs, some of which gave a spasmodic jerk and smacked him
right in the face.

"Scab flapping boil pocking what is your problem?" he growled at the
brat, whose filthy bare feet remained inches from his nose. The brat
only laughed: an unnervingly adult laugh, though high in pitch.

Fred rubbed his eyes for a while. That was mostly to cover his face. He
didn't want to risk betraying his thoughts, all of which were variations
on: *hoy, brain, tell me again why the three hells I decided to do this.* But
soon he'd drunk some leftover tea with Dok, and let her scrape his
ill-shorn hair back into place and dust bits of mattress stuffing from
his beard stubble, and then without many more words the two of them
crawled from behind the boards across the shopfront and back out onto
the dim street. Two of them? No. Fred looked over his shoulder and
wasn't a bit surprised to see the brat following.

"Ah, the wee dawnlit hours, easy pickings time," said Dok, with a lilt
in her voice. She was wearing her sash as a scarf now, and had tucked
the bodice of her robe down into the waist of her pantaloons to make
it a skirt, under which the fake bosom was repurposed as a kind of
bustle that changed the very outline of her figure. "Let's go down to the
waterfront and see what's lying about."

What lay about was sailors. A surprising lot of them had not managed
to crawl or stumble the short distance back to their ships' boats;
instead they slept peacefully, faces pressed into the cobbles or boards
or whatever other surfaces had presented themselves at the moment

when cheap rum won out over duty. Some of their mouths hung open, drooling; on one memorable victim, the chunk of maidenroot she'd been chewing was half in and half out, and a singer's codpiece remained clutched in her hand.

"Ugh. Hope she chewed enough to stop her getting one of *those*," said Fred, tipping his head to indicate the brat.

Dok crouched to empty the sailor's pockets, stashing the loot in her bustle. "You don't think maybe your alter-ego Rodge caused a few brats in his time?"

"The hells I ever did."

"That you know of." Dok grinned to show she was only joking, but a few sailors later she asked: "Really though, *have* you got anyone who'd care if you were knocked on the head? Coastwall is a lot rougher than the Isle of Gold." Her slantwise glance dared him to ask how she knew where he'd come from. *Not a lot we don't hear.* In reply Fred only shrugged, but he had to hand it to the Grand Constable: the fellow certainly knew how to plant a backstory. Frednick Casmarr. New in town and already notorious.

"Fred Casmarr looks out only for himself. And Rodge, of course."

"Glad to hear it. Listen. You and the kid keep clawing up this garnish— I'm going to pay a call on a learned gentleman's private estate." Dok winked and pointed one elbow at a locked-up booth some distance down the wharf.

With daylight a scribe would arrive, accompanied by a guard and carrying a cashbox, to open the booth and set up for business. Waterfront scribes mostly wrote the paperwork required for ships to legally transport passengers and cargo; every stroke of ink was another penny in the de Brewels' coffers. But ink was valuable, and so were quills, and so was paper— anyone clod enough to leave his booth on the

134

waterfront overnight deserved burgling. With a rustle of her bustle, Dok strolled toward her goal by a winding path.

Fred was left with the brat. He really couldn't tell if it was a boy brat or a girl brat. In fact the whole child was disconcertingly nonspecific: pale or dusky, dark-eyed or light, young or younger, it defied description. The tongue it stuck out at Fred was pink, at least. He stuck his own tongue out in return and then, to show how a professional operated, he pulled a face that made the brat burst into more of its strange cynical laughter. In fact, the brat laughed so much that it attracted the attention of— boils. The sun, bursting from behind the hazy outline of Brewel Hall far across the harbor, threw a long, deep, menacing shadow over Fred. The shadow of three Coastwall Harbor guards. They reminded him of the imported laborers back in Good Market.

"Up from there, fella." The first one spoke in a monotone.

"Whaddaya doin, huh?" demanded the second one, spitting her maidenroot only a an inch from Fred's head. This was no accident, he was sure: her kind could spit with supernatural accuracy. *Hoy,* he thought, *I'm His Honor, the Esquire of Good Market!* The nerve of —

There was no time to think further; the brat, clearly under some delusion that this business involved only Fred, had continued ransacking the slowly awakening sailor, and was caught red-handed by the third guard.

"Gotcha, ya gutter bug!"

Fighting in the woman's grip, the brat let out a shriek that could have peeled the paint off a dinghy. Fred, the guards, the sailor, even the brat itself were all knocked back for a moment and Fred seized the opportunity to turn his face into a mask of fatherly anguish.

"Let my baby go! Sh— he— *my baby* was only checking to see if my wife had any money left for us! She drinks it all away, the heartless shrew. Baby!"

He whirled to address the brat, calling upon his theatrical training to bring a flood of tears to his eyes. "Oh, Baby! Tell me you didn't lose any of our things! All our precious things, crammed in our pockets, all we have left now that your mother drank away our cottage and our carriage and our donkey and our doggie and our..."

"Aw, pus buckets. Fine. Gwan and drag ya wench home— ya look as if ya could manage it. Beefy clod."

The guards strode away down the wharf and the sailor groaned, "I'm not your wife, man. And that ain't our baby. Is it?"

A din of jumbled shouts and splashings arose from the harbor. Fred left the sailor lying where she was and ran to go see.

A limp, wet, fully clothed man had been fished up out of the water and now lay motionless on the wharf, attended by the three guards and, kneeling beside the man's head and bending down to blow a lifesaving breath into his lungs, Dok.

With one hand Dok pinched his long nose shut and with the other, pried his mouth open; she poked her fingers down inside to clear his throat and then she dug something long, thin and fleshy out of the fellow's mouth. She stared at him for a moment and then cried out in horror, leaped away, hitched up her makeshift garments and ran. The fleshy thing remained on the wharf. It looked like a piece of pinkish-gray rope.

The guards were confused: should they chase Dok? Should they examine the fleshy, ropy thing? Should they keep trying to revive the drowned fellow, or at least try and figure out why his lips had abruptly turned such an unnatural purple? By the time they'd decided, Dok was gone.

Fred had an idea where. He hurried back to the crooks' boarded-up den and found her just outside it, kneeling in the gutter, eyes vacant with fear, taking great mouthfuls of rum from the handsome silver flask and spitting them into the gutter. Then she stared at her hands, holding the flask, as if she'd caught them doing something terrible.

"Fred!" she cried. "Thank Ye Gods you're here. Pull my bustle out and use it to hold this flask, all right? Pour the rum over my hands, and then throw both things away. Never mind the loot in the bustle. Hurry."

In a trance Fred lifted the hem of Dok's robe-skirt, right out there in what was fast becoming broad daylight. Well, she'd asked him to. And there was no one on the street to see them. He freed the linen bundle and held the flask with it, turning it bottom-up to let expensive alcohol pour into the gutter. Dok scrubbed frantically between her fingers and under her nails. Finally she nodded, and Fred flung flask, bustle and that morning's take far away into a pile of other trash. Dok leaned on a lampless post, tucking her skirt back into place, and finally she spoke.

"That wight didn't drown. He got mounted on a signboard."

"What's— how do you know?"

"If you'd seen his mouth, you wouldn't have to ask! Only one poison in the world turns lips that color. And inside his gape I found—" Dok shuddered— "the tail of a rat."

"Well, come on, though. That's the tastiest part."

That actually brought back her smile. "Oh, ho! But why the sign? Who'd want to announce to the world that he'd snitched? Because who'd he snitch on? And what about? Lub should never have been near the harbor anyway. He hates water. Hat*ed*."

137

"You knew that wight?"

She met his eyes and there was silence.

"Was he your…"

"Lubber Howell? No! I only know him because he works for Hamflesh."

"Really? Not for money?"

She smiled again. Pretty smile.

"You're a quick thinker. I like that." She patted Fred's shoulder as she stood up; the blank pages still pinned to it crackled. "But it's true, no one gets much money working for Hamflesh Fliss. The gentleman is a notorious tight-fist. Maybe Lub just finally decided a few pieces of news were worth a few pieces of silver…" her voice trailed off.

Fred had the strongest urge to put on an expression of deep concern, lean forward and whisper "…to Granny?" and see where that got him. But there was a chance it might get him a set of purple lips. So instead he just shook his head and said, "Poor miserable wight."

They strolled. The sun peeking out from behind a crumbling tenement was idiotically cheerful, as if it hadn't just risen over a gangland murder. Again Dok's voice had changed, her gait had changed— now she seemed smaller, closer to Fred, more sincere. They turned a corner into a cleaner part of town.

"Miserable, you said it. Not a bad sort but his life's probably a lot happier now that it's over. Hoy." Dok held out her hands. They were shaking. "Wish we still had some rum left— that threw me off my stride. I mean, some waves have been rocking the boat around here lately. I just never thought any of 'em would get so close to *me*. The thing is, Fred, that I'm—"

"You. The wight with the blank Guild papers."

A peacekeeping officer of the Municipality of Coastwall was with them. Before Fred knew it there was a manacle around his wrist and as for Dok, she might as well never have existed.

CHAPTER 25

OVERLOOKING A GREAT OPEN PLAZA IN the genteel part of Coastwall stood the Station House, a massive sandstone edifice whose tall bronze doors were held open by a pair of marble seahorses. Above its portico was an inscription, in the old scholarly dialect Coastwall had once shared with the Isle of Gold. It read: HERE DWELLS JUSTICE.

Deep in the guts of this handsome building throbbed a jail— a tumor of sandstone cells where strongarm bailiff wenches wrestled crooks down and gentlemen officers wrote them up. There iron bars would clang, brass keys would rattle and the crooks would chill their cheeks, awaiting their turns before a district magistrate. The jail was loud, and rowdy, and crowded, and Fred was heartily glad he'd never so much as seen the place.

Instead he sat in a chair upholstered with sea-green leather, sipping brandy from a glass shaped like the De Brewel seahorse, and watching the Grand Constable's face as it shone with the light of a gray-whiskered man feeling young again.

"A rat's tail, you say? That's one I remember from way back! It's a sign, branding someone an informer— a ratmouth. Get it?"

Fred yawned and rested his freshly shaved chin on one soap-scented hand.

"Ratmouth," chuckled the Grand Constable. "Now. This Dok sounds interesting. Tell me more about her."

"I'd have more to tell if you'd left me with her. It was just getting good."

"You mean getting risky. Danger comes later, Murd. Right now you're still wet behind the ears."

Fred tipped the seahorse up until the last drop slipped down his throat. So smooth.

"Well, my ears were drying up fast. What a deep-damned minute to pull me out of there! She'd just started talking about a male crime boss, this Hamflesh fellow. I could have learned—"

"You could have learned what the bottom of the harbor looks like. Or what the blade of a knife feels like."

Fred clenched his jaw. He knew very well what the blade of a knife felt like, probably far better than the Grand Constable did: just beside his navel, there was a frightful scar to prove it. All right, so he didn't want a second one. With a sigh, he set the empty glass on the Grand Constable's desk. "What next, then, my cautious overlord?"

"You're going to observe a construction project. While you and I were developing your cover, the de Brewels started building a farm. Now something shady's going on there— and sure as the Great God made little red currants, Granny must be behind it. Many roads lead to her, Murd. Just do as I say and one of 'em will take you there."

CHAPTER 26

F LOUR, BUTTER, SUGAR, AND SALT. THAT'S what bread is made from—
shortbread, that is, which must obviously be the simplest kind,
reasoned Buddy Dabroo.

There was no library at their new farm, so Buddy couldn't consult *On
The Practice of Agrick-Culture* by the eminent Grandmaster Bharr for
instructions on growing flowers, or peek into Parafu's immortal work
Stuff and Whatnot for the alchemical composition of butter. But he
had plenty of neighbors who were constantly leaning on the rustic
post-and-rail fence that encircled the Dabroo property and offering
heartfelt advice, so he decided to go ask them.

Buddy's feet rattled about within his heavy new workboots as he walked.
No, make that strode. There was something racy about it— striding
instead of sauntering, through grit and mud instead of over silk and
wool. It made him feel as though he were tearing down some sort of
barrier, a barrier he'd never realized was holding him back.

"Hoy there, neighbors!"

The neighbors laughed a bit amongst themselves, as Buddy had
discovered the Poor were wont to do. One of them, a stout woman with
a single eye, chewing on the stem of a clay pipe, gestured at him and
croaked, "Looky there, if it ain't Donny Fill in his shore-goin' rig."

Everyone laughed, Buddy included, because of course she was wrong.
She never got the name right, this one.

"Good day to you, Spyglass." He nodded to the others as he strode
over to lean on the fence with them. "Good day, Jaine Hushmouth,
Quickfinger Maggie, Shoogy Britches. I'd like to ask you a few questions."

For some reason, this request made the neighbors nervous. They backed a few steps away from the fence and for a moment Buddy thought they'd leave. At last the squat, muscular Shoogy Britches stepped forward. "What kind. A questions."

"Agrarian ones, mainly... about flour, and butter, and sugar, and so forth."

"Hain't got. No flour. Never saw. No sugar."

"Except in yer britches," suggested Spyglass, and of course everyone laughed because this referred to the stylishness of the garments the fellow habitually wore. Buddy decided to have one of his tailors run him up a similar pair. They were strikingly unlike anything ever worn back at Brewel Hall.

But Shoogy Britches looked unhappy about the baking ingredients, so Buddy reassured him: "Oh, I'm not asking to borrow anything. Heavens, no. I mean— hells, naw. I want to grow some bread here, on the farm, and all of a sudden I think to myself, well, scab scratch it! I really don't know nothing 'bout flour, butter, sugar and salt."

Jaine Hushmouth made a cryptic gesture, pressing the palms of her hands together and twisting them. Next she held her fists a few inches apart, squeezing them alternately in the air; after that, she waved her upraised hands slowly about, twiddling her fingers as if to indicate a multitude of tiny flying things. Her final gesture was a shrug.

"Nah, woman, he said sugar, not honey," Spyglass admonished her. "And salt is from the sea. Don't ya know nothin, ya half-burned dip?"

Jaine Hushmouth took a swing at Spyglass, who dodged and knocked Shoogy Britches to the ground. He scrambled to his feet and swatted at the women. Quickfinger Maggie, ever the kind soul, leaped across the fence to protect Buddy from violence, but of course that wasn't necessary. He helped her climb back over and a few minutes later everything was sorted out.

It seemed that flour came not from flowers at all but from wheat, which was processed in some kind of mill— much like a steel mill, probably. Butter, meanwhile, originated in animals such as cows. Sugar had to be refined; in this, thought Buddy, it was clearly similar to other ores such as iron and gold. And lastly, the sea was full of salt— this, he knew. He'd just forgotten it, in the excitement of being Poor.

"Thanks a bundle, good neighbors," he called out when at last they went their separate ways. As he strode back to his hovel, the summer breeze blew construction dust into Buddy's eyes and he reached into his sleeve for a handkerchief. Funny— he could have sworn he'd brought one.

"Did you learn anything, Butterpat?" Ro-Ro asked her man as he rattled open their home's sagging front door. "I've just been outside having a lovely chat— I mean, a good old jaw session— with the ladies delivering bricks. They are truly the most dedicated workers! Apparently bricks disappear if left unattended. I had no idea. We must build the garden wall faster, I suppose."

"I imagine they dissolve, because they're made of salt. Rock salt."

Buddy was proud of himself for remembering there were two kinds of salt— such facts weren't as blindingly obvious as, say, the vowel shift in Hwardelian loanwords or the declension of nouns in ancient Vonnish. To emphasize his new worldliness he kicked his boots off, one at a time, and watched them fly across the room to hit the unlit cookstove.

"What's for supper, Ro-Ro? I could eat a horse." Inwardly he hoped he would have to do no such thing; they'd only brought the two ponies, and Ella doted on them.

"Well... I'm not sure we have anything at all. The peacock confit and truffle rolls are all gone, and I still can't figure out how to use *that* thing." Ro-Ro threw a surly look at the cookstove.

"It's all right, babe. Long as we're together. We'll just... tighten our belts and make do."

Buddy strode across the room in his stocking feet. He embraced his wife and they stood, holding one another bravely, for a minute or so until Ro-Ro whispered, "That was perfect. I'll order something to eat." And she dispatched two little servant girls with a big basket, a fistful of paper money notes, and Babou, who was now wearing a collar that read "HANG IN THERE— IT'S ALMOST COPPERDAY."

LATER THAT EVENING, THE DABROO family sat in the dirt farmyard on a pile of logs. Ella had arranged these for maximum aesthetic effect, and also to afford a diverting view of the departing workers, who were helpfully hauling building materials— as well as an ambitious selection of the Dabroos' personal belongings— to an undisclosed location for safekeeping. Privately, Ella thought there was a chance the workers might trade one or two of these items for wine; artists like her saw the world with unflinching clarity, not shying away from the dark side of human nature. But she said nothing of this to her parents. They looked so happy.

"Pappy. Maw. Want me to sing a song?"

Buddy raised his head from Ro-Ro's shoulder and turned to look up the log pile at Ella. "I hope you didn't write it— I won't have you riling up your mama."

Ro-Ro agreed. "Hear your father, little miss. Just because we're low-class doesn't mean you can be vulgar."

"I promise I didn't write anything. Petey did. He sent a bard with it just yesterday."

"Oooh, what fun! Sing away, dear."

Ella reached between some logs and brought forth what had once been a tea crate, with a whitewood stick glued to it that held a tightly stretched bundle of tail hairs from the buckskin ponies. It made a series of planging and twanging sounds as she plucked it rhythmically, singing:

"Dazed awake this mornin', bumped down from my bunk.
Searchin' for my silver, tore apart my trunk.
Prayin' for a penny— good god give I might
Find more than
the drinkin' can
I fell into last night.

I'm in them been down by the tavern too long grooves.
Every empty tankard only proves
I'm lower than the shoes of ponies,
where they wear their hooves.
I'm in them been down by the tavern too long grooves."

"I can't imagine how Petey knows so much about liquor," groused Ro-Ro. "He's a *student*."

"Indeed," agreed Buddy, though with somewhat less conviction.

As the sun sank below the ridgepole of the Dabroos' barn, a final knot of workers straggled out through the gate with quick furtive glances and bulging pockets. That left only the family, who were much too wrapped up in yet another song to notice the workers' departure— otherwise they'd certainly have waved goodbye. In the end, night fell upon the Dabroos: still singing, still swaying, delighted to be down and out.

147

CHAPTER 27

THE SKY RIVER SWEPT CORVINALIAS AND his new companions, the cranes, into its irresistible current and pulled them eastward across the world.

Hours became days, and days had their nights, and onward flowed the current, a massive lane of wind in the vanishing, lofty air at the edges of what Corvinalias could only imagine was the known universe. The Kingdom soon disappeared far behind them, but they were not going southeast toward the Warm Ocean, and the Herb Islands, and any of the other places Corvinalias had been with Ata Maroo. Instead they flew only over land. Within days the Uman settlements passing underwing grew small and far apart and the squares of green and brown and gray they surrounded themselves with began changing shape: smaller, more broken, more tightly applied to the sides of landforms that became steeper the further they went.

They stopped periodically to roost and to hunt for frogs and lizards, but never for very long. "We will join the fer-lock very soon, magpie gent. Fer-lock are not really our people, but they are friendly." At this explanation the crane's mate nodded and the red skin of her face paled a little. "Friendly enough," she agreed.

"Why aren't you following your own people?" asked Corvinalias, stripping and quartering a frog faster than he'd ever had to do in his life. The cranes were already wiping their beaks and setting their feathers right in preparation for another plunge into the sky river. In their behavior, they were as driven as doves, who magpies considered a neurotic and overly punctilious race; and yet the cranes spoke as if they were in no hurry at all. They were difficult to understand.

"Our people dead," said the male crane mildly.

Corvinalias stopped eating with a frog's foot still hanging from his mouth. "What?"

"Long time now," said the female crane as she smoothed her last rectrix back into place. "We are very old. Last ones of us. We will nest a pair of egg." She and her mate did a quick ritual movement, flipping their heads up and down, singing a duet in trumpet blasts. "You ready, magpie gent? Up we go again. Soon we will see mountains."

Corvinalias thought he'd been seeing mountains, but within a day, such places as they'd passed seemed quaintly flat. The lumps of land beneath them grew sharp. The jungles covering their sides grew dense. Uman settlements grew scarce, separated from one another by huge green and brown fins of earth, until only the most nearly invisible tracks wove through the low spots between them and then there were no longer any Uman settlements at all. Now the fins grew more brown than green, and the jungles began to fail. Ancient, jagged complications began revealing themselves on ridges of naked stone. When Corvinalias and the cranes stopped for meals, the air was difficult to get satisfaction from. All was harshness: thin rivers as cold as ice, holding small wary fish; here and there some spots of meltless snow; now and then a lonesome ibex crawling up the face of a rock. Once, Corvinalias thought he spied a massive gray shadow with spiky-feathered wings and a shriveled head like that of a parched, dead snake, following them— but when he looked again, it was gone. This country made him shudder.

"What's this place of yours like?"

"It is a valley. Last valley before mountains."

These still weren't mountains?

And then one evening, at the closing of a cloudless day, Corvinalias looked up from his usual rapt attention to the ground below him to behold the limit of the earth.

In front of him, the setting sun blazed upon a monumental wall that reared up almost vertically, damming the sky, its dark stone face streaked with ledges holding fields of snow lit red and gold. Somewhere high in the dome of night, the upper edge of the wall was a faintly visible streak of purest white. Or were those stars?

"Now we at mountain," shouted the male crane. "Just below here is valley. That is where we find fer-lock. Follow us."

And then, as if it were perfectly normal to have reached the edge of reality, the cranes folded their wings and dropped out of the air current. Corvinalias hurried after them; down they all fell, descending into a long, deep slash of darkness at the foot of the wall, where thousands of warm red candles were glowing.

The darkness was a blueneedle forest, which had grown up around a slender stream of water, and the glowing candles were the flock.

Corvinalias had been in the Whellen Country in autumn, so he had seen the leaves of the sugartree in their full brilliance. Up until that evening he would have called those leaves the most luminous red found in nature: an utter purity of translucent scarlet, most of all when it was lit by the sunset. But these birds— and here he had to look again: yes, they were living birds, like mild-eyed eagles with long, long tails— they weren't being lit at all. They were the ones shedding the light.

Whether it shone from their feathers, or their eyes, or from some quickening of the air around them, Corvinalias could not say, but each one burned at its own brightness, some harsh and some dim; they sang sweetly, and spoke flowingly, in soft tones of a language Corvinalias couldn't understand. He sagged against the trunk of a blueneedle and rubbed his head under his wing a few times, shook it, opened and shut his mouth and when the vision did not go away he decided simply to believe it. He'd seen lots of strange things already. What was one more?

"Now we finally rest," said the male crane. "No broadcat can come here, no longwolf. Here we have only one enemy, and we not see it."

Corvinalias wanted to ask what that enemy was, but the cranes were busy striding into the stream to do another song and dance. When they had concluded it, the female crane trumpeted: "Good night, magpie gent. We enjoy trip with you," and there was no further talk; the pair had already tucked their heads under their wings and fallen asleep, each standing on one leg.

The air smelled like resin and the night was not dark: it couldn't be, lit as it was by the luminous flock. They looked like a vast bed of embers. One of them walked past Corvinalias, so closely that he might have reached out with a wingtip and touched it, might have called to it— but already he felt himself becoming drowsy, and could not speak a word.

Unaware it was being watched, the bird sank down into the duff of blue needles on the forest floor, head drooping, eyes closing, light dimming. Within moments it had burned down to ash and a wisp of wind, wandering in somehow from among the scented trees to touch nothing on earth but that lonely little pyre, breathed into it, rekindled it, lit the ashes warm and pink; Corvinalias fell asleep looking at what seemed to be a deep red stone, set in a ring of flame. A stone that trembled, and cracked, and let a gleam of light shine out from within.

CHAPTER 28

FRED'S HANDS WERE SORE. THEY FELT permanently hooked, like the pincers of a scorpion-crab, and his gloves had done surprisingly little to protect him against deep, flesh-rending blisters. But barrows of gravel didn't wheel themselves, and a surprising amount of gravel was being wheeled at the construction site where the Dabroo family farm was supposedly taking shape.

It hadn't taken him long to notice that the same barrows were traveling back and forth between the same points, never actually being dumped out but diminishing steadily nonetheless. Fred was fairly sure it was being taken away in the big water-butts the workmaids seemed to drink so many of, but he had no proof— they hadn't let him in on their scheme. Instead the workmaids had closed ranks against him, seeming to dislike his temerity in pushing gravel while male. They also compared him, quite within earshot, to some local boor named Shoogy— and Fred didn't always come out on the plus side.

But after all was said and done, he *was* fighting crime. And better still, he was near Kestrella.

The first time he'd wheeled a barrowful of gravel past her, Fred had admired how stunning she could make even a threadbare hempen overcloak, tied with a piece of twine. In fact his admiration had made him spill the barrow, which was all right because the longer it took him to pick the gravel back up, the more glances at Kestrella he could steal.

She had set up a tripod table in the middle of the busy work site and was sculpting something. Just what, Fred didn't know or care; for him it was enough to watch her fingers, smoothing and slipping through a lump of clay, pressing it, squeezing it, smoothing it, drawing out little protrusions and tucking them back in. Lucky, lucky clay.

When at last he'd scooped up the gravel, hurried to the dump site, and eagerly made a return trip, he stopped beside Kestrella's table. The Grand Constable had warned him not to let any of the de Brewels recognize him, but the temptation was unbearably strong: surely Kiki— perverse, beguiling, maddening Kiki— wouldn't be such a killjoy as to blow his cover. But he mastered this desire, hoisted the handles of the barrow in his smarting grip and rolled on, assuring himself that she certainly *had* been about to say something to him.

Back and forth, back and forth with the gravel. Then with cobbles. Then with bricks. Each walk past Kestrella was a torment. At last Fred rerouted himself so as to pass Felip de Brewel, who stood leaning on the fence talking to some wenches and... hells afar, what kind of ugly breeches was His High Honor wearing? and Dame Irona, who was busy learning some sort of peasant dance from a crowd of workmaids' brats.

So, so many workmaids. It seemed to Fred that even with all the nothing they were doing, there were far too many of them. Could the Guilds really support so many, outside of ridiculously overfunded projects like this one? And then, just like a flying trapeze artist swinging in at precisely the right moment to pick up a partner, the back of Fred's mind handed his conscious thoughts a fully formed, helpfully vivid memory of the Bumpy Fellow, selling his fake cantrips on the streets of Good Market, and the forged Poets' Guild license pinned to his shoulder.

It had not been blank, like the pages Fred wore when he posed as a street Fool. The Bumpy Fellow's license had been neatly inked; if Fred hadn't already known him for a charlatan, it would have deceived him. The Haulers', Pavers', and Brickers' Guilds didn't know all of these wenches. There might not be a single real Guild member in the lot. They were all just thieves, busy making off with whatever they could, and that would doubtless bring good brass. *But the papers,* thought Fred. Any hands could steal, but only learned hands could write. Forged Guild licenses. That's where the real crime was.

"Gonna go on break here," announced Fred, setting a barrowful of bricks neatly beside a pile that had grown and dwindled at least three times that he knew of. His alleged supervisor scowled and pulled a three-minute glass from her satchel. *What a buncle of boils,* thought Fred as he made for the latrine. As if she can control how long a worker squats.

The latrine was a three-holer and no one was happy when he barged in alone and pulled the door shut, but once he pushed the bolt across there was nothing they could do about it. He drew a length of twine out of his pocket and, climbing into a somewhat precarious spot on the seat, poked it between two boards so it dangled out through the wooden wall. After taking care to utter a few pitiful groaning noises, he went back to work and waited for one of the Grand Constable's men to come with some excuse and pick him up.

But first he poked his supervisor's meaty shoulder.

"I did my emergency business back there," he loud-whispered, pointing none too subtly at the latrine. The supervisor bunched up her nose in disgust.

"No, not that! I meant the business with the string. I poked the string out the corner of the shithouse." Fred waited for her to ask him what the hells he meant by that, and interrupted her before she could. "Isn't that the signal? For when we see a pig rooting around?"

Now he had her attention. "Because listen, I think a pig noticed *this*." He plucked at his own Haulers' Guild papers, hunching his shoulders as if he were trying not to be seen. "I think a pig's gonna pick me up in a minute. Wait till I see that seeping Jimmey Scribbles— he'll wish he'd never dipped a pen." He gave the big brick-red wench a look that said: *and I'll kick him once extra for you, would you like that?*

She was baffled, just as Fred wanted her to be.

"Who the pock's Jimmey Scribbles?"

Fred showed surprise. "Jimmey Scribbles. Him. Who wrote our..." he indicated his license again, and threw in a quick look around for the approaching officer.

"Bad luck for you, beefcheeks. Mine's not from any Jimmey Scribbles. Ya ask me, *he's* the one better be afraid. If Hamel Fliss finds out there's another bent inkfinger in town— your Scribbles is gonna end up packed in a barrel."

Jackpot.

"You!"

A healer had joined them, clad in goggles, gloves and mask. He caught Fred's arm in the crook of his cane and gave it a painful twist. "We've had a complaint. You're coming to the Coastwall Sanitary Home."

CHAPTER 29

THE BRANDY DIDN'T TASTE SO GOOD this time. The sea-green chair was not as comfortable. Fred felt like smacking the mustachio right off the Grand Constable's gullible face. Never, never in a thousand years would he have thought the fellow could be such a star-blinded idealist. And yet the man saw fit to shout at him:

"Crooked scribes? Preposterous! You're getting cynical, Murd."

"I thought *you'd* be the cynical one. Didn't you write the book on crime?"

"I did. But I'll tell you something— the only reason I'm up here today, and not down in the cheap cells, is because of scribes. Scribes took pity on a thief's little brat, Murd, and that was me. One of 'em caught me burgling his booth and instead of raising a hue and cry, he took me to his Guild and they gave me a future. Now, I know you learned to write from the holy fellas in—" the Grand Constable looked at something scribbled on a tablet. "Huh. That's a backwater if I ever heard of one. Well, you might not know this about scribes, but they swear an oath—"

"You don't think *monks* have a deep-damned *oath?*"

The Grand Constable consulted the tablet again. "Well, says here you washed out of being a monk. *Nine* tries at the exam? But back to scribes. Their oath isn't to some bunch of maybe here, maybe not gods. It's to learning itself, to the power of the mind..."

Here the Grand Constable's mustachio actually trembled. He stared reverentially at the wall of books behind Fred as he concluded, "...so I'm not just puffing smoke in your face when I say scribes are on the level. They have hearts of gold."

Fred twisted around in his sea-green chair and looked at the books too. Every one of them had a title like *Soothing Embrocations for the Spirit, How to Amass Allies and Sway Supporters,* or *The Seventeen Behaviors of Extraordinary Gentlemen.* He shook his head.

"Times might have changed. Today that gold might be in their pockets, not their hearts! I tell you, the workmaids all have fake papers from a wight called—"

"Enough, Murd. I sent you to watch that site for the Almantree gang, not veer off on some pocking tangent. Unless you follow my orders, I'll drop you from this mission— I bet Rhonso has an apprentice, or something, who'd like to ask the de Brewels for a favor."

The thought of some other fellow spilling his gravel at Kestrella's feet was more than Fred could stand. He clenched his jaw, met the Grand Constable's stony eyes and nodded, a resentful nod that might as well have come with a warning label. But it placated the Grand Constable.

"There! Glad to have you aboard again. Now. Here's the plan for tomorrow."

He pushed paperweights, empty teacups and a lumpy little vase full of quills across his desk to make space for a diagram. "I'm hiding one of our Documentary Artists in this shed here. Right by where they're building that brick wall. Tomorrow when the town bell rings four, I want you to be at *this* spot— exactly here, do you see?— buying a load of hot materials from some bent worker. I don't care what materials they are, just make sure you hand over some cash for them, with you palm facing the Artist, all right?

"After that, my officers will bring your worker in here and show her the picture of an undercover man handing her money. That always makes 'em talk, Murd! Forget the ratmouth you saw this morning— if you pull this off, we'll have our very own ratmouth. And..."

The Grand Constable seemed to have thought of a witticism. "...this rat of ours— ha ha, she might tell us a very interesting—"

With a friendly, cooperative expression— and pinpoint timing— Fred finished the Grand Constable's sentence:

"Story?"

THE NEXT MORNING, FRED ARRIVED at the construction site wearing a boiled white linen infirmary smock marked with a big, purple circle of disinfectant powder. Despite this advertisement that the Coastwall Sanitary Home considered him disease-free, everyone avoided him and he spent his day hauling materials all alone, under the distant eye of his big ruddy taskmistress. Fair enough. But what really annoyed him was how, every time he got near Kestrella, she'd pick up her clay and hurry off somewhere else.

The sun reached its height. The cicadas got so loud they threatened to drown out the clang of the district bell tolling noon. As the workers took a break from their assiduous thieving, Fred sat on his wheelbarrow, grabbed the back of his collar and yanked off his disgraceful sweaty smock of shame. He was just turning it inside out to hide the purple mark when he heard a familiar peal of deep, melodic laughter.

"Hoy, cover that up, fellow! It'll give me nightmares."

The woman in front of him, pointing at his bare midsection, was a perfectly convincing Brickers' Guild supervisor. The way she stood, the dust on her face, everything was right. Except, of course, he knew who it really was.

"What, this here? It's nothing. I had a little accident."

"Sure, with a pack of rabid highcats." Dok laughed again.

Her laugh gave Fred a ticklish feeling behind his scar. Somehow that brought to mind Kestrella's hands, stroking her sculptures, and that was embarrassing and the embarrassment irritated him and he recalled, with some indignation, the way Dok had run out on him at the Harbor. She'd just disappeared. She could have at least waved goodbye. The officers arresting him would never have noticed it.

Taking care not to look at her, Fred crawled back into his inside-out smock and marched away to one of the water butts. Dok followed him.

"What are you doing here, Frednick? Why aren't you singing or fooling or doing something you're good at? 'Cause you might be strong enough to push that barrow but you sure as all hells draw some attention to yourself. And your fingers don't seem to have been the least bit frolly."

Fred drank a dipper of water from the butt. Two. Three. Thinking of what to say. At last he wiped his mouth.

"Can you keep your gape shut? I came here to lift a few of *these*." He reached down the collar of his smock and unpinned the false Haulers' Guild license the Grand Constable had made up for him. As he re-pinned it on the outside, he continued: "But yesterday I didn't have the nerve, and now that I've been in Sanitary, I can't get near a soul. I may as well bag it."

Dok dipped herself a drink. "Aw, poor Fred. Listen. People here are clawing up so much garnish it's outrageous— I think you deserve to get in on a certain operation I'm running here. Interested?"

"Tell me more."

"Word is, there's a really good price going on some bricks. Want 'em?"

Bricks: perfect. Afraid Dok might see his expression of delight, Fred wiped his legitimately sweaty brow with one sleeve; by the time he uncovered his face, he looked as unruffled as any career crook. "Depends. How many? For how much? Who's selling and where at?"

"Maybe a few hundred. Price is a silver bit. I've never met the moll who's moving 'em but I hear she's all right— name of Zigzag Bess. She's been meeting buyers by the new wall. Do you know where that is? Bring a cart."

Fred made his reply sound casual. "Fine. Can she be there when the bell rings four?"

"They say she's always there. Bring the money and she'll find you."

Dok threw the dipper back into the water butt with a well-practiced flick. She gave Fred a wink and was half a dozen steps away when he called after her. He wasn't really sure why he did it; his voice just somehow slipped the request past his better judgment.

"Hoy, brickmaid. Later on, will *you* find me?"

"That depends, barrow man. If I see you doing good work around town, then I might invite you to join my very, very selective Guild. Have fun shopping."

The fourth peal of the bell was just dying away when Fred dragged a handcart to the place where a surprisingly high brick wall was being constructed. A wench with crossed eyes approached him, walking in fits and starts, never quite headed in what seemed the right direction, but nevertheless reaching him quicker than he'd expected her to.

"A friend said you'd loan me a silver bit," she said from one corner of her mouth.

"That's right. Got the collateral?"

"Right in that whip," said Bess from the other corner of her mouth, looking down but pointing up.

Above them, in a cable sling dangling from a great wooden crane, hung a pallet loaded with bricks. The crane was run by an operator and four wenches in a treadmill; with a startling lack of expertise, they swung the pallet over so that it hung directly above the cart. And Fred.

Of the numerous Fools' Guild certifications he held, the most recent was in Funambulism, otherwise known as walking on a tight rope or cable. The very first question on the examination was about how to recognize a properly affixed cable— and this one was decidedly not. Fred's heart gave a skip of fright but then another, calmer and wiser internal organ took over. *Fake*, said his gut.

In a flash, both of these systems checked in with his brain and its extensive training in the art of charlatans' tricks. *Correct*, agreed Brain. Someone's giving you the old IFC, the illusion of a free choice. Someone wants you to step out from under this pallet, over to— oh, perhaps that convenient empty spot there beside the wall.

Instead of moving, Fred froze. When the wall crumbled and crashed down to bury the convenient empty spot, he was too stunned even to flinch. But in less than a moment he regained his senses. He legged it the smoking-hot hells out of there, while the dust was still flying, so fast that the Documentary Artist in the building opposite never got his picture at all.

CHAPTER 30

IN FIFTY-ONE YEARS OF RULING THE Whellen Country, Dame Elsebet had always considered her people's holidays well-nigh holy and she was loath to disturb them.

But she had slept poorly, awakening to the same ugly, churning feelings that had plagued her dreams. Her breathing exercises had done nothing to help. Neither had bathing, dressing, breakfasting, riding; after some unhappy hours, Dame Elsebet had decided to seek out the advice of the knight Lady Verocita at her estate not far from Whellengood.

As she approached Blackbud Cottage, riding her freckled gray gelding, she let the reins hang loose and patted the animal's neck. The estate was named for its little house beside a certain immense, ancient, almost completely hollow blackbud tree, and Dame Elsebet meant to let her horse lower his head and get a good look at it. Hollow trees could be frightening; she wasn't surprised when he flattened his ears and snorted.

Suddenly a girl child swung down from a branch by one leg, aiming a toy crossbow into the hollow, and shouted, "Don't scare the horsie!"

The gelding spooked, dropping low like a cat and then leaping sidewise with all four legs at once. Dame Elsebet's lifetime in the saddle kept her seated, but only barely.

From inside the tree a little boy's voice wailed, "*You* scared it!" and the wail was followed by a writing slate, which he flung at the girl. Then came Lady Verocita's powerful voice from the cottage:

"Behave yourselves, you little— ah! Medame!"

This was, of course, not the first time Dame Elsebet had seen her trainer without her mail and helmet on. But it still was a surprise to behold the fierce Lady— normally so grimly devoted to showing her mistress the best possible way to heft a broadspear, hurl a javelin, swing a sword, or rain down a paralyzing torrent of twinstaff strikes— step out into the courtyard wearing a tunic printed all over with boisterously cheerful flowers and stirring a bowl of something that made Dame Elsebet's gelding point its ears, sniff the air and whicker.

"Forgive me, good Lady. I am so sorry to intrude upon you. I just... I just..."

Lady Verocita turned and shouted at the tree again. "One of you get over here and take Medame's horse. And stop that! A crossbow isn't a toy."

"But this one *is* a—"

"I said stop it." As the children led Dame Elsebet's gelding away, it threw a last pleading look back at the bowl.

"Whatever is wrong, Your High Honor?"

"I... that is... some days ago I killed a meldragore."

Lady Verocita tilted her head to one side, as if she were a puppy. "But that's wonderful. No matter what your age, Medame, you should never lose the playfulness of youth— excuse me a moment. *Straight* to the paddock, do you hear me? Don't let him graze there!" She raised the bowl and shook it menacingly. "Who wants me to throw this away instead of baking it?" Then, with a last glare at her brats, Lady Verocita turned her attention back to the distraught Dame Elsebet.

"Forgive me, Medame. So. You slew a meldragore. Did you find it with hounds or did you lay a bait for it?"

"It was trying to eat the Queen."

164

"Ah."

"And her baby."

"Ohhhh..."

"And I was the only thing between it and the King. Who froze into some sort of frightful trance. And now cannot recall a single thing about the day."

Lady Verocita was struck into silence for some time before she could half-whisper "Small blessings?"

"I suppose I should thank my god that His Majesty doesn't seem to remember. And yet, I..." Dame Elsebet's pale hands rose and fell in a gesture of miserable resignation.

Somehow Lady Verocita had led her into the summer kitchen of the cottage. In one corner, a domed oven added its heat to that of the day; from overhead came the fragrance of drying herbs; and through a broad window lay a view of a neatly fenced paddock where the gray gelding pawed and posed as he introduced himself to the rest of the Blackbud herd.

Lady Verocita pulled a bench up to a cheerfully painted table upon which sat a dew-beaded pitcher of tea. "I understand. You hoped to show His Majesty the best of our country." She poured two glasses, offered one, and waited.

"Some wonderland I showed him. A nasty monster and a whole lot of nothing."

Outside, the horses milled about and tossed their heads. Lady Verocita's chestnut mare barged to the front of the herd and began an elaborate series of threats, beginning with an arched neck and expanding into pawing, head-shaking and the presentation of an upraised hind foot.

Although the women at the table watched silently, both of them were on the edge of the bench. Finally Lady Verocita took her eyes off the unfolding drama and said: "What did the Queen think?"

"Why, I can just imagine. The attack came when we were riding in my coach—I told Her Majesty to hide in the seat locker, of course. Afterward she took the King away and, if you can believe it, *she* tried apologizing to *me*. I insisted that there was no need, that it was absolutely my privilege to have protected them... but that only seemed to make her so disgusted with me... I haven't seen them since." Dame Elsebet covered her face with her hands.

"Does Her Majesty practice an art?"

"An art? Do you mean— a combative art? I don't suppose she would. She's." Dame Elsebet didn't say the final word, but through a gap between her fingers, one of her eyes was a dark, despairing void.

Lady Verocita downed the last of her tea and set the glass down with a sharp click. "Now there, Medame, you might just be surprised. I understand Her Majesty comes of the Vonn Country nobility, a fine old branch keeping good old ways, and I doubt any of their ladies would neglect their training. Even if they were blind. We all learn techniques for night fighting, don't we?"

Something overhead clanked and a cool breeze blasted down onto the women. Lady Verocita's husband, a handsome, slender gentleman with ink-stained cuffs and a magnifying lens hanging from a ribbon around his neck, leaned into the room. "Perplexing how you constantly neglect your comfort, dear! The temperature today is— ah, how do you do, Your High Honor. Surely you prefer the fan, Medame, do you not? If *you* would rather perspire in an insalubriously overheated chamber, simply say so and I'll disengage the mechanism."

Lady Verocita pretended to be annoyed with him, though Dame Elsebet could tell that was only for show. She had taken up the spoon and bowl again; the dough she mixed smelled sweet. Honey. Might it attract a meldragore? If so, Lady Verocita would slash it in two with a broadspear and go on about her business: despite their mechanical comforts, the Whellen Country still had a streak of wildness and its people a pioneer spirit. The Isle of Gold, however, had long since been tamed. In the few days she'd spent there, Dame Elsebet had formed the sense that its only remaining dangers were played-out gold mines and too much feasting. Surely no woman on the Isle ever had to perform her sacred, ancient duty to stand fast and defend...

Dame Elsebet had a thought. At first she shied away from it, much as her horse had shied from the hollow tree. It was just too arrogant. But the thought worked alchemically upon her, as though it might hold a crystal of truth, and finally, brushing away a snowy streamer of hair that the rotary fan kept blowing back across her face, she gave voice to it.

"Do you think, Lady Verocita, that perhaps... perhaps... if she weren't the Queen, mind... if Margadet de Vonn were just an ordinary woman... that perhaps I might be... mistaken about just who she's disappointed in?"

Lady Verocita dropped the honey dough by spoonfuls onto a steel tray. "Disgusted, I think, was the word you used. Well, far be it from me to guess what royalty might be feeling— but if a monster was about to eat *my* family and I had to rely on someone else to fight it off..." She shook the spoon extra hard to dislodge the final lump of dough. "Medame, I suggest that at our next training session, you invite Her Majesty to join us. I know of a very effective art that works for anyone with a sense of touch." Then, keeping the spoon for herself, she handed her mistress the empty bowl.

Although Dame Elsebet had not touched food with her bare hand since before Lady Verocita was born, somehow it felt perfectly right to pull off her glove, brush the inside of the bowl with her fingertip, scoop up some dough and lick it away. Again and again she did this, gathering one streak after another, letting its flavor carry her back into a world of youthful sweetness. In the midst of wordless memories, she remembered something the Queen had said.

"Thank you, Verocita," said Dame Elsebet softly. "Somehow I think it will be all right— I think Her Majesty meant it when she called me 'friend'."

Outside the window there was a commotion. With a squeal, the chestnut mare touched her nose to that of the gray gelding; together the two of them broke from the herd and all the rest followed, dancing across the paddock in joyful unity.

CHAPTER 31

ALVERT DIDN'T SMILE TOO OFTEN, BUT when he did his teeth were big
and square and all of the same perfectly even pale ivory. His eyes,
too, would become less round and more the shape of Peaceful Ocean
people's eyes— at least for a moment— and flash dark gray like a rain
cloud. The stone face of the One Who Listens never did any of these
things, and so Ata Maroo treasured them all the more as belonging
only to her.

She also treasured his voice, with its thick overlay of the Yondstone
accent that she associated with crumbly white cheese and silver birch
forests and colorful woolen pompons. When Alvert spoke it was as
though a little bit of the other side of the world were visiting her. And
it gladdened her heart most of all when both of these happened at the
same time.

Alvert came bounding through the yard of spice vines surrounding the
Ata home's feasting terrace, slapping road dust off his pigskin shoes,
grinned broadly and announced: "I made it all the way to the top o'
Mount Grumble without a stop, Maroo!"

From the earliest days of their marriage, Ata Maroo had noticed that
unless Alvert was clearly, demonstrably good at something he wouldn't
let anyone know he did that thing at all. Swimming, for example.
Somehow, during the course of his harsh former life zigzagging up and
down the clay roads of the Kingdom with a bag around his neck and
not a moment to waste, Alvert had managed to steal enough time near
the Midland Sea to teach himself how to swim like an otter; she'd never
have known it, except that she caught him diving for pearls to bring
her. So no doubt this new announcement about Mount Grumble meant
he'd not only reached the overlook where lava glowed and ashes flew,
but that he'd swept up there at a Trade Road flyer's impressive pace. She
embraced him and kissed the prow of his nose.

"That wonderful, *ipo!* Sound like you good as new again! Look here, what my mother and I doing. We getting main dish ready for big dinner tonight that celebrate our return. I will feed extra delicious piece to my tough mountain man."

Ata Steera murmured "Maybe you'll tell me what you and your *ipo* are talking about."

"Oh, I'm just congratulating him on a personal achievement. And promising him the most delicious piece of this *pweleloka*." Ata Maroo smoothed one hand, well greased with coconut oil, along the unsplit side of a tender, middle-sized sea-hog— from its fierce tusked snout, past its plump shoulder and meaty loin, to the nubby spot where the scales began around its dorsal fin, and all the way down its metallic-blue side to the glittering forked tail that showed how very fresh it was. The cooks stoking the domed brick oven on the feasting terrace had bought the sea-hog that morning from a fisher who'd harpooned ten of them; this was the most perfect one, and surely it would make the guests all clap with delight to see it emerge from the oven crackling crisp and hot. Those who liked fish would eat the tail, those who liked pork would eat the rest, and for those who liked neither, the feast would offer plenty of other dishes to choose from.

One of the cooks stepped in with some thick sennit twine. She began folding and tying the sea-hog's two legs and as she did so, Ata Steera said: "Those strings are soaked in rum, aren't they? So the shanks will have that sugar char flavor?"

"Yes, just as you say, Medame Ata."

"Let me do it, Yuni. We need more twists here. I want it extra delicious." Ata Steera took the twine and began wrapping it the way one wraps an air-cured sausage. "Maroo, will you please help? Take that string and tie the other shank, just like I'm doing, do you see? No, no! Not like that. Undo it. Watch me. Nice and even, like *this.*"

Ata Maroo was undoubtedly clever with her hands, but she hadn't prepared any of her own food in years and was hardly surprised to find that her hog-trussing skills didn't meet her mother's standards. Still it cheered her up to feel the two soft pats that Alvert gave her shoulder. When she looked at him, she saw a kind of humorous commiseration in his round gray eyes.

Ata Steera saw it too.

The last twist she gave the twine was much tighter than the others, causing an unsightly dent in the meat, and she addressed the cook without looking at her. "Yuni. Choose me a pineapple."

While the cook stepped away to a teak sideboard loaded with ingredients, Ata Steera wiped her hands on her apron and said: "So. Your *ipo* had a personal achievement. How very nice. But of course, his best achievement was being nearby when you were in a marrying mood."

Ata Maroo was genuinely confused. "What brings this up?"

"Only that tonight's guests will wonder why you didn't wait and let your father and me choose for you again. Of course it's because of your *ipo's* face, I know— it isn't every day you come across such a perfect way to remind the Empire of who you are. You had to move fast, before some upcountry girl stole him away by showing off her butter churn."

"Mother, that's not how it was at all! I'll tell you the whole story sometime. Maybe tonight, if you want. But I assure you, I didn't choose Alvie as any kind of symbol. He proved he was kind, honest, generous and well, yes, he *was* in the right place at the right time. I wanted to come home already remarried because..." she hurried to finish before the cook came back. "...because I wanted to spare you and Papa. I thought you might be..." and here she made a gesture that she hoped her mother would understand as: *embarrassed about the way the first one went.*

Ata Steera swept the pineapple from the cook's grasp and shoved it into the sea-hog's mouth all in one motion. It was definitely off-center, but she didn't adjust it.

Ata Maroo's hands felt unpleasantly idle. Fortunately the cooks had already set pottery tubs of salt and clay and ash on the cooking table; in clumsy haste she scooped these into a bowl, wet them from a pitcher of water and began smearing the resulting paste onto the tail of the sea-hog. When Ata Steera plunged her own hands into the bowl, it was as though four crabs were fighting in a pottery arena.

"You wanted what, child? You wanted to spare me from my *duty*? There's a fine thought! I've always done everything properly, exactly as it should be done. Even your first husband, rot his soul, how could I have chosen better? Who could have known that the jewel child of Wahayee's premier family— an even older name than Ata, if you can imagine that— who could have guessed he would turn out to be... bad? Well, if you'd read the very first *ow pala* I sent, you'd know how I—" and here Ata Steera stopped smearing the baking crust— "you'd know how very, very lucky it was that someone took a dislike to that man for whatever reason and shot him in the back with a hog dart. That solved everything, didn't it? You could have come home immediately. Instead you took a terrible risk. If your last breath as Headmother had gone out into winds that weren't those of the Peaceful Ocean...*ai!* The chain would've been broken. That's never, never happened. That would have been like— like the ocean turning upside down."

A breeze ruffled the feathers in the green crown. Ata Steera pushed away the tickle of them, leaving a gray smear across her forehead.

"Now you'll have to make up a lot of lost time not only refreshing your grasp of the language, but learning all the cultural traditions and local practices that let you carry out your diplomatic function. You'll learn them eventually, I imagine— and until then, don't worry. Owa Lulu has assured me that it's perfectly proper for me to continue as acting Headmother." She inclined her head at Alvert, who was still standing

172

silently by. "But you might want to start with your husband. Lucky face or no, he should learn something about our people... Maroo, I think this crust will bake the tail perfectly. Will you please ask him to bring us the roasting cage?"

Ata Maroo did so, and followed that with: "I *am* teaching Alvie about us, Mother. Every day. You'll see."

"Pour a bowl of water, let's wash our hands. Well, I hope you'll teach him more. Because back when he took that chicken leg from the offering platter— do you remember that day? Oh, my!" Ata Steera laughed. "Oh, the poor gentleman who'd come to consult me, I thought he would die of horror. Of course you remember! You had to explain it to him yourself! Ha ha, how your *ipo* only took the chicken because he wanted to taste it, and not as a holy sign telling the poor gentleman he was up against a meat problem. Oh, that was so funny!"

Something deep inside Ata Maroo's stomach began twisting. Her voice was small when she said, "Mother. You still have a smear of clay on your forehead."

"Wash it off for me, *ipo*, there's a good little girl. And ah, yes, to a mother, her child is always little. We don't see age at all. I suppose neither do you and your boy."

"My...boy? Do you mean Alvie?"

"Why yes, who else? It *is* a bit delicious. People like it, your age difference. It gives them a thrill of scandal."

"But Mother! You and Papa—"

"Oh, but in our day it was different. Back then prestige was the key— it overrode personal qualities like age. Your father's parents met with mine on the very evening I was presented at the ball. They didn't wish to wait. The big Re shipping business, the illustrious Ata name, what a match! But nowadays a boss may marry her exotic outlander servant. Modern times."

Alvert came back carrying the iron roasting cage, wrapped in bentfruit leaves so as not to mark his arms or chest with any grease. As he laid the device on the table and unwrapped it, Ata Maroo looked him over with the eyes of a stranger and was dismayed to realize that her mother was right: poor Alvie *was* an obvious outlander. Back in the Westlands he had been far too tall; here he was only a bit too tall. Peaceful Ocean people were three times as thick as he was. And most of them had smooth black hair, not light wavy hair like Alvie's— that was only for the people of the Feud Islands, and even so the Feud Islanders' skin was an ordinary golden brown, not pinkish tan like pigskin... oh, why had she thought of pigskin? Alvie didn't resemble a pig at all, at *all!* He was her treasure from the other side of the world. He was a god.

"Ah! I thank you." Ata Steera bowed to Alvert. Of course he couldn't understand her, but Ata Maroo heard her use all the correct words. Her "I thank you" had the *I* of the host, the *you* of the friend, the *thank* of the relative. It was entirely proper, just like the way she showed him how to open the cage, and how she directed him to help the cooks lift the sea-hog into it, and how she walked behind them all as they carried it to the brick oven and swung out the spit and set up the counterweight.

By the time the sea-hog was roasting merrily away, with the cooks down on the terrace turning the spit to the rhythm of a song and Alvert upstairs floating with Ata Maroo in yet another cool bath, she couldn't remember just what it was that had left such a feeling inside of her: a feeling like a waterlogged rock that, having somehow found its way into the oven, later— and may we hope it's when no one is passing by— explodes.

CHAPTER 32

THE GRAND CONSTABLE THREW A STACK of drawings across his desk and barked at Fred from under a bristling mustachio. "Ten... twelve... twenty... twenty-two pictures, Murd, and not one of 'em has you in it. What a perfect waste of an opportunity!"

Fred riffled through the drawings: the cloud of dust in front of the collapsed brick wall. The initial shock. The arrival of an infirmary wagon, hauled by a big brindled mule. Workers and healers all scrambling to clear the bricks from the mangled body underneath. No body there at all. Mild commotion. Piling bricks on a handcart: could each worker really carry so many? Fred stared at this picture for a few extra seconds and then went on to the next one. The mule, in its boredom, picking up a brick in its teeth and flinging it into the air. The brick falling back down on the mule's head, hardly bending the animal's long, furry ears.

At this one, Fred stopped riffling. He frowned.

"*I'm* not the one who wasted the opportunity— looks like your artist did that for me. I mean, come on, the extra-strong workers were a stretch, but an indestructible magic mule that can bounce a brick off its face? No judge would believe these for a minute. Talk about creative liberties."

"Creative liberties? Not a chance! Documentary Artists are pledged to put down the absolute truth. They swear an oath—"

"You and these oaths. Is it some kind of fixation with you, or...?"

The Grand Constable was on his feet, leaning across the desk, his face red.

"If a Documentary Artist lies, the Guild glues his eyes shut for a year! No sane man would get creative with that over his head! Those bricks are obviously fake— pumice and plaster. It's an old jail-breaker's trick: a bent mason builds a cell out of featherweight fakes, then later on the crooks kick it down and leg it. Just like *you* legged it, Murd! Why? If you'd stuck around like you were supposed to, we'd have had that Zigzag moll on selling both stolen *and* adulterated goods. She'd be squeaking her scaly tail off and we'd be getting somewhere! Instead you come running back here with your wild theory."

Fred closed his eyes and took a moment, then replied with exaggerated mildness. "Come on, now. You didn't exactly give me orders on how to react to a murder attempt."

"Oh, lay off it. Some hunch about a bad knot isn't attempted murder. That wight back at the harbor must have you imagining things. Running scared."

Ignore that, Fred told himself. Noblesse and so forth. "Well, I do apologize, Mesir Doak. I've only been in one other attempted murder. I suppose I panicked."

It all might have ended there, but the Grand Constable just had to say:

"So get your head straight, Murd! There's no place for panic in undercover work! I thought you'd be good at improvising, what with having been a Fool. Huh. Should've paid attention to my notes: seems you washed out of that, too. Although *how*, I have no idea— it's got to be the world's easiest job. Forget all the stunts and wisecracks, all you really have to do is botch things and let people laugh at you. Well, I'm not laughing."

At that, Fred got to his feet. He spoke more mildly than ever.

"Do your notes mention a municipality known as Good Market? It isn't a big municipality. Or a fancy municipality. It is in fact the smallest of

176

the Whellen Country's municipalities. But it's a municipality just the same, and governed by an Esquire. You can go look it up if you like. It's on the books."

"And? Are you setting up some kind of joke?"

"I am not. I'm describing my fief, which was granted to me at the whim of Her High Honor, Dame Elsebet de Whellen. Do you see where I'm going with this?"

The Grand Constable's mustachio stopped bristling. Instead, it drooped.

"You're absolutely right," continued Fred, strolling around the office and examining the bookshelves, the curio cabinet, the sideboard with its decanter. "I *don't* mind people laughing at me. In fact, I laugh along with them. It amuses me when commoners do ridiculous things like disparage my efforts to help them, or fail to address me as 'Your Honor', or not bother finding out that I'm a nobleman. They have no idea they're doing something that might make any other nobleman say something to his liege, who might say something to her cousin Felip, who might say something to his wife Irona."

Fred's back was turned to the Grand Constable, but in the reflective curve of a silver tea pitcher he could see the man subsiding into his chair, dazed. The silence was delicious, its profundity marred only by the buzzing of bugs through the window grate. Fred fought back a smile as he continued, "You seem to have plenty of ideas how to run this investigation, which all I do is botch up."

"Please, ah, Your Honor..."

"Oh no, do call me Murd. Or Brother Malfred. Or Fred Casmarr. Or Rodge. Take your pick, I'm a Fool of many faces."

And then Fred played a character. From the decanter he poured himself a single sherry Lorosso, carelessly leaving the stopper to drip on the bare wood of the sideboard. He took the louche posture favored by one of the Old King's most dissolute and whimsical courtiers and turned around, chest hollowed, eyes hooded, bored with the world. Was a yawn too much? He decided to play to the back of the room. "In fact—" yawn— "I've had enough of this game. Maybe you should find that apprentice you talked about last time, and use him instead. I think I'll try working on my own. I expect not to be interfered with."

Oh, what a priceless reaction!

For the first time in his life, Fred felt the rush of command, of power. No more scheming or fighting for respect: the title did all the work. He even *felt* like a gentleman now: slim, slouchy, self-assured, like all the nobles he'd known since childhood...

And something dawned on him. He really *had* had enough of the game. Grimy streets, poison rats, murder bricks— what a lot of nonsense. They weren't necessary; never had been. A commoner like the Grand Constable might need to risk his neck in exchange for Irona de Brewel's indulgence. But if Fred wanted to walk in the garden with Kiki, talk Art and hold her hand— he could just ask her. He was of her kind.

CHAPTER 33

THE FOLLOWING DAY WAS FILLED WITH exertion and want, both of which the Dabroos thoroughly enjoyed.

Buddy began his morning bright and early at the bell of ten, with a long, shivering stretch and the announcement "Well, Ro-Ro, sun's up. Time to get out there and hunt down another penny!" following which he rubbed his eyes and scratched his backside, just as Ro-Ro had instructed him to.

"That's how they do it on stage," she explained, "to show the character preparing himself for his daily toil. Meanwhile I arise, throw on a simple wrap— like this one, no, this one— wait, make it this one. This one is the simplest, don't you think? And now I shuffle over to the cookstove— see how I shuffle, Butterpat?" Ro-Ro approached the iron cylinder with halting steps. "It shows I'm groaning under the weight of *my* daily toil. We both toil, you see. Thank you, dear." This to one of the brats the departing workmaids had left behind, who was holding out a freshly prepared cup of quince-jelly tea. "And now I sup my scant sustenance with a grateful heart, knowing that, although we have little in the way of possessions—"

"—we've got each other," finished Buddy, to Ro-Ro's beaming approval. His eye fell upon their daughter's empty hammock. "Hoy, where's Ella?"

Ella was outside, busily digging a pit. As she plunged her spade repeatedly into the earth, the rough fabric draping her bodice swung like the tail of a trotting pony, nearly but not quite offering a series of glimpses within. When she stood, rubbing the back of one large leather glove over her glistening forehead, Shoogy Britches leaned eagerly on the fence.

"I could. Dig too," he offered.

At this, Spyglass and Quickfinger Maggie whooped with laughter, while Jaine Hushmouth made a series of bawdy gestures.

"That's it, Shoogy," chortled Spyglass, pulling her pipestem from her mouth and picking a fleck of smokeweed off her tongue. "You and Kesteroil da Brool. Dream big."

But the group had caught Ella's attention, and she waved to them.

"Oho, Neighbors! I'm going to fire some ceramic! Want to help? I could pay you in sculptures!"

Shoogy Britches was eager to help, already climbing between the fence rails. "Be there. Right away. Pretty lady."

"What the hells is sculchers?" Quickfinger Maggie asked Spyglass, who could only wry her mouth to one side, shake her head and say "Dunno, but anyone who wants to go on livin' better give Granny her cut of 'em."

The long, oppressively humid day crawled by. A series of strange visitors, most of them gentlemen, came and went from the hovel to discuss some business with Ro-Ro and Buddy. To pass the time Ella sketched some clothing designs for Jaine Hushmouth, who really did have a most elegant tall and strapping figure. As the sun began its downward arc and the late afternoon light turned golden, Ella decided to dig open the makeshift kiln and see what had become of her sculptures.

"Where in the world have my gloves got to?" she wondered.

"I'll loan ya mine," replied Quickfinger Maggie, offering her a startlingly similar pair.

The sculptures glowed red-hot in their nest of charred, smoking trash— the neighbors, reasoning that a good bonfire ought not go to waste, had thrown a startling amount of household rubbish in with them. Ella approved: it gave a variety of exciting colors to the ceramics, only half of which were broken.

As the neighbors went home they crossed paths with the day's final visitor, a gentleman who was dressed far more elegantly than any of the others had been and in fact sported combed hair, a fresh shave and something indefinably familiar about his bearing. Ella stopped rolling out a rope of clay as he approached.

My god, Kestrella is in peak form tonight, thought Fred. The smudges of soot on her face were in just the right places to accentuate its foxy angularity. Her gown was the most exquisite scrap of roughspun that had ever hung from the slim shoulders of a stunning miniature minx. And her hands... rolling on that pliable cylinder...elongating it...

"Well how do, feller. Here to see my Maw and Pappy?"

"No, Medamselle." Fred bowed. "It's me. Brother Malfred, from back at Brewel Hall. You drew my portrait. I caught your snake."

Kestrella looked him up and down for longer than he might have hoped.

"I don't quite recall, but if you're a lover of Art I'm pleased to meet you. I have the most wonderful plans for a mural. When those snobby Prophessors at the College of Justice see it, they'll drop their spectacles! You see, my recent work has been deliberately provocative. I find myself teasing open new avenues of thought, and repeatedly thrusting my ideas into the consciousness. Because I strongly feel— don't you?— that Art is nothing unless it upends society's tender vulnerabilities and violates them."

This sizzling barrage of double entendres sent a thrill coursing through Fred. He'd heard such remarks from her before. Recalling them sometimes kept him up all night.

"Oh, but *now* I remember drawing your portrait!" exclaimed Kestrella. "I really was surprised. Such well-shaped perfection— I simply had to hand it to you—"

The sunset over the barn roof threw a bar of hot-pink light across her face. In the middle of the dirty farmyard the Dominelle de Brewel glowed like a soulcomet, and let the warm breeze ruffle her gown, and set Fred's heart on wings.

"—I mean, they usually don't ripen until weeks later." She looked at him expectantly. "Had *you* ever seen such a beautiful pomegranate?"

Ah yes, thought Fred, recalling that magical day when he'd held the leathery red globe as a prop, lying on that divan in the eight-sided underground room, watching her fingertips glide all over his body, there in the charcoal portrait. It could happen again. Now was the time to ask. He'd trade equivoques with her; she'd understand. They were so much alike: nobles, wits, sensuous souls.

He edged closer to Kestrella and tried to be handsome. "I'm sure you know I long, I ache, I hunger, to model for you once more."

"Why, how very kind of you! Some gentlemen find the poses, well, unexpectedly hard. I use them once and they seem pleased— they promise to come again— but then they find they can't manage a second time. I suppose it's all right: I do have a wooden model to use when the gentlemen aren't up to it."

Fred's pulse began to pound. He rested his hand on the clay. "You were pleased with me, I think. You didn't say it in so many words, but... you painted me quite a vivid picture."

A narrow line of concentration appeared between Kestrella's brows. "I believe you're mistaken, Brother Malfred. I distinctly recall using charcoal."

Fred struggled to guess what she meant by that. He pressed his fingers into the clay and tried again.

"So you did. But your intentions were... clearly outlined."

"Well, yes and no. I do sometimes utilize linear elements, that's true. However, overall I rely chiefly on the use of value."

This was simply too baffling. Fred decided to bring out a sledgehammer.

"Another portrait would... satisfy me deeply. Next time we do it, I hope you'll prepare a suitable surface, lay my figure roughly in position, and then make a thorough study of me, using a variety of sensitively executed strokes."

Damn it deep, couldn't he have said it without blushing? But now the gauntlet was well and truly thrown. He gripped the clay and braced himself for her reply.

"Oh, yes, absolutely. Contact my studio assistant any time, she'll set it up."

Fred fell silent. Kestrella sculpted. He tried again.

"So if... if I wanted you to explore my structure... to, ah, further scrutinize my..."

"Just drop by. If I'm not there, Teesha will make you an appointment."

Fred was stunned. Try as he might to convince himself otherwise, it was painfully clear: Kestrella had no idea what had been going on.

His brain raced through its well-worn stash of Kiki de Brewel memories. From this new point of view, they looked alarmingly different. Could *all* of her double entendres really have been unintentional? And if so, then how about her gowns? Those arousing arrangements of fabric, always seemingly on the verge of giving way... was it possible that to her, they were just interesting drapery? And her clay sculpting. Was it *not* meant to demonstrate the power of her fingertips to squeeze, tease, and tantalize, but just... shaping a lump of mud? Was Kestrella de Brewel— hot, sharp, hornet-stinging Kiki— an innocent?

Suddenly Fred was filled with self-loathing. He yanked his hand from the clay as if it were a trap about to snap shut on him, and took a huge step backward. Two, three. You know what, it was probably a good idea to keep going. He made a few more backward steps, tripped on a brick, caught himself with no attempt at any acrobatics, then turned and got the smoking-hot hells out of there. Night was coming and he wanted to hide in it.

CHAPTER 34

L ITTLE WISPS OF WOOD BARK FLOATED through the air of the shipyard Re Ata Pako was showing to his son-in-law. The old gentleman stood perfectly straight and strode with the light step of one whose life had never lacked for physical activity; he moved fast. When a bit of the floating bark stuck in his hair, Alvert had to reach out quickly to brush it away, or else Re Ata Pako would already have turned a corner past one of the great wooden levers that workers were using to bend heated planks.

"Thank you, son," he said. "Very breezy today. I expect it's because of a storm brewing off to the northwest. You see, there's a zone here where strange weather patterns arise, especially when seasonal temperatures are changing. Some people suggest that a shift has taken place in the location of this zone, as evidenced by records preserved in the Cultural Archive..." Alvert's face was cheerful and attentive, but Re Ata Pako was really only talking to himself.

"So back to the ships, observe how this crew is bending these iron-teak planks with steam: they'll cool in position and, if all goes well, this method will produce a craft with an extremely capacious and efficiently utilized hold, being ballasted entirely with the goods being transported. We have high hopes for this method of construction. It's become quite standard in the Herb Isles, and my eldest sister is already in talks with a firm there to lease a tract of forest producing top class iron-teak— although if they can't get it we are also testing cypress, a wood that while not as strong is extremely rot-resistant. Fascinating, isn't it? And in the next shed I can show you yet another method we're investigating, this one from the Warm Ocean. You'll notice that here the planks are *not* pegged with dowels and caulked with bark, but rather sewn together with sennit twine..."

Re Ata Pako kept up his continuous drone of technicalities as he led Alvert from one experimental craft to another. Big as the shipyard was, he felt as if there couldn't be enough of it. Eventually he'd run out of ships to talk about, and then he'd either have to retrace his steps and repeat all of them or else he'd find himself thinking about what had happened at the feast.

The great antique tortoise punchbowl had done yeoman duty for the 1,055th time in its storied career. The music had been delightful, the fire-dancers thrilling, the call and reply of the two poets haunting and beautiful. The tables teemed with colorful place mats and delicate shell-handled dining tongs, and the head table had featured Owa Lulu in the center as the oldest honoree, Ata Maroo on her right and Ata Steera on her left— true, there had been some small struggle there, but in the end that's how they sat. And then Alvert beside his new mother at one end, and Re Ata Pako beside his daughter on the other. All was well. The sea-hog was a thrilling success: when the cooks set it on a bench and opened the roasting cage, the delicious cloud of steam that had risen from it was more invigorating than all the incense any healer could prescribe. Ata Maroo chose Alvert the very best bite: a piece from that part of the loin where the forequarter joins the tail, a beautiful piece that glistened like an amber bead on the bed of pink noodles in his bowl.

And then, despite the noise of the guests and the pulse of the drummers and the lilting of the flute players, Re Ata Pako distinctly overheard what Owa Lulu said to his wife:

"Forget that mistake your daughter made earlier, Steera— no Headmother's first few years are perfect. She comports herself beautifully. It's *time*, my old friend. I believe I'll make a toast..."

"*Ai! Ai! Ai!*" Ata Steera leaped up as if shot in the rump with a barbed arrow. Her hand swept out so fast, no one could have seen what was in the bowl Ata Maroo was eating from. The bowl flew out in front of the head table and bounced off one of the drums: an ear-splitting boom accompanied the splatter of pork and fish and noodles.

"No! No! My daughter! No!" Ata Steera had one knee on the table, reaching for Ata Maroo's mouth. Owa Lulu would have fallen off her cushion if Alvert had not moved quickly to support her. Guests leaped to their feet.

"She ate it! I saw her eat it!" wailed Ata Steera.

The next few moments were a horrific blur. Ata Maroo sat frozen in shock as her mother screamed and wept, tearing her hair and sarong in frantic grief. "It was a seven-leg spider, *ai, ai,* woe, oh woe to us all, I saw it right there in your noodles and you've eaten it now, oh my child, you—"

When Ata Maroo insisted "No I didn't," Ata Steera's ranting soared to a whole new level.

"How can you question me, now of all nows, when your life hangs by a thread? Oh! *Ai!* Help us, help! Is there a healer? *Is there a healer?*"

And so the feast had degenerated into a panic, with a healer found only after Ata Maroo had been escorted away, and Owa Lulu left behind in the confusion. In the end there had only been a few sad tweets and booms from down on the terrace as the musicians packed their instruments and left. The poison of the seven-leg spider— which was not really a spider at all but a long-legged, long-stingered flightless wasp that pollinated a certain special and very expensive variety of fig— would either be fatal by the next evening or not at all.

"I didn't even take any figs, Mother!" Ata Maroo had shouted from her bed. "You can tell the healer to leave me alone. I don't need any leeches! Certainly not this many! Get them off me and—"

"These will be the worst hours of my life," moaned Ata Steera. "Oh, if only I'd eaten that poison bug instead!"

"For the last time, I didn't—"

"Oh, what horrible words! 'For the last time'? *This* may be the your last night on earth! Oh, and how I had meant to hand over the Headmother position to you the very moment you proved you were ready for it..."

"Ah! *Ah!* At-last-yes!" Ata Maroo cried, pushing the healer out of the way and standing up out of bed. Her beautiful silk sarong, sash and apron were all wrinkled now and the tall pale-green wrap around her hair was askew. "I see what's going on! Don't try and make me doubt myself— I know I never ate any spider. Owa Lulu told you to say I was ready, isn't that it? She wants you to let me start. But you don't—"

"I don't *what?*"

Alvert surged across the room and seized Maroo's hand. Before he could say anything, she shook her hand away and blasted him with a wave of Westlander language that was fully as powerful as the native ones Ata Steera had leveled at Re Ata Pako over the years. And then she turned back to her mother and finished:

"You don't think I'm up to the job yet!"

A little something like relief passed over Ata Steera's face before defiance replaced it.

"Correct, my little girl. Don't imagine I've enjoyed all this responsibility, mind you. But how can *you,* who still hardly remember how to behave here, possibly find your way through the... the absolute maze of customs the Ocean Empire has? Settle our particular disputes? Come up with solutions to our kinds of issues?"

"I'll have you know, Mother, that back in the Westlands— or let's be perfectly proper and say *the Federated Kingdom of Midlandis*— back in Midlandis I didn't just flog some oxen up and down a road. I did work like Papa's sisters do. Contracts. Road access. Insurance matters. Personnel. Acquisitions of equipment and land. By the face of god, Mother, one thing I'm really good at is coming up with solutions."

This whole time, the healer had been edging toward the canvas door; he almost reached it without stumbling, but at the last moment he'd blundered into a potted orchid on a stand and his noisy pratfall had reminded Ata Maroo that she was still under treatment, her arms blanketed with leeches.

"Get these blood-suckers off me!" she'd shouted, picking frantically at them. And then Ata Steera's face had turned deeply old and sad, and she'd only had to half-whisper, "Ah. And this is how the Headmother controls herself in the face of difficulty?" to make her daughter emit a sigh of rage and barge through the door, bleeding from a dozen spots, with such a flounce that Re Ata Pako almost thought he'd heard canvas slam.

This, then, was what he had rather repeat an entire shipyard's worth of technical jargon than remember. In fact, he preferred technical jargon at all times. It was interesting, harmless, and correct.

"What was I talking about, now? Oh, yes. The sennit twine used in order to— that's it! You've got it, exactly!"

While Re Ata Pako had been in his unpleasant reverie, Dragonsson Ata Alvert had picked a few scraps of wood from the floor and begun imitating the work of the shipwrights. There was a tricky knack to tying the planks together, but he had done a nearly perfect job.

Re Ata Pako's heart glowed with pride for both his clever new son and the clever daughter who had found him. He reached deep, deep into his trove of knowledge for a few words he'd learned from the carpenter of a Westlander ship: "Right square, mate," he said. "Right good."

Alvert's pale ivory smile was wonderful to see. Whatever trouble was between their wives, it didn't have to trouble them.

"Ah, my dear boy," said Re Ata Pako, more to himself than anything, "I'm sorry you had to see all that the other night. And yet, you'll be seeing it plenty, because you've joined the family business. We make things, you see: Steera makes scenes, and I make... myself scarce. Ah, well. In our day, a name and a fortune were the perfect match."

They turned and began their stroll back toward the boat dock; Re Ata Pako wasn't walking quite so fast anymore, and he reached up to put his hand on Alvert's back.

"But I'm glad about this thing I've heard, that my little Rooey chose you because of love. And I'm glad she's home— don't get me wrong. But I hope life here doesn't put anything between you two. Because if I had to choose between having my little Rooey home but unhappy, versus having her in love, and succeeding, and being herself, somewhere halfway across the world... even if it meant I'd never see her again... well. Well." He cleared his throat. "Right good," he repeated in the Westlander language, and again Alvert smiled.

Their boat was drawn by only one whale, a bull calf known as Re number Eight-four-seven. Alvert had learned that while Cloud Whales did have proper names for one another, no human could ever begin to pronounce them, so identifying numbers were used instead. In much the same way, rather than shout in their puny human voices, drivers used an instrument with a penetrating sound, known as a whale-pipe, to blow commands— Alvert had tried using it several times on Ata Maroo's team with hilarious results. Cloud Whales, however, were excellent mimics. They could, and sometimes did, embed facsimilies of human speech into their calls.

Now, as he and Re Ata Pako boarded their boat, eight-four-seven began acting up. He splashed with his big black-and-white snout, patted the boat with his tail and committed other such youthful mischief. Re Ata Pako bore it all with patience but the last straw was when the calf surfaced, opened his mouth to show a tongue like a pink mattress and gave a great, reeking belch.

Re Ata Pako fanned the stink away with the hem of his kilt and blew a sharp rebuke on the whale-pipe.

Eight-four-seven's oxlike eyes narrowed. In a sulk he slipped the harness over his stubby tusks but not before uttering a humming, buzzing, crackling squeal, deep inside of which was buried a short phrase of complaint, common among Peaceful Ocean children.

"None o' your sass," snapped Alvert upon hearing it. "Da an' I *do* know what's funny. That just weren't it." Of course the whale had no notion of Yondy speech, but Alvert was glad he'd stuck up for proper behavior.

The sun shone. The wind blew. Re Ata Pako said, in his halting Westlander: "Whale was say we no fun."

"Well Da, I hope you told 'im— there's times for fun, and times for work."

"Yes, I was tell it."

Re Ata Pako was proud of himself for knowing a bit of his son-in-law's language. Surely this nice young man was still half a stranger. Ah, but someday— he said to himself, and who knows when it will be, but someday— he'll understand us.

CHAPTER 35

THE ENEMY OF THE CRANES WAS the vulture, Corvinalias learned. Also that the red flock glowed only in darkness, and that the immense wall of mountains, which cast a deep, cool shadow over the whole valley until midday, was known as the Breathless Heights.

"Nothing has ever crossed them," the male crane assured him as he and his mate waded in the stream and Corvinalias walked on the bank beside them. "No air is there. Too high." The crane turned to his mate, who had just plucked up a frog and swallowed it whole.

"How long we making this travel? Thousand years?"

"Yes. Something like that."

Corvinalias thought there might be a bit of an error in translation there.

"Any way, magpie gent. We making this travel where my wife lays pair of egg for very long time, and we have never heard it ever happen that someone crossed Breathless Heights. Up there nothing can live."

Corvinalias gave a Uman chuckle. "If you've been coming here for a thousand years, you must have an unbelievable crowd of descendants. Back home I have two sisters and two brothers from my own clutch, and eleven more from earlier, and I'm the baby of them all, ha ha. My Da is the Prince of Limberlimb and his oldest brother, who I'm named for, is Corvinalias Elsternom e Rokonoma the Third. Our, ah, King." He was a bit ashamed of himself for having injected this last vanity; by way of distraction from it, he kicked at a bit of moss beside the stream. Fortunately the cranes did not notice. The female crane had begun striding about, picking up rushes and twigs and stacking them. There wasn't a lot of such material in this forest, but it didn't seem to bother her.

"We have no chicks, magpie gent," she said. "We are last of us. We come here end of every summer, I lay pair of egg, vulture eats them."

What.

"A vulture eats them? Every time? But— but why?"

"They are our enemy. And hungry. And mean. Many reasons why."

In his astonishment Corvinalias couldn't help being rude. "But why do you keep doing it? Coming here and laying eggs? Why not go somewhere else?"

"Any other place, we would not have lived thousand years."

"But what's the point?" cried Corvinalias, gobsmacked. Why did the cranes come here every year only to— to— and the thousand part, that just had to be wrong.

"Maybe there is not point," agreed the male crane. He strode to his wife and let the tips of his wings droop down like black rain from a white cloud. She did likewise. They strode about one another, flipping their bright red heads rhythmically, forming sculptural shapes with their bodies, singing. Their motions had a meaning they clearly understood; it went on for a long, long time. Finally the male wrapped his neck around that of his mate: they twined together like vine flowers and he said, very softly, "I love you very much as ever— but this travel, it has become tiresome to me. I wish not to make it any more."

"I feel same. I have felt same for some time. Thousand years is very long. I too wish this to be last travel."

Corvinalias leaped into the stream between the towers of their long reedy legs and tried pushing the cranes apart. "Wait, wait, wait! I didn't mean you had to change your lives or anything! Forget I said it! I'm sure you know what you're doing! It's a tradition! Please don't— don't—" He didn't know what would happen to the cranes if they stopped coming to the valley, but... no, that was wrong. He knew.

"It all right, magpie gent. We very old and this never was our own fer-lock."

Corvinalias lay on the water and floated like a dead duck. "But... but what happened to your own flock?"

"Who knows?" the male crane shrugged. "So many years, we forget."

THE FOREST WAS SOLEMN AND dark until at noon the sun finally cleared the Breathless Heights and began its trip westward; then the forest was solemn and slightly less dark. Corvinalias traced the stream to its source. He had nothing else to do.

The crystalline flow grew quicker and narrower the further he followed it. Finally he discovered that it issued in a swift gush from a cleft in the base of the Heights. The cleft looked interesting, generously sized, and surprisingly tame. Corvinalias stepped inside.

Stuck in the ceiling of the cleft, one red feather cast a warm light. Underfoot the water danced with a jaunty motion. Corvinalias didn't know why, but it inspired him to whistle a tune: the first line of the House of Elsternom's anthem, "From Boughs On High We Hail to Thee".

From the water, a bubbling noise answered him.

This would have been surprising enough— but the noise had a rhythm. Unmistakably, the rhythm of the song's next line.

Corvinalias jumped like a startled cat, hit the wall and fell half into the water. Something laughed into his submerged ear. In his wild scramble he touched something. A long, white, eyeless fish.

The bubbling noise continued but he could hear words through it; in this way it was like the language of Cloud Whales. His failed speech to the Scientific Institute on that topic seemed to have been a lifetime ago. Corvinalias didn't want to interrupt, but he couldn't help himself.

"How did you know the song I was whistling?"

"I know all."

"All?"

"All."

So they were quiet for a while, there being not much more to say.

"Who are you?"

"Whoever you think I should be. If you're frightened of me, I am the Wyrm of the World. If you find me amusing, I am White Leaf, the trickster. If the thought of a fish swimming in the veins of the earth, growing its every scale and barbel in a solution of the Stuff of Magic and so coming to embody eternal wisdom, fills you with wonder— then you may call me the Perpetual One."

"What do you call yourself?"

"I don't."

And they were quiet for a while longer; Corvinalias had nothing else to do.

Finally he decided he might as well ask this wisdom fish some questions.

"Are you real?"

"As real as you are."

"And how real is that?"

"Real enough for you to believe in."

"Do you always talk in riddles?"

"These aren't riddles! I'm answering you in a perfectly meaningful
fashion. What's bothering you, Vinnie?"

"How did you know my family calls— oh, right, you..."

"Yes. So I really don't *have* to ask what's bothering you, except that I
believe you'll benefit from hearing yourself say it out loud. Take your
time, Vinnie. Then tell me."

Corvinalias thought. He thought for quite a while, since he had nothing
else to do, and at last he said: "I'm not sure, wisdom fish. A lot of things
are on my mind, but which of them bothers me, or at least which of
them is, ah, the most... uh—"

"Think it over and come back tomorrow, Vinnie. I'll be here.
Until I'm not."

"Aha. And when will you stop being here?"

"I have no idea."

"I thought you knew all!"

"Well, every one of us has things we cannot know we do not know. The
only difference is that with me, I know about them."

"I'll come back tomorrow," groaned Corvinalias, sloshing through the water.

"Leave the feather burning," bubbled the fish after him. "It keeps bats from coming in here. Tedious noisy twits."

CHAPTER 36

THE COMBAT-PRACTICE ARENA AT WHELLENGOOD HALL was an impressive room, complete with sand and benches and racks of weapons, but of course the Queen could not see much of it. Three of its walls were made of glass and steel, so perhaps she did see the afternoon sunlight pouring through them; she also might have been able to make out an array of silhouettes on those walls; but it was unlikely that she could recognize the silhouettes as trophies of the monsters Dame Elsebet had fought and slain in her youth. Ten firewyrms, with their razor-sharp scales and flaring halos of horns; fennemums and meldragores by the dozen; twenty bat-serpents; a coily-tusked, perpetually angry-looking bhabairus; and an artistically rendered presentation specimen of the dread ramphaleon. Instead, the Queen recognized these creatures by touch.

"Margadet be careful it's sharp you want to stay away from it my grandma had one of these she warned me to stay away from it she said it's dead but it's still sharp no Margadet don't touch it don't—"

"It's all right, sweetheart. I'm wearing gloves and Elsebet is helping put my hands on only the... the..."

"You're touching one of the firewyrm's horns. His Majesty is quite correct: one does not want to rub a firewyrm in the wrong direction, without gloves on. The hunt would end with you grated to shreds. But truth be told, no one in my country has seen any need to hunt the firewyrm in the past fifteen years: its light, if you recall, is now manufactured in one of those mills we saw before the Heart—" oh, no. She had been trying so hard not to mention that frightful day. Dame Elsebet was glad Margadet de Vonn couldn't see her cheeks and ears burning dark red, but the falter in her voice was plain enough.

The Queen stepped bravely into the fray. "I would very much like to feel an example of the monster you were so kind as to save us from."

"I have a number of their pelts hanging here, Your Majesty. You'll notice that the coat is soft, but underneath it the hide is extremely tough."

Behind Dame Elsebet the sand floor of the arena gave a thud and scatter as though a small sack of potatoes had been dropped on it. This was followed almost immediately by a squall of rage from baby Prince Nedward, now down in the sand, rubbing his bottom. Over him the King stood blank-faced and swaying, arms dangling, both hands wide open, obviously unaware he had dropped his son; if he could see anything at all, thought Dame Elsebet as she whirled to face him, it was the wall of meldragore pelts.

Queen Margadet was already halfway to her husband when a memory jolted Dame Elsebet: Fred, saying *Don't touch him— that'll make it worse!* Oh gods no, she thought... but the Queen must have had the same memory. Just a step away from the King, she stopped.

"Enrick. Turn around, sweetheart. Let's go." Her voice was casual, light, sweet, desperate.

"Let's go let's go it's a good idea I think that is a good idea let's go."

"Take my hand. Here it is. Is it near enough? Can you— that's it. Now lead me back to our rooms, will you please? Elsebet: you'll bring little Nedward, won't you?"

That evening the Queen sent one of her maids to Dame Elsebet's chambers: a plain-looking woman in a black robe blazoned with the stripes and magpie of Castramars, who had the most unexpectedly beautiful and delicate voice. "Her Majesty begs Her High Honor's forbearance, saying she is aware of what an unfortunate guest she is showing herself to be. She wishes that she might rejoin you and try the arena again."

"Why, of course— of certainly," babbled Dame Elsebet, who had already begun taking apart her hairdo and removing the face paint which her own maids insisted upon slathering her with whenever she appeared in the guise of a hostess. "Shall we plan a, a, time for..."

"Elsebet," came a whisper from behind the maid. "It's me, Margadet. I changed my mind— I couldn't just send a message to you. Enrick is all right now, he's with some of our people, and— I'm so sorry about all the disturbances we cause—"

The doll-eyed girl, forty years Dame Elsebet's junior, who had crept alone down a long corridor with her hand against the wall: that was her Queen. Her heart filled with pity; she pushed it away as disrespectful; back it came, with an addition of embarrassment at making the poor girl look at a messy-haired old woman with half her face smudged and smeared. Then, of course, Dame Elsebet remembered she couldn't see her at all. Was that better, or worse?

"A few more moments, and I'll be ready to do as your Majesty wishes. Meanwhile, may I offer some tea?"

"I'd like that. But please, I'm Margadet. At least for now."

WHEN THE QUEEN, DAME ELSEBET and Lady Verocita next entered the arena, there were no observers with them. The wyrmlight globes were glowing and the walls were nothing but reflections.

Lady Verocita removed her sword and her dagger and set them neatly in a rack. She guided the Queen down a short flight of steps to the sand; here the three of them stood in a circle, and the knight spoke with the quiet authority of one who is in her element.

"So, Your Majesty. You were taught to swing a broadspear. A fine old tradition, excellent for health and coordination, and the appropriate tool for one who must perform an execution in the, Ye Gods forbid, rare case of high treason. But there is a devilish knack to the use of it, for its pole is long and its blade develops extreme speed, so with all respect, Your Majesty, I don't feel you should waste any more of your precious time on broadspear training. Noble weapon though it may be. Neither do I think it will benefit you to practice the twinstaves—" here her motionless stance took on a certain pointedness, as though she knew Dame Elsebet would take a breath to speak, think better of it, and hold her tongue. The half of Lady Verocita's mouth that faced the Queen rose up in a little smile.

"—fond though Medame is of them. And let us not even consider the stately sword and its frisky companion: the old tale of the blind swordsmaid is a fanciful one. No, Your Majesty, for you I suggest something far more effective. Something in which cool thinking is rewarded and eyesight counts for very little. If I may, Your Majesty, let us begin."

And then, with the precision of an artist, she took the Queen's wrist in two iron fingers, turned it outward, and with one touch of the other hand pulled her sovereign down to the ground.

CHAPTER 37

Sitting as it did in the quiet but never completely forgotten presence of Mount Grumble, New Port Ata seemed caught in a double identity. On the one hand, it was a very settled place. It had departed from the ancient tradition of building lightly in preparation for the inevitable, and now sported all sorts of permanent stone structures of the kind found in places like Nikibi Loop, where volcanoes were a thing of the long-vanished past. But on the other hand, people did know there once had been an *old* Port Ata.

Every other generation or so, Mount Grumble would utter an ominous vibration or display some wanton midnight glimmer, and then a considerable number of citizens would propose moving everything elsewhere; after a few months of controversy, stodgier heads would prevail, such proposals would come to nothing, and New Port Ata would go on as before. But one thing *had* been moved: on a small island apart from the city stood a building covered in fireproof imported slate, housing all the records and artifacts documenting the Ocean Empire— except, of course, for those that had been lost, or were housed elsewhere, or had never existed in the first place.

"You remember this place, don't you, *ipo?*" Owa Lulu asked Ata Maroo, gesturing at the remarkably small front door of the Archive.

Ata Maroo regarded the building, which looked like a scaly dark-gray tortoise.

"Absolutely. I remember coming here with Mother." Just looking at it made her recall being very small, marveling in the dimness at shelves filled with *ow palak* and grabbing one. Then, of course, came the memory of Ata Steera slapping her hand away with a warning to ask before we touch. Well, she hadn't been wrong. The archivists with their fireproof lanterns certainly wouldn't have appreciated a child disorganizing all their work, future Headmother or no.

"Not just with me. Lulu was with us, too," injected Ata Steera. "In fact she and I often came here to study— even as you got older and spent all of your time at your father's shipyards and terminals. Though to be fair, you must have learned something there, too. I imagine. Probably."

"I learned enough to navigate all the way to Midlandis singlehanded."

"Ah. That does help everyone who plans to go on living *here*."

Owa Lulu raised her arms in a universal gesture of frustrated peacemaking. The long decorative bodice of her apron, pinned over her shoulder with a bronze clip shaped like a pentapus, fluttered in the lazy wind. "Children!" she snapped. "I've enjoyed enough of your not-so-hidden argument. I didn't suggest this outing just for some fresh air. I thought the Archive would make a good starting line for the challenge I'm going to put to you. We need to decide this Headmother issue, so we can all move on into the future."

Ata Maroo and her mother expressed surprise, but really both of them had sensed such an announcement coming. They deliberately avoided looking at one another as Owa Lulu went on.

"The Headmother is more than someone who's memorized as much of this—" gesturing at the Archive— "as she can fit into her head. She is the queller of disputes, the pourer of sweet perfume on foul waters, the impartial voice whose wisdom goes among the Hundred Clans like fish go among the corals. Now. I'm old. Don't start with me, Steera, I was no suckling pig when we met! Flattery is one of the diplomat's tools, but even the world's best hammer won't boil soup!

"As I say: I'm old. In my day I've seen many a problem made and solved. When I was the last Headmother's advisor, we went through a stretch of about ten years where it seemed like the problems multiplied faster than ants— most of them meat problems, really troubling ones. Right now we're living in a time of relative stability. But! There's one country in our Empire that's never known peace. Even its name is trouble. Yes, I can tell you know where I mean, so I'll just come out with it: I challenge you to reconcile the Feud Islands.

"Each of you will offer a solution to the rulers of their two factions. The one whose solution satisfies both sides— *she* has the skill to be Headmother of the Hundred Clans. Either I'll bless the long-awaited transfer of power to the one who took up the breath—" Owa Lulu patted Ata Maroo's hand— "or else I'll decree that it stays with the one who's been doing the job." And she nodded decisively at Ata Steera.

Both of the women opened their mouths; here Owa Lulu held up one withered old hand. "I assure you, such a contest is perfectly proper."

Both of the women looked doubtful, and here, Owa Lulu raised her leathery old chin.

"There is ample precedent— why, almost this same thing happened only six hundred years ago. You can go right in and look it up. Now. Let's head back to the boat. I brought a basket with me and there are four cold chicken buns in it: one for you, one for you, and two for the old lady who's keeping this ocean Peaceful."

CHAPTER 38

THE DABROO FARM WAS BACK IN action.

The strange visitors who'd been coming to see Ro-Ro and Buddy had made various proposals regarding the development of salt, butter, sugar and flour. These proposals now being agreed to, the gentlemen— for they were mostly gentlemen— lost no time installing equipment and personnel.

The first proposal was for a crew of brats, whose fingers were known to be tiny, to craft superfine nets with which to harvest salt from the sea. The principle, said the architect of this proposal, was similar to that of commercial fishing, which one and all knew to be a sound and time-honored venture. Ro-Ro's eyes had lit up at the thought of the adorable, industrious little net-knotters and Buddy liked fish, so it was a go.

The second proposal, a set of well-crafted, extra-large butter churns, depended upon the availability of plenty of milk. For that, a number of female animals would be required. A team of advisors, helpfully billing by the three-minute glass, argued the merits of sheep, goats, vicannas, dray-deer, cattle and hogs. For a time it looked as though the gentleman recommending hogs had the upper hand: it was incontrovertible that sows had far more teats than any of the other creatures and thus could outdo them in terms of sheer volume. But at the last moment Ro-Ro opined that their milk might taste like bacon, so they had better go with the traditional cows. Yes, it was regrettable that forty fine milking hogs had already been ordered, but the Dabroos were willing to absorb the non-refundable deposit on them if it meant a better-tasting loaf of bread. Once this decision was made, the approval of the butter churns was a mere formality.

Sugar was similarly straightforward. Buddy had heard of sugar crystals, and sugar refining, so he was confident that the sugar mine they were being advised to consider was in fact the real thing. The engineer assured them that the mine was productive, shipping over a hundred tons of rock candy per year; certainly the Dabroos would need nowhere near so much sugar for their bread-baking project, but as the excess could be sold, the mine really was a fine investment.

That left only the flour mill. The designer of the flour mill was a stocky gentleman of few words; though most of the Dabroos' furniture was long gone, one table remained, and upon this the he unrolled a number of diagrams that did all the talking. As Buddy followed the gentleman's charcoal-stained index finger, he quickly grasped how the facility resembled a steel mill: molten wheat would fall through a handsome brick furnace, forming a mass of dough at the bottom which would be extracted and moved to a forging stage, where millers would knead it with rolling pins until all the impurities, such as crumbs, were forced out. Buddy admired the efficiency of it and authorized two, so that the millers could work in shifts. Wheat would be easy to source: all they had to do was buy it.

Brats arrived. Cows arrived. Workers came to build the flour mills. The Dabroo farm hummed with busy excitement, and the workers' camp became the scene of much playful activity in the way of card dealing, dice throwing, and even a spat over the favor of Shoogy Britches, which turned into a prize-fight when two factions of workmaids, each backing their champion, pooled some coins on a blanket and said winner take all. Ro-Ro put in ten silver bits because she liked excitement, and was saddened when the women resolved their differences at the last moment, disappearing with the blanket, coins and all— though no one was more saddened than the forsaken Shoogy Britches.

"Well, Butterpat," said Ro-Ro one evening as she settled down with Buddy, sprawled on a quilt in the corner, their heads nestled together on their one remaining pillow. "How do you think we're doing?"

Buddy thought back on the day. It had been rich with experiences. A cattle stampede, both flour mills on fire, ten brats with the spot-rash and a message saying part of the sugar mine had caved in. Well, no one ever said life was a lawn bruncheon. He turned his face toward Ro-Ro's and discovered that she had turned hers toward him. Their foreheads touched, then their noses, then their lips. "I'd say we're doin' all right," murmured Buddy. "I'd say we're doin' fine."

CHAPTER 39

A S PLEASANT AS POOR LIFE WAS, eventually it dawned on Ro-Ro that the farm might have crossed some line. It might actually be harboring rascals, rogues and scoundrels.

She didn't want to alarm Buddy, of course. He was a tender soul, not having attended as many theatricals as she had and therefore not as deeply exposed to the grit of life. But once Ro-Ro had seen the crooked dice game at the workers' camp, she could not unsee it. The dice were completely irregular and so, she suspected, were certain other workers' cards, and their fascinating little puzzle made from three teacups and a pebble, and the ring toss game she'd played all day but simply could not seem to win. None of these seemed to be, as she'd heard it put, "on the square"— and she was fascinated, *fascinated!*

At first the roguish workers would not let her in on their secret. But eventually she wore them down. The first time Ro-Ro fleeced a mark out of two suns and a moon— that is to say, cheated a victim of two brass pennies and a silver bit— the delight she felt at her own cleverness was indescribable. She'd heard it said that this was what men felt, constantly, and suddenly she understood why they so strongly guarded their place in society. Compared to that exhilaration, feminine activities such as combat were no more than the dull doings of animals.

While Buddy busied himself with the mechanics of the farm, Ro-Ro dug yet deeper into the ways of the scoundrels. She found that swindling was not their only skill; no, some of them flat-out stole. This was shiveringly naughty. Ro-Ro felt like a glamorous villainess up above the footlights every time she pinched a scarf from some passer-by outside the gate of the farm, or told a neighbor brat that to hand over a basket or a bit of ribbon or what have you. Eventually it all became so exciting that Ro-Ro let Ella into her confidence, ready to hear words of disapproval since, looking back, the girl really always had been rather a prig. But to her great surprise Ella was, as the rogues themselves put it, down with that.

Ella's own joy lay in having discovered the system of fashion the women of the underworld had developed. It differed greatly from that of the artists and free-thinkers she'd been emulating. On the surface, the rogues' clothing did not seem to break any new ground— no gowns or slippers or jeweled hair here— but to those in the know, every piece had a meaning. The drape of a robe's lapel, the way a boot top was folded around a pantaloon leg, the use of a scarf as a sash, all spoke a complex language which could brag, taunt, cringe, accuse or mourn. Thus attired, Ella joined her mother on forays that started out only at the very perimeter of the farm but later ranged further and further. Soon they were out in Coastwall proper, doing crimes left and right; whenever Buddy asked where they'd been all the live long day, they would exchange knowing glances.

Mother and daughter had never before had such fun together. Ella was just helping Ro-Ro filch figs from a vendor's barrow when a peacekeeping officer strode up and clapped the rowdy-bracelets onto both of them.

"Oooh, Ella," cooed Ro-Ro gleefully. "It's finally happening! We're going to jail!"

CHAPTER 40

DEEP IN THE SLIMY SHADOWS OF an illegally operating tavern, Granny's hefty servant groaned. Finally off work for one night— just one night to not have her head on a swivel— and here this wench sits down right beside her and spoils it.

"I tell yer, this wight works the benniest angle I ever seen! The quality fling their money so thick you won't believe it. Ret up yer togs and come have a look."

"All I want's one mumping drink in peace. That ain't exactly no nullicorn wish."

Granny's other servant, the wiry one, made a contemptuous gesture with her pewter tankard, spilling grog on the reeking floor. "This rumbucket won't blow away. But the wight with the benny angle might— he might take his show on the road. It'd be a shame to miss."

The hefty servant grumbled and heaved herself out of her seat.

She had been at Granny's side for years beyond counting: this was because she really couldn't count. But if she could have, she would have counted the streets she and the wiry servant crossed. One, two, ten. The closer they got to the better neighborhoods, the more excited Wiry became. She reached out and picked a handkerchief from a passing gentleman's pocket, to wipe her boots clean with, and even rubbed her teeth clean with one corner of it. "Ret up yer wig, sis," she advised her companion. "Smooth yer sash. Don't draw no tension to yerself."

"Hoy, you sweet on this wight or somethin'?"

Wiry didn't answer, so the hefty one knew. There she went again— always ogling any wight with a brain in his head. They turned a corner.

Under a stretch of merrily burning oil streetlamps was a crowd gathered around a Prophessor.

He was young for a Prophessor, no more than mid thirty, although the hefty servant would not have known how to put a number to it. He had sea-green spectacles and a dense little pointed beard, and he moved about with uncommonly active grace, sweeping back and forth through the ranks of his fascinated listeners, his black robe sweeping behind him as though it were trying to keep up.

"But wait, halt!" cried this agile young Prophessor. "I shall continue my lecture, good people, never fear. And yet I cannot in conscience ignore the terrible vibrations I sense— from—" he wandered into the audience, bowing his head in concentration and waving his arms. "Someone here. Right before me. Who is it, the one hiding an inner rage behind an *amicafaccium falsiobius?*"

"He reads their minds," Wiry explained to the hefty servant. "He hears 'em thinking in the Mystical Language and then he looks it up in his Book of Books. See? There! Told yer."

As the Prophessor worked his way through the crowd, peppering them with a patter of exquisitely erudite questions, he consulted a small gray volume and told the listeners things about themselves they never even realized were true until that very moment, in words that they could understand almost perfectly, with startling accuracy except when he made completely forgivable mistakes. He flattered the ladies in the Mystical Language, made the gentlemen feel as learned as he was, and discreetly left one of his old-fashioned sleeve pockets open for the tuition his grateful students slipped him.

The hefty servant was startled to find herself wondering exactly what lay beneath the agile Prophessor's dark velvet robes. Flustered, she posed a gruff question: "Ain't his University gonna say a thing or two, when they find out he stole that book and went workin' a side job?"

"Yer think that's any of *our* business?" growled Wiry. "Me, I don't know whether I want to follow this fella and lift them coins off him, or ask him to di-a-nose my case of Five-Minute Fever."

The hefty servant resented the way Wiry always assumed wights preferred *her*. She clenched her fist and said, "I say we take him to Granny. Not tonight, ya fried oaf! Pus buckets, ya think I ain't been her right-side wench for how long? I mean later. For now, let's just watch him."

Wiry knew when she was beaten: a whole lot of bones, muscles and fat said so. She slouched a bit but soon cheered up. "Watch him a few days, ay. Make sure he don't leave town. That's fine by me. Still wanta go back to that rumbucket? No? What'd I tell yer."

FRED'S SLEEVE WAS DELIGHTFULLY HEAVY as he made his way toward the ferry landing where Coastwall's wealthier citizens crossed the Denna. It really wasn't the money that he cared about; it was the applause. It felt good, oh so very good. For a moment his mind's eye flickered upon an image of Kestrella applauding— but a wind of humiliating memory blew grit into his mind's eye and it winced shut.

With the Dabroos away, Brewel Hall had become very quiet. He and the other guests had seemed to drift about in a haze. At first Fred had passed the evenings playing cards with various nobles and scholars, and the days playing tennez with their children; then, finding that they took the games either far too seriously or not seriously enough, he had exchanged games for lying flat in the sun, drinking punch and doing nothing, until he thought he might die of boredom. Eventually he'd helped one of the gentlemen's sons improve a poem, and showed one of the old ladies a dance step, and then one thing had led to another and Fred had put on an entire show in the gazebo. He could no longer deny it: he simply had to Fool. And so, with one of Donn Felip's Mitsa-Konig University robes and a pair of his spectacles, one of his memo books and a scrap of velvet cut into the shape of a beard and glued on with pomade, he'd been hitting the streets anonymously every evening, in search of the alchemical potion he needed to keep his soul alive.

This last night had been a real winner. The crowd had shown its delight with a copious outburst of coin. He was on his way back to the ferry when he heard two sets of footsteps behind him: one heavy and hostile, one small and sinister. Fred turned.

"Ladies."

"Phesser."

It was the fat one who'd spoken. The scrawny one only nodded, staring at something that was decidedly not his face.

Impulsively Fred reached into his sleeve. "Do you like money, ladies?"

The wenches were taken aback. "Hells a whistlin', zat some kinda trick question?" asked the scrawny one.

"Not at all, not at all! I simply find that I have more than I need. I do not practice the ob-fuscatonical arts for mere pecunitarian consideratoria, good ladies! What sort of a man of knowledge should I be, if I— ah, yes, that's right, help yourselves."

"Where yer penned up, fella?"

As the scrawny one asked this, she scooped Fred's last coin into a hidden purse. The fat one met his eyes sadly, as if to say: see what I have to put up with.

"I beg your pardon?"

"She's askin' where ya live, Phesser."

Fred blinked at them. "Why, at the Scholars' Inn, obviously. I'm visiting from Mitsa-Konig. Go Meldragores!"

The scrawny one spat on the cobbles. Well-dressed pedestrians turned to glare, so she lowered her voice to a menacing scrape. "Think maybe yerd rather give us yer extra coins again tomorrow, instead a havin' rumors go round at Mitt-Ser-Ka-Nick about yer side job?"

"Oh. Ah." Fred's mind raced. These crooks might follow him all the way back to Brewel Hall. "I don't think rumors could do me any more harm. I was, ah, encouraged to go teach elsewhere." Hmmmm. *Should* they follow him to Brewel Hall? Should he lure them there, and have the de Brewels' gate guards bundle them up for the law?

Suddenly Fred heard the Grand Constable's voice again, loud and clear: *Wild theories. Waste of an opportunity. Justice doesn't let cowards take her by the hand.*

A shiver shook him, as though Lily had slithered down his collar. If he went back to the Grand Constable after all this time, with nothing to show but a pair of common thugs— no. There were two ways to be laughed at, and that would be the wrong one. Indeed Fred was flooded with the most desperate urge to show up the Grand Constable, to maintain the superiority he'd so masterfully shown when he put the wight in his place. But how, how?

And then he had it. He would prove his wild theories correct. He'd find that Fliss, if it took all year.

He waved his hands about. "I'm... I'm getting a tazmic vibration from you two. It's— let me put it in plain terms. I sense that you have a, a friend or an enemy of some kind. I'm sensing a letter..."

"We don't know no letters," said the fat one, sadly. "I met a wight once taught me to write a bee, but I forgot how."

"A sound, then. A fluh, or a flih, or a..."

The women exchanged glances.

Fred reached into his other sleeve, pulled out Donn Felip's memo book, and flipped wildly through its pages. "F—loss? Fleece? Fliss?"

The scrawny one fell back a step. She turned to her companion. "He's heard."

Fred licked his thumb with a showman's flourish, slowly turned one more page and then, pointing at the spot where Donn Felip had written *forehead massage: ?benefits?*, he cried: "Aha! Here it is. The Book of Books tells me that this person is a powerful— oh, dear, he is a criminal of the most pro-tracticated exotanity. His emblem is that of the cured pork shank..."

"Great God Almighty in the lightest brightest Heaven," whispered the fat wench, making a superstitious gesture. The scrawny one stared at Fred in what looked very much like fear.

The thrill. The indescribable thrill of it. Fred felt like doing a triple flip. He wanted to sing, he wanted to shout. Instead he slapped the book shut and whispered, "I'm sensing that you want to— kidnap me. To take me to this horribsome, devianic, skoi-lodical person. Please, good ladies, don't do it!" he cringed and covered his face. "You've already got my money. I'll— write you poems. Long poems. With your names in."

"Naw, fella," said the scrawny one. "It's all right. We've got nothin to do with him. In fact, here." She gave him back one dented coin. "So— where *are* yer penned up? We know it ain't no Scholars' Inn." She paused and gulped down her fear. "We'll walk yer home—less yer wanta go home with *me*."

"Hoy!" groaned the fat one.

"Very kind of you, but…" said Fred, weighing his options. He'd rather eat rat tails than go home with the wench. Brewel Hall seemed an unlikely place for a disgraced Prophessor to be spending the night. He no longer had any money for lodging…

The answer, when he thought of it, felt like something he'd always known.

"…but I already have someone to, how do you say it, pen up with. Ha ha, your slang term conjures an image of livestock. But this person offers fine hospitality, I assure you. Such a comfortable mattress. I hope it won't take me long to find the place."

CHAPTER 41

THE FEUD ISLANDS WERE NOTHING BUT trouble, in two different flavors.

Since ages long forgotten, its two factions had pitted themselves one against the other in eternal battle over the burning, cataclysmic question of whether a drinking straw, thrown into the waters of the— no. That was not the origin of the feud.

More likely, it had begun because of a piece of twine, accidentally caught in— no, that can't be right.

In the dim light of the Archivists' fireproof lanterns, Ata Maroo and Ata Steera dug deep into what people had written about the Feud Islands, back when anyone dared to visit that terrifying archipelago. Ata Maroo had stifled a cry of triumph when she learned the truth: that the feud was about how many hens would fit into— no. That was not it, either. Likewise Ata Steera, in her excitement, nearly cut herself on the ragged edge of an old, old *ow pala* when she discovered that the feud had begun when two brothers, each convinced that he would win the hand of the fair— no. The timing was all wrong. That couldn't be it, either.

One thing they both learned was certain: the battles fought in the Feud Islands were horrific. Eyeing one another over stacks of *ow palak* and mounds of folded parchment charts and crates of scrolls, mother and daughter both read about fields trampled crimson under the stamping feet of warriors, about weapons aimed straight for the heart. In the Feud Islands, young and old alike fought with great abandon. It was shameful to lose: those who fell on the field of battle, who were lost— and there were mind-boggling numbers of these— were banished to the Place of Shame, there to spend the dark night of their afterlife. Each time the factions met, there was a bloodbath.

And yet these proud people bore their lot in life with no complaint. They had never applied to the Headmother; indeed, on the rare occasion that Feud Islanders showed themselves elsewhere in the Empire, covered with scars and arrayed in whalebone armor, they made no mention of their troubles.

This, then, would be a difficult egg to crack. Ata Maroo and Ata Steera began asking people around the city whether they had ever met any Feud Islanders. They took to visiting the Cultural Archive earlier and earlier each day, trying to outdo one another. They stayed in separate wings of the Ata house and spent all their time thinking about the challenge. One night Ata Maroo sat with Alvert on the veranda of her rooms, listening to the rumble of an approaching thunderstorm, combing his hair with the tortoiseshell comb she had used as a child.

"Alvie. Feud Island people have hair like you, ah? Color of tall grass in dry season, wavy like swell east of Wowmi harbor. You think maybe in time long ago, you ancestor same people? Do people back in mountain have feud?"

"Nothin' like they've got." By now Alvert had heard all about the Feud Islands. He almost felt like he'd been there already. "There were some talk, way back, 'bout how some rich family might o' got its start not strictly honest, like. They took a lot o' knocks for it. But it never become nothin' like what you've been a-tellin' me every day wi' breakfast, and dinner, and supper, and bathtime, and—"

"Ah yah, all right, I sorry. It just so much on my mind. This big problem, ah?"

Alvert was silent. He knew when he could help, and when he couldn't, and this was the second kind of situation.

Ata Maroo put down the comb and buried her hands in the waves close to the back of his head. "You hair getting so long, ah." She nestled her face down into it, smelling the ginger and coconut dressing she had combed in. No one back in the Kingdom would ever have recognized Alvert now. He was transformed.

Am I transformed?

Her mind had spoken to itself. It had used actual words. She'd just heard them.

Out in the darkness beyond the veranda, beyond the rooftops of New Port Ata and the trees that ringed the harbor and fringed the streets, the clouds jittered with light. A long, low, roaring boom bigger than the roar of the ocean came growling toward her. It was no kind of answer to the question she'd asked herself.

Soon she'd be the Headmother. That was a kind of transformation, wasn't it?

No, her self answered. *It's not. You always were Headmother, weren't you? The old Headmother's last breath was your very first one, and you've been carrying it with you ever since. This is just going to be you turning into what you always were—*

But that didn't seem right. Ata Maroo tried following the thread of reason.

If I'm about to become what I always was...

Well now, wait, she told herself. *About to?* There was no guarantee she'd win this challenge. Of course she was extremely confident about her chances, but still. Mustn't get cocky. So, if it happened that she lost the challenge, then she'd be transformed into... into Ata Maroo. There. Into what she'd always been.

But that wasn't right either. Once she'd been the Ox-Train Queen. Sometimes she felt she still was, sale of her business or no, coming home or no. Or was home the place she'd left?

What am I doing here?

A big, cold wind swept through the treetops of the city, just the way Ata Maroo's comb had swept through Alvert's hair. More lightning, more thunder, and a mist of wetness on the next wave of wind.

"Alvie. Help me close shutters, ah? There is... something I want us to do."

Ata Maroo turned the lamps low. She spread a cushion on the floor.

"You sit here, *ipo*. Do not worry about straighten you kilt. For this clothes not important. Also not important whatever you hear from me. Just ignore, ah?"

Ata Maroo scrounged about in the trunk at the foot of their big teak bed and found some things. She came back and put them on the floor in front of Alvert: a piece of jerky and a raisin. And then, as a whole skyful of rain began hissing down the roof like a waterfall, Ata Maroo kneeled and spoke to The One Who Listens.

I'm speaking to God, not Alvie, thought Ata Maroo, because of course Alvie can't understand my language. That's all right. He doesn't have to. We put out an offering, and we hear ourselves talk, and we think.

CHAPTER 42

AFTER WHAT SEEMED LIKE EONS OF wandering Coastwall's filthy innards in the company of the two wenches— and the scrawny one was rapidly losing her awe of him— Fred finally found the street where the thieves' den lay: that crooked sign dangling from the defunct inn on the corner, that broken spot in the gutter where scum pooled. There were many boarded shopfronts; Fred hoped to all hells that he could identify the right one quickly enough to convince his escorts that he really did belong there.

And then from somewhere along the rotted boardwalk came deep, bright, tuneful laughter.

"Why, if it's not Prophessor Doktor Magistre Frednick Casmarr! Welcome back to your laboratorium, Doktor. I see you've discovered two new species of parasites."

The fat wench turned away almost immediately; the scrawny one stopped in her tracks and glared at Dok. Dok, for her part, only smiled more brightly and said: "But seriously. Fred. You can't bring those in here."

Although everyone heard the scrawny wench's knuckles crack, she knew she was beaten again, and so she gave Fred a little shove in the back as she left, snarling, "Good one, Eireen. Next time pick up yer own trash."

All the way across the noxious street, Fred was on a cloud. Somehow he'd never felt so good in his life. Why? Why?

By the time he reached Dok he had it.

"You recognized me," he said.

Dok laughed again and drew close to him. Gently she peeled off his velvet goatee and re-applied it to his forehead. Then she slipped Donn Felip's spectacles off his nose and put them on herself.

"Of course I recognized you. Why wouldn't I? You think I'm fooled by disguises?" She pulled the spectacles down and peered over the top. "I mean come on, me benny, brainy, mally Fred— you're an extremely special man. In this whole wide world there's only one of *you*."

Fred's knees went loose. The life story written inside of him turned into curlicues. He decided he didn't give a damn if she was a thief, or a grifter, or a cheat, or that she'd never sent anyone to find out whether he'd been smashed flat in a brickalanche. None of that mattered, compared to this. She knew him. She saw him. *There's only one of you.*

By now, Dok's frolly fingers had lifted his Book of Books; she held it up, pretending to read it, but of course it was upside down.

"I hope those gutter bugs didn't get grabby with you, Fred. I'd have to go kill them if they did. But really. I'd say you were asking for it, dressed like that. We wenches just can't resist a learned gentleman."

She angled her head toward the den behind the boards, where the brat was rubbing its belly, licking its lips and beckoning. "Let's go, Prophessor. There's food."

BEAUTIFUL DAYS PASSED, FULL OF delightful thieving and delicious swindling. Little by little Frednick "Booksy" Casmarr became known to the local crooks; they esteemed his skill and gave him a wide berth out of respect for the woman he knew as Dok, though of course she had other names. Brewel Hall and everything in it disappeared from mind.

As the Month of the Peaches gave way to the Month of the Pears, merchant sailors returned from voyages, their pockets full of brass and silver as they stumbled along the waterfront every long, hot evening. The famous Lantern shone from its tower high above Coastwall Harbor, while crooked card games and rigged contests and lessons by the learned Prophessor Booksy earned bales of benny garnish. Where it all went, Fred didn't know, but Dok took it to someone. He knew he ought to ask who, and thus move up the ladder of crime until he reached the goal he'd set himself— triumph over the Grand Constable, vindication of his hunch about Fliss, the eradication of a menace to society. But every night he put it off because, no matter how hot it was or how sweaty and rank he might get between dips in the Denna, Dok never told him to stop sleeping with his back against hers.

He grew to know its every bone and bump. He could tell what kind of mood she'd be in the next day just by how square she kept her shoulders, how far she sagged toward him, whether she murmured if he chanced to pull away. Once, one of her elbows had drooped behind her waist and lain on Fred's hip for what seemed like hours, slowly drifting downward until, every time he breathed, the point of it brushed against the outermost tendril of his scar. Seven hundred twenty- two times, it brushed. Well, give or take.

All those weeks, the skies over the Brewel Country remained an oppressive, solid blue. Even the filth in the gutters began turning to dust. The cicadas found one another, paired off, and died. And then finally, after a night when Dok rolled completely over and fitted herself around Fred like a cupped hand, Granny sent someone for him.

A PAIR OF THUGS BROUGHT him into one of Granny's blacked-out warehouses and pulled the blinderbag off his head; they took up their places behind her, jawing their maidenroot and cranking their crossbows. Through the halo of the single oil lantern standing on the table, the mistress of Coastwall's underworld could just make out her guest: a common-faced bull-bodied undistinguished wight, though she knew he sometimes passed himself off as a learned man. Granny spat on the cobblestone floor. She'd soon know how learned he was.

In the past few weeks her network of crooks and informers had been busy painting her an ugly portrait of her onetime protege, Hamflesh Fliss. Granny's crying little ratmouth in the Fliss clique had been mounted on a signboard, a bald announcement that Fliss knew the lines were drawn. And it was now clear that the only reason her crooked workmaids had all managed to latch themselves into such benny wheezes as that idiotic so-called farm in the middle of the city was because they'd been wearing fake Guild licenses, bought from bent inkfingers run by— who else?— Hamflesh Fliss. The thought of literate criminals chilled Granny's blood. It was as though some ominous star, that up till now shone only for her, had begun to fall from its heaven.

She stared through the lantern glare at the peasant-looking mock scholar who, if he were one of Fliss's gang, would leave the warehouse only as a cask packed with flumbers' flesh.

"Neh then, me benny. I'm Granny— may thaz'll tek a little drink wi' me." And she nodded toward the tray at her elbow. On it stood two stoneware bottles that had been specially prepared by Jaine the Brain, a wench who, as a brat, had spent a year impersonating a novice monk and thus knew the secrets of the written word.

Granny pushed the tray across to her guest. Jaine the Brain had labeled the one with the red stripe around its mouth AIL and the other one, PYZN.

"Just fetchin' glasses, me benny wight." And she made a show of shuffling to a sideboard half-hidden in the gloom. There were indeed a pair of chipped stoneware glasses on the sideboard but, more importantly, there was a discreet mirror.

Fred's mind reeled. Why, why had he gone up an alley that morning and got separated from Dok? Of course, Dok had nothing whatever to do with this... wait, why did he even feel the need to think of that? Stop, stop, think of what's happening right *now*, damn it deep. These bottles of AIL and PYZN. This test. What kind of test?

Fred had always been clever, but nowadays he thought like a crook, a sharper. He saw the angles all at once. And of course there'd always been that voice within him, the one that sometimes just said: *fake*.

It's not about which bottle you choose, the crook and sharper in him saw. It's about how. About whether you can read them at all. Granny's rivals, a gang of literate crooks— this test is to see if you're one of them.

Fred gave the tray a half-turn as though it were only common sense, when toasting with crime bosses, to never take the drink put in front of you. He did it blindly, unwittingly, the way a wight who'd never cracked a book in all his life would do it, and added a few hammy touches such as glancing about in worry; then, with all the confidence in the world, he picked up the bottle marked PYZN, hoping desperately that he'd chosen right and that Dok wouldn't have to find his purple-lipped corpse somewhere. Or at the very least, that she'd be horrified if she did...

When Granny brought the glasses, and somehow dropped her bottle of AIL so that it broke on the cobblestone floor, and shared his PYZN, Fred broke into a smile.

When she told him she had a benny plan in mind for him, which was for him to go spy on Fliss, he broke into a sweat.

CHAPTER 43

ORVINALIAS HAD GONE BACK TO THE cave the next day, just as instructed. But he still hadn't known what was bothering him.

"I give up, wisdom fish. Can't you give me a hint?"

He'd never known a fish could snort.

So he'd said nothing. He'd watched the shapes of the burning feather's light on the rapidly flowing water, and traced one wingtip in it beside them, until at last he'd called it quits.

One day became the next and the next, and still Corvinalias wasn't sure what to tell the fish. On some days he was troubled, but on others he really couldn't say anything was bothering him at all. There were plenty of tasty foods to eat in the forest, and the fiery birds were not unfriendly; the cranes had laid their egg...

There was only one egg. Try as the mother crane might, she said a second one was not to be, which probably was a good thing: one less egg for a vulture to destroy.

"How can you be so calm about it?" Corvinalias had wailed upon hearing this. "Why don't you fight? Why don't you hide your eggs somewhere? Why don't you..."

"Magpie gent. You act as though chick would grow up and have fer-lock other than family, stranger to find mate among. But we are last of us. Egg or not, chick or not, it does not matter."

Magpies don't have teeth, but they can grit their bills.

"Then why lay eggs at all?"

The cranes had shrugged. "We are alive. We must fill time with something."

That night Corvinalias had gone to the cave late. The sun was setting; the forest was growing dark; the fiery red birds had begun to blaze, like the Wyrmlight lanterns back in the Whellen Country.

The Whellen Country. As he slipped into the crevice of rock, Corvinalias thought about Dame Elsebet. She was a nice old lady. Was Fred helping her make friends with the King? He hoped so. Maybe he shouldn't have flown off so hastily, just because the King's baby had squeezed him. Maybe he should have stayed to help her.

But how would he even have done that? He really did care deeply about all of these people— the cranes, Dame Elsebet, Ata Maroo and Alvert and yes, even that blasted Fred. But he was an outsider to them all.

And then he'd known what was bothering him.

"Hoy. I'm back."

"Greetings. It is a beautiful night. And no, one does not need eyes to see beauty— in fact, it can be far easier to do so without them."

"That's deep, wisdom fish."

"I know. I've got plenty more like that."

Just outside the cave, something pale flickered by, something that had the most beautiful grassy smell.

"Ah, another one of these," said the fish. "They grow up drinking from this stream. I know you're curious— go have a look at it."

And so Corvinalias had hopped closer to the opening of the cave and beheld a nullicorn.

It looked like an antelope the color of a moonlit pearl, with a vast cape of mane and a spiraling beard, which is its particular treasure. It is said that, should a virgin pure of heart touch the beard of a nullicorn, the wishes made then will come true.

Corvinalias was a fine-looking young noble and he'd romped about plenty with court ladies; and even if he hadn't, his heart held strongly mixed emotions; and anyhow, he'd never have been able to reach the creature's beard. That helical pale-gray tassel, over countless years grown oh so very long, lay soaking in the water, swept away downstream. So the nullicorn was only for looking at, and eventually Corvinalias had looked long enough.

"I know what's bothering me. I feel so— useless? Helpless? Meaningless?"

"Pick one, Vinnie."

"I can't pick just one. It's those and more. I mean— I wish I actually had some power to help people who deserve it, you know? *Good* people. I don't mean by telling them how to live, or making decisions for them, but just— some real thing I could do. To help them survive. Or something. It was clear in my mind a moment ago..."

"I know it was." The fish's head rose out of the water.

The fish was white as cloudwisp, and eyes it had none, but on its forehead was a silver spot like a mirror, which the firelight of the red feather picked out strong and clear. It swam to the edge of the stream and lay comfortably against a stone worn smooth by the ages.

"Do you know what lies at the heart of creation?" it said. "Just joking. I know you don't."

Here the fish drew what would have been a breath, if fish had any use for such things, and went on.

233

"It's... by the way, feel free to take this metaphorically if you prefer. Some people find it a bit much. Ready?

"When the universe began, it was so small there wasn't enough room for it. And then suddenly it became too big for itself, so it went away. It's about to do this a long time ago. Do you follow me?"

"I think so."

"Hmmm. Then I must be dumbing it down too much. At any rate, the Great God Almighty— which I know you've heard of and actually *is* the universe— has one emotion, and utters one word. These are as follows: awe, expressed as a single tear, and a word that means "my wish comes true". And what's really convenient, Vinnie, is that these happen to be the exact same thing: the gem that lies at the heart of creation."

"An actual gem?"

"Are you taking this metaphorically or not?"

"I'm... not sure."

"Well, I can't make your mind up for you. Although when you do, I'll know. Go ahead, I have time."

The water splashed for a while. The nullicorn went away. The fish raised the mirror spot on its forehead as though it were an eyebrow, then continued.

"Slowly but certainly, the gem at the heart of creation is wearing away. And the dust grinding from it is the Stuff of Magic, which flows in the veins of the earth. Now someday, Vinnie, the gem will be ground away completely. And then the Stuff of Magic will fill the universe, causing everything to stop existing and instead start becoming, so that it can concentrate on having been. So you see..."

"I really *don't* see."

"Well, neither do I, obviously. But my point, Vinnie, is that everything is possible. In fact, it's inevitable. The only question is whether the one experiencing it happens to be you. Well? Are you?"

"Am I what?"

"Unless you're paying attention, I really don't know why I bother with this. No. Strike that— I do know why."

Corvinalias stretched his wings until they touched the walls of the crevasse, shook his head and raised the feathers along his back in a rippling stretch. "I think that's enough for tonight, wisdom fish. I only came to tell you what was bugging me, and now I can't even remember it anymore."

"It's all right," said the fish. "You don't have to— I'll remember. Until it's time to forget."

CHAPTER 44

F RED WAS IN A COACH FLYING toward Spireburgh, the City of a
Hundred Towers, which Granny had learned was Hamflesh Fliss's
new headquarters. Made sense. Spireburgh wasn't just a historic town
with a strange skyline— it was the home of Mitsa-Konig University, and
among the hordes of academics who flocked there from all over the
Kingdom, an aspiring literate crimelord would no doubt find some who
loved money more than learning.

Granny had made it crystal clear that Fred was being sent there to do
one thing, and one thing only: prove to Fliss that he was trustworthy,
join his gang, and wait for instructions. The other two occupants of the
coach were tasked with making sure he didn't deviate from this plan.

They were not Granny's fat wench and her scrawny one; he had become
used to that odd pair of flunkies, quite a common sight among the
sharpers of Coastwall. The women now on the seat opposite Fred were
new. They reminded him of the stuffed and mounted monsters on the
walls of Dame Elsebet's combat arena back at Whellengood: motionless,
menacing, chillingly strange. Fred kept his eyes on their compact
crossbows and not on their faces.

He hadn't said goodbye to Dok. How could he have? Immediately after
hearing the plan it had been on with the blinderbag, crossbow butt to
the back, a wandering march he couldn't memorize, the smell of horses
and four steps up into something whose sprung wheels had crunched
on gravel. Then the gravel noise had given way to the rhythmic click of
stone pavers, the blinderbag had come off and here he was— out on the
old Ve Hamilia, the arrow-straight stone road built by ancient people
who cared about travel by land as much as the de Brewels cared about
commerce by sea.

Fred watched the parched, gray-green landscape flashing by and hoped Dok would care, at least a little, that he was gone. That was as much as he dared to think about. The presence of the menacing bravos across from him was not conducive to the thoughts he would have preferred to spend the next four hours with: of how it had felt to yawn awake that morning, draped in something warm and heavy, and discover the something was one of Dok's arms and one of her legs. How it had felt to lie still for what he wished could be forever, feeling Dok's heartbeat against his spine, the feather touch of her breathing and the whole long interior curve of her, wrapping and cradling him— with a start Fred realized he *had* been able to think of it, after all.

He stretched a bit and rearranged his robe. The menacing bravos made no sign of caring what he thought or did, so he tried again but this time he couldn't so instead he clenched his jaw hard and decided to speak up.

"I'm going to need to take this Mitsa-Konig patch off my collar. Granny said I was supposed to make friends with Hamflesh, but he'll see right through it if I try to pass myself off as local faculty. Instead I'm going to be a visiting lecturer from Isladorro University— because in case you hadn't noticed it, I have an Isle of Gold accent. Hear it? Hear how I say 'hope you're not going to follow me everywhere', with that little, you know, zing? Just like when I pronounce 'because that would ruin everything' as 'and Granny wouldn't like that'?"

The bravos showed no sign of recognition. Fred opened his mouth, shut it again and turned his attention toward the patch embroidered with Mitsa-Konig's motto— "Thirst for the Sweetness of Knowledge"— and its mascot, a coiling meldragore whose legs represented MKU's sixteen Colleges. Slowly, slowly from his sleeve he withdrew the pen-case he'd lifted on his first pickpocket outing. He unbuttoned its flap, opened it wide and showed its contents: an amber quill-grip and a pretty little tortoiseshell penknife. As he touched the knife his heart sped up.

"Now, look, this is just for the patch, all right? I'm not going to— ah!"

This last ah, halfway between a sigh and a cry, was occasioned by the terrifying stiletto that the left-hand bravo had flashed out, in a sleight of hand to rival that of any pickpocket. It was aimed directly at Fred's neck; under its scruffy stubble his face went pale. Wordlessly the bravo leaned forward and picked away the stitches holding the patch to Fred's collar, skewered it and flicked it through the window with lazy expertise. She held out her hand; Fred put the pen-case into it; the coach rolled on.

FOUR HOURS AND NO LATRINE stops. They crunched under the drop-gate of Spireburgh's beautifully preserved ancient wall, down a street lined with square-pillared porticoes, under a banner reading WELCOME, FRIENDS, TO THE SYMPOSIUM, through the magnificent quarter of Spireburgh given entirely to the University, and on into a section of town which, though it could not possibly rival the seething grubbiness of Coastwall's unsavory bits, was nevertheless an advertisement that even here, there was crime. The coach stopped in the middle of a square with greasy cobbles. When its door opened, Fred shot out down an alley with the bravos in hot pursuit. "All hells, woman!" came his cry from behind a dilapidated fence.

He reappeared on the square with a red face, pulling the fall of his breeches back into position, and let them march him back to the vehicle. There, one of them unlashed a trunk, the other one threw him the pen-case, and they left him with one corner of his supposed baggage immersed in a puddle of something. As he picked up one handle of the trunk and began dragging it up some street, Fred was finally able to draw a deep, if stinking, breath.

Eventually, with his hands smarting like they had from the wheelbarrow, he arrived under the banner welcoming friends to the Symposium. Although Mitsa-Konig was almost certainly in a constant state of hosting some gathering or other, he was still grateful for the timing. And if this event was anything like those held at Isladorro, he stood a chance of blending in.

As youths he and the King had once sneaked out of the Palace and pretended to be students, with the unsuccessful object of getting the waxen young Prince Enrick to loosen up and have some pocking fun for once. Looking back, he knew they'd been carefully guarded the whole time; but the jaunt had shown him something of academic life and now he scoured his memory for details that would add to his characterization of a Prophessor of Poetic Literature who was unhappy with his position, disgusted by his colleagues, and heavily in debt from betting on crooked highcat races.

Men and boys passed Fred in clusters, all wearing robes like his own, arguing and chattering, trading books and papers, sipping from not-so-discreet flasks, whipping out abacuses, waving handkerchiefs emblazoned with meldragores—or in the case of visitors, bulls, lorro leaves, or the sun. Fred targeted a boy whose flask had clearly done yeoman work that day and lifted his hanky, which bore the sun of Isladorro.

"Scuse me!" he shouted to no one in particular, using a deaf-old-man voice like that of Enrick's late father the Old King. "Scuse me! Where's a gentleman to get lodging? I've been walking in deep-damned circles, just like the... the..." a phrase Fred remembered from somewhere popped out of his mouth. "...the Spiral-Striding Fakirs of Pharendolia!"

In a cluster of students just at his elbow, an unfortunately tall boy with the large extremities that promise worse to come froze, turned around and cried, "Oy, *hoy!* Who else is studying the Fakirs?" and before Fred could regret his words he was face to face with Petir de Brewel.

CHAPTER 45

A YEAR OR SO EARLIER, WHEN FRED had made the acquaintance of the young Seigneurin of the Brewel Country, Petir de Brewel had been a winsome, peach-faced, slim and bookish lad, taking strongly after his scholarly father. But growth had shunted him onto a different path altogether, and now he bore a disquieting resemblance to Dame Irona. He was already taller than Fred and his shy, intellectual voice had become a bull-calf bellow, issuing from under an incipient mustachio. Nevertheless he had plenty of friends gathered round him, and they all crowded to gape at Fred.

"How extraordinary!" bugled Petir. "I thought Doktor Kwaga and I were the only ones studying the Fakirs! Will you be at our talk? We're presenting our paper tonight at the bell of seven! Under the Broad Portico! There'll be drinks!"

At this point his friends burst into a fracas of whooping and gesturing which assured Fred they'd been to a few such events already. "But please excuse me, Doktor! My name is Petir! I'm the captain of the Esoterical Confounders! I see you're an Isladorro man! If you were at the debate this morning I really have to apologize for the thrashing! But we also thirst for the sweetness of victory, you know?"

Fred's mind raced, wondering whether he should trust in the blandness of his face or take this infant bull by the horns. Feeling as though he were diving off a cliff, he chose.

"Young man, let me tell you something about those Fakirs," he said, and seized Petir's collar. Into one big downy ear he whispered: "Petey. Listen. It's Brother Malfred. I don't want any attention drawn to me. I have reasons." *My god be good,* thought Fred, and let this kid have a brain in his skull.

Fred's god was in a rare agreeable mood.

"I'll play along," Petey whispered. "*Hoy!*" Fred's eardrum nearly burst. "That's fascinating! Please join me for supper! I'd love to hear more!" and Petey managed, in a surprisingly natural way, to dismiss all of his friends.

SUPPER WAS SERVED IN PETEY's dorm— that is to say, in a grand building adorned discreetly with a seahorse motif and a plaque identifying it as The Residences, Dedicated to the Memory of Onri de Brewel. There were in fact nearly a hundred other students housed there, and Petey's rooms were by no means more than five times as large as theirs: a surprising show of modesty, Fred thought.

They were alone now, at a table and benches set on a balcony overlooking the square where reveling students had, among other things, wrapped a knitted toy meldragore around the neck of the famous "Mother Mitsa" statue. Petey surprised Fred by ordering a small orchestra sent up to the rooms with their food; the musicians stood in a solid wall behind the two of them and kept up a rollicking din of old Vonnish tavern songs with their um-bah-bah beat.

"It's so no one can overhear us," Petey explained, glancing behind Fred at the player of the Bass Tubehorn. "*They* can't even hear us. So tell me, are you here because of the mystery? I wrote home about it, but what I didn't tell Mumsy and Da is that I'm working on the case. I really think I know who stole them— I'm just terribly torn as to what I should do."

"Stole them? Stole what?"

"The Tacular Specs, of course."

242

That sounded familiar, but Fred couldn't place it. Something about the tiled boathouse? An eel mermaid? The thought hovered at the edge of his mind.

Seeing Fred's blank look, Petey lowered his voice still further. "You mean your reasons are something else entirely? Not about the Specs? Do you want me to explain? Right.

"Well, Brother Malfred, I don't know if you follow the physical sciences, but MKU has been at the forefront of research into what used to be known as spellbound objects— magical things. The new term is 'preternatural initiators'. For instance, the Twin Cans, those drinking cans my parents used to own, that repeat sounds between them. Or the Everso Dice, a pair of gambling bones that seem to affect the outcome of certain events. Or the— good, I see by your expression that you've heard of the Specs after all. I'm glad you follow me.

"Well, researchers here have been making impressive progress toward their goal of understanding the mechanism, but for the past few weeks it's been a hush-hush thing that the Tacular Specs are missing. Gone. Hocka, bocka, dominaka. And so— oh, I'm sorry. I thought you knew. The Tacular Specs, Brother Malfred, are a pair of what look like sun goggles. But when a wearer puts them on, he sees a replica of what's to come: about five seconds' worth of the future. You do see, don't you, how that could be very, very— exactly. I'm so glad you're a perspicacious gentleman, Brother Malfred. One grows so tired of fools."

After a pause in which they both ate cold lobster, Petey pushed the plates away and cut to the heart of the matter.

"So. I'm fairly sure I know who stole the Tacular Specs, because last evening he got drunk and as good as told me. This fellow says he's 'in possession of a sought-after item that gives the user a refreshing, forward-thinking outlook' and he 'wants to place it with a well-funded, highly discreet private institution'. And, well, what comes next is a moral decision for me."

Upon hearing this, Fred suddenly realized that young Petir de Brewel's face no longer looked silly at all. Young, yes, and unformed, and oddly caught between the features of his mother and his father— but a deadly serious and very intelligent face. Fred raised his eyebrows in anticipation.

"The thief is Doktor Kwaga. My own mentor, the gentleman whose name is linked with mine in the groundbreaking research I was hoping would define my future. I don't know how it is with monks, Mesir, but here at the University our reputations are very much tied into those of the Prophessors we support. So I don't know which path to take, Brother.

"Should I turn Doktor Kwaga in anonymously? That way I'd avoid any ugliness, and it's a proper enough response. But somehow it seems craven. I'd feel as though I were trying to protect my own reputation by keeping the whole thing a secret, when of course I don't give a fig for that— I'd rather do the virtuous thing, wouldn't you?

"But on the other hand, I know Doktor Kwaga well. He's no thrill-seeker. He can't possibly have thought up, or carried out, a brazen crime like this all on his own— he must have some kind of partner in the background, perhaps a dangerous partner. So if I make my moral stance plain by denouncing him publicly, do I risk angering this person? Because I'd rather not give Mumsy and Da and Kiki anything to worry about.

"They're such innocents, Brother Malfred. It sounds ridiculous for a brat my age to be saying so, but it's true. For all their power, for all their authority, they're completely unable to imagine evil. They've only heard stories about it. A, a *crime boss*, for lack of a better term, could send an assassin straight into Brewel Hall and they'd offer her tea. Sometimes I feel it's a wonder it hasn't happened already."

A roar sounded from the square below, and what looked like comets began flying: someone had tied kite tails to stinger bolts, those blunt, lightweight projectiles sometimes used in crossbows to disperse crowds. The decorations twirled and swirled; factions of students chanted, sang, clapped and stamped; um-bah-bah played the old Vonnish tavern songs. It was all very cheerful.

"So there's my moral dilemma. What do I *do*, Brother Malfred? I suppose I'll take the first option— people might say Petir de Brewel is a coward, but pocks to that. As if I care. But then I think: Mumsy and Da, they'd hear about it forever— whispers of oh, you raised that Petir— that kind of cruel talk might hurt them even though they've done nothing wrong. And then I'd be doing them an injustice, wouldn't I? So which is worse? Which do I protect them from?"

In despair Petir laid his head down on the table, and as he did so, an uncanny emptiness washed over Fred.

No thoughts, no words; only the sense that a world without him in it was approaching— quietly, inexorably, the same way it approaches everyone, and that while he could, he should leave something good in it. He bent down and wrapped his arms around the boy's meaty shoulders.

"Your High Honor. The solution is easy. I'll go buy those goggles for you." And if that made Granny rush him to the end of his world, so be it.

Petir turned his head. "Oh, no, Brother Malfred! Don't trouble yourself. You have your own mission. Whatever you came here to do must be work of great value— far more important than helping me."

Fred wasn't expecting a lump to fill his throat. But it was just as well. There was either far too much, or nothing else, to say except: "Trust me. It's not."

He and Petir sat up, and something colorful raced directly into the spot where their heads had been.

The Bass Tubehorn player gave a howl of agony. Blood spurted from the back of his hand. A standard-issue crossbow bolt had gone straight through it, pinning it to the brass coils of his instrument.

A fluttering tail of ribbon led from it over the guardrail in front of them, already dangling so that neither Fred nor Petir could tell which of the dormitory's other balconies the shot had come from.

CHAPTER 46

FINALLY CORVINALIAS CAME BACK FROM A visit to the cave and met evil.

The vulture had come, just as the cranes had said it would. As that ragged gray brute the size of a deep-damned ox bent to stab the hook of its bill into the cranes' egg— their only egg, their single and precious final egg— Corvinalias didn't hesitate for a moment. He launched himself at it, his only thought being a kind of indignation that the filthy rancid seeping red birds were nowhere to be seen, the useless bastards.

The cranes' egg lay broken, bleeding out its golden heart, and that would have been bad enough but then Corvinalias saw the worst thing he'd ever seen, anywhere— and he had seen a hurricane sweep an entire island away. In the moment before he hit the vulture, he saw that it had killed the parents, too.

And now the young Count of Upper Cloudyblue— who had never in his life so much as pecked a nest-mate or called anyone out in a duel or even uttered the words "I hate you"— threw his soul open to show a furnace of rage.

He clawed for the vulture's only weak spot: its reptilian eyes.

One of its wings smashed Corvinalias across the temple. His head whipped painfully back and his ears rang. He lay hurled into the grass and felt the brute leap onto his keelbone, crushing him, twenty times heavier than he was, more; its weight alone would have killed him, but it was impatient. It tried snatching Corvinalias up in one of its talons and somehow he slipped its grasp and rolled away, out of sight for a moment, until the vulture spotted him face-up and slashed down at him with its frightful blade of a beak. Corvinalias gave a desperate squirm; the beak slashed not him but the nest beside him; and his outstretched fingers, clawing blindly, connected with something. One of his fingernails had caught in a fold of the brute's bare, shriveled head. Corvinalias fluttered up into a wild hover.

Fighting not to lose this tenuous hold, he brought the tip of a second nail to join it. Then a third. Bend the fingers, bend. Frantically he scrabbled beside them with his other hand— and he had it. He had it. By every god in every heaven, he had hold of the bastard.

Corvinalias pinched all his nails together and felt the tips of them really begin to dig. The vulture screamed and whipped him in every direction. He almost let go, but at the thought of the cranes and their egg, his fingers became iron; a sudden release twanged under them like leather being punctured and then they were slipping, slipping through a pulpy wetness, passing one another as they scraped the bone of the vulture's skull and jutted scarlet from the leather opposite. Corvinalias was clenching his fists so hard they shook.

The vulture's eyes bulged. It was blinded with its own blood. Try as it might to pin him and strike him a killing blow, it couldn't; each time it clawed at him, it clawed its own face, and in the feeble atmosphere of the high valley every attempt cost more energy than it could spare. Reduced to rolling on the ground and flailing in panic, well aware that it had lost the advantage, the vulture pulled a fiendish final move: it rocketed into the sky, dragging Corvinalias along with it, meaning to fold its wings and fall upon him, to crush him like an eggshell.

But adrenaline is a fearsome elixir. It sped Corvinalias's mind like fuel. He guessed the vulture's intention and instead of fighting its upward trajectory, instead he aimed it at the stony wall of the Breathless Heights. *I'm taking you where nothing can live,* he promised it. Not me, not you, nothing.

They collided with the rock. When the vulture closed its wings and fell, it crashed not to the earth far below but only onto one of the Heights' shallow ledges. With each spasmodic struggle, Corvinalias used the brute's own momentum to fling it up onto the next higher ledge, clinging to his enemy's head like a gruesome bloody wig.

It became a kind of meditation. Sometimes he hurled the vulture and sometimes he found the strength to pull it— again, again, as the sky above them turned darker and darker under a sun that burned blindingly pure.

Finally, to his own surprise, Corvinalias landed on a sheet of ice.

Before him, a slope cascaded away earthward in a gradient from white to green. The murderer hanging in his fists was long dead, stiff and cold, so he peeled his frozen fingers out of its flesh and watched it slide away— down, down, down into the trees until it was gone. And then he lay on the ice and cried.

He cried for all the obvious reasons, but in frustration, too.

Was that all I have to give? he sobbed. Revenge? Taking revenge didn't help the cranes. All I wanted was some power to help good people survive... but I missed my chance to get it... there I was, an inch away from a nullicorn, right there in the stream it grew up drinking from, standing in the very same water that floated its beard full of wishes...

It was a long time before Corvinalias had the strength to half-flutter, half-slide down the slope of snow. Even longer before he reached the treeline. Longer still, until he managed to roost for the night.

It was the next day before he realized he did get a power, after all.

He could cross the Breathless Heights.

CHAPTER 47

QUEEN MARGADET DE VONN, DAME ELSEBET de Whellen and the puissant Lady Verocita had spent the tail end of the Month of the Peaches training together, learning the ways of the oldest combative art of them all: the art practiced by the mother bear, the soldier ant, the falcon upon her nest.

It was the art of touch, of grip, of cling and hold and bend; a contest of strength against an opponent who also clung and held and bent— but a contest of wits as well, for strength applied incorrectly was worse than useless, while a modest touch at the right moment, in the right place, could turn the fight. And most of all, it was the art of courage, because without a weapon the entire battle hinged upon one thing: the ability to get close to an enemy, by speed or guile or patience— close enough to sink in the claws.

Margadet de Vonn proved surprisingly good at this. She cared not a whit, for example, whether her assailant attacked her eyes. She was not distracted by extraneous motions. And having lived all her life in a world of blurs and shadows, she could tell where objects were located by the way sounds moved around them. The first time she managed to maneuver Lady Verocita from the open arena to a position wedged against one of the pillars used for training horses, the knight had cried out in triumph: "That's the way, Maggie!" And as the days passed, her confidence grew and grew.

The King was happy to stay away from these sessions. "You might not know it to listen to him," explained the Queen, "but Enrick has an extremely vivid imagination. He says he can't bear to watch us even pretend to be hurting one another," she explained one day as she and Dame Elsebet took part in the ancient practice of *ren-teri,* or playful sparring. By now some of the movements were so natural that the two of them were able to have a conversation as they threw attack after attack upon one another, countering as best they could and feeling their way toward an understanding of what worked when. Dame Elsebet was surprised to learn that some of the unconscious movements of horsemanship— for example, the little unbalancing push one gives when asking a horse to raise one of its hoofs for cleaning— had analogues in the nameless art. Both of them learned, some days more than others but always steadily, under the tutelage of the fierce Verocita; they sparred, they drilled, they listened to short explanations of theory and undertook strengthening exercises like the almost forgotten ones they'd taken when they were young and just beginning to really grow.

All of this made the students feel stronger in many ways beyond the physical. One evening Dame Elsebet came down to the arena alone and, in secret, set up a practice sheaf, mounted her broadspear on its longest handle, and attempted the three-stroke *kuaga-losha* cut that had been her bugbear for years. Sweep, sweep, sweep: the blade whistled uninterrupted through the bundle of straw tied around white oak dowels, and for what seemed an eternity the sheaf had stayed perfectly still before falling apart into four exactly equal pieces.

"My god within," she said out loud, filled with equal parts of pride and horror. Pride, because she had finally done it perfectly; horror, because the *kuaga-losha* cut was the one used to execute a traitor. If ever one were to arise— and she prayed one never would— she would have to face such a person alone and dispense justice. Such was the law in the Whellen Country.

Meanwhile the Queen found the strength to speak to her husband.

Margadet de Vonn was no fool. She knew that, had Enrick of Castramars been a typical mannerly, learned, self-composed noble gentleman— why then, her parents who ruled the ancient, prestigious Vonn Country would have swum the whole length of the Denna to marry their other daughter, the one whose olive-green eyes could count the spots on a fawn a hundred ells away, to him. Margadet's was the last laugh, of course: somehow it happened that the King's eccentricities were no burden to her, and they loved one another dearly; yet she'd learned that in a world full of dangers— such as the freakish one they'd faced last year, and the meldragore, and who knew what might come next— love was not enough.

She broached the topic one morning as they sat in the garden outside their suite. They were sharing a pleasant silence, listening to one of the Whellengood maids clank about amiably in the rooms, chatting with their own servants and cooing to the baby as she cleared the breakfast dishes.

The Queen could tell that her husband was facing away from Whellengood Hall. She'd noticed that, from the very first day he'd ventured out through the pair of doors opening onto their own little plaza, he tried his best never to look back at the wall their doors opened out from. The songs of birds, the hum of bees, the chatting of gardeners, all seemed to resound brightly upon this wall and so she surmised that it was made of glass and that the King wanted to avoid the very sight of it.

She reached out to him and was correct about the location of his hand. "Sweetheart. Please tell me something. Are you bothered by the glass wall?"

"Yes."

"What don't you like about it?"

"I don't want to talk about the wall I don't like glass buildings stop asking me about it."

So she knew. It reminded him of the humiliating scene on the day of their arrival.

"Please tell me what would happen if there were another emergency, and you needed to pay careful attention to something you didn't like."

Then she waited for the long thought she knew he would give this request. The breeze blew, the birds sang, and the King's answer came from a throat full of approaching tears.

"I had to do that once you remember and I don't ever want to think of it again oh Margadet I don't even like to think about that idea it almost makes me feel like I'm going away inside the way I sometimes do when everything is too much..."

"Nothing like that is happening now, sweetheart. Don't worry. But I ask because Dame Elsebet and Lady Verocita and I have been learning to face danger unarmed, and soon I'll have finished the first course of lessons." She reached for his other hand, felt around until she found it. "And then, dear, we're going to have an examination. A test. We will fight Lady Verocita, and— sweetheart, I can tell you're turning away from me. I don't mind that, but it's exactly what I want to talk to you about. Someday we both might find ourselves facing danger again."

"I don't want to take those lessons no Margadet that's for you to do not me I am not meant to do that it makes me want to go away I hate the glass and I hate that monster and I hate thinking about danger—"

The soft crushed stone of the patio began to crunch rhythmically under his feet. The Queen knew what that meant. She moved her hands into another position, something she didn't even realize she'd learned from the training, and somehow the position was soothing and as she held it his feet slowed down.

"You won't have to look at any glass or any monster. But will you look at me?"

"I am looking at you Margadet you don't know it but I am looking at you I have improved that people used to say I don't ever look at who I'm talking to but I have improved that I am looking at you right now."

"That's wonderful, sweetheart. But I mean: will you come and watch me take my examination? I'll ask Lady Verocita whether we can have it in a garden, a perfectly peaceful garden. Will you watch me face a little danger there? Because if you do, that will be an enormous improvement in your courage."

"I don't have courage Margadet."

"Yes, you do. You've only forgotten it. Reawaken your courage. Watch me fight." She squeezed both his hands: would he flinch away?

He did not. To her great delight he squeezed back.

CHAPTER 48

RHONSO DIMACHI, THE MAJOR-DOMO OF BREWEL Hall, pressed his
closed eyelids harder. Wherever his fingertips went, they made
flashing blobs and black-ringed moons on the dark field of his
frustration. A moment's escape. But he could only delay for so long.
Finally he opened his weary eyes to behold his mistresses the Domina
and Dominelle de Brewel, now housed in a commodious private cell at
the Coastwall Station House.

This cell, built many years before as potential housing for prisoners
who were friends of a certain corrupt magistrate, now deceased, had
never actually been used; upon the arrival of the de Brewels, the Grand
Constable had put them in it rather than down in the guts of the
Station House with the common run of crooks. But the cell was so clean
and handsome that Ro-Ro and Ella had ordered the addition of some
dirt, a dented pewter drinking can, and a musical instrument known
as a blow-harp. As Ro-Ro clanged the can against the plastered wall,
Rhonso pleaded with her.

"Medame. I urge you to give this up. I've brought enough money to bail
out an army, although a single word from you would be enough. Or a
word from His High Honor Donn—"

Ro-Ro paused in her banging. "Don't go bringin' Buddy into this!"

"That's right, don't you dare tell my Pappy!" cried Ella, frantically
folding her sleeves into a pattern requesting any crook who saw it to
try smuggling her a weapon, and her pantaloon cuffs into one insisting
she'd been framed. "Freedom!" she cried, snatching up the blow-harp
and tooting on it to great effect.

"But Medamselle! Medame! I'm telling you, you *are* free! You may go at
any time! Mesir Doak. Open the cell, do."

Ro-Ro thrust her hand between the bars and swatted away the key for the dozenth time. "No, no, no! Do you not understand how this is supposed to work? We must repine! Repine, I tell you, in durance vile! You cannot simply let us go. I demand we—"

"Do a long stretch in the jar," offered Ella. "Rust away in the pokey. Get a pinstripe suntan."

Rhonso threw his hands into the air. "I simply have no idea what to do, Mesir Doak. My training does not extend to this. I believe I need to go away and consult my bureau— forgive me, consult the book in my bureau." He rubbed his eyes some more. "You have no idea how many other things are on my mind."

"I understand, Dimachi," said the Grand Constable in a beaten-down voice. "I'll have my men row you back across the river to the Hall. Look in your book and come back when you can. We'll still be here, I'm sure. If anything changes, I'll send a note by messenger."

"Very good, Mesir." Rhonso bowed wordlessly to the ladies and hurried away.

The Grand Constable pulled a chair up beside the cell, threw himself into it and cradled his head in his hands. After some time he looked up through his fingers.

"Medames. One last time— it's open. Please come out."

"Nice try, pig!" growled Ella, adding: "But in all earnest, Mesir Doak. We'll escape on our own, thank you. Mumsy is right. Helping us would be *cheating*. When we break the law, we want to do it by the rules."

CHAPTER 49

THE GRAND CONSTABLE BROUGHT IN THE Dabroos' supper— gruel, which they'd insisted upon, even though gruel hadn't been the standard fare in Coastwall penal facilities for the past thirty years. For form's sake he put a few slices of jailhouse cake (coarse bread, spread with soup-grease) on the tray beside the sea-green porcelain bowls of gruel, and as he marched toward the room that held their cell, watching his feet in their neatly polished uniform boots appear and disappear under the tray— left, right, left— he practiced how he'd explain this menu addition to Medame and Medamselle.

Left, right, left. Step over the threshold. Inside the room now. Deep breath. Get set to look up. Feel that great, big evening breeze blowing through the little barred window— holy hells.

The little bars of the window lay detached in the midst of a heap of rubble. The breeze was blowing through a great, big hole. The Grand Constable let the tray smash to bits on the floor, leaped through the unlocked, but untouched, door of the cell, fell to his knees in the middle of the heap and dug through a mass of cloud-light stones and fragile plaster. Under it all was the blow-harp, clearly scratched from use as a pry bar.

The Grand Constable didn't know what to do. And then it hit him that he didn't have to do anything. The country that Ro-Ro and Ella were running loose in belonged to them. *Maybe all I need to do*, thought the Grand Constable, is just sit here and laugh.

BUDDY WAS WORRIED ABOUT RO-RO and Ella. They'd never been gone this long before: the sun had set. The ponies were still home. They hadn't been in the workers' camp. The neighbors were nowhere to be found, so he couldn't ask them if they'd seen his old lady and his li'l sunshine, and as he leaned in the dark door of the hovel, he thought maybe he ought to go out and find them himself.

But at the thought, his heart sank. From hearing the citizens who came to his levees, he understood that Coastwall on foot was vast. And what if the womenfolk had wheedled a vehicle, hit them wide open roads and made for other places? It struck him that the only places he really knew were Brewel Hall, the University quarter of Spireburgh, and certain parts of Cousin Elsie's estate, Whellengood. How could he possibly hunt down a headstrong, imaginative wife and a persistently contentious daughter?

In the darkness, something soft passed under his hand. "Good boy, Babou," he said to it. But the growl that came in reply was sharper and higher-pitched than that of the family highcat. And the growl wasn't even over when another of exactly the same kind joined it. Buddy gave a start. The tag of Babou's collar clanked, there was a shuffle of paws and three sets of golden-green eyes stared up at him.

"Grrrrow? Rrrrrow? Prraow."

As he went to light the lantern, Buddy was pushed softly back and forth by the animals' heads. The light flared on the familiar Babou— but also on two strange female highcats who bore the most unusual markings: their spots bled one into another forming a set of horizontal stripes, far more black than gold; on their faces, the stripes that led from their eyes down to their jaws were doubled. Around these cats' necks were collars so dirty and sun-faded that Buddy had to coax the creatures close to the lantern to read TRACER and TRACKER.

Out onto the streets of Coastwall strode Buddy Dabroo, with a strong hold on three crude rope leashes and a pillowcase full of Ro-Ro and Ella's gloves and socks. Thugs and cutpurses stepped aside for them. Hardy bravos whistled in admiration and fell back into shadows. Buddy was pretty sure that, in one particularly dark and gritty alleyway, Tracer bit someone, but he didn't slow down to learn more.

Then finally, as man and highcats reached a dust-choked street leading down to the harbor, Tracer and Tracker made a lot of eager noise. Before Buddy could tighten his grip the ropes jerked free, his palm burned scorching hot, and all three cats flashed away, black-and-gold under the gibbous moon. Faster, faster, they accelerated, their bodies reaching and stretching, spots and stripes and white tail-tips streaming out behind them like the wakes of racing yachts, with Babou the fastest of all; when he reached his owners he pounced joyfully upon them and Tracer and Tracker took his example. The whole pack collapsed into a laughing, purring pile. As Buddy came near enough to hear her, Ro-Ro sang out:

"Butterpat! We've been having the most incredible adventure!"

"We're the voice of the streets, Pappy!" Ella pointed at a splintery fence where, with a stick dipped in a pot of tar, she had drawn a mural featuring the Grand Constable's glowering face, under which wept a pair of doves in chains. "And Maw give some bandit two bent shins and a mouthful a Coastwall marbles!"

"It was nothing— she sassed off to Ella so I just grabbed a stick and did what any lady would do. I mean, done what any wench oughta. For her young-un."

The moon glowed on the gutters, the stars twinkled over the trash, and Ella said, "It's a beautiful night, Pappy. Let's stay out here in the hot, beating heart of the city."

"It *is* hot," averred Buddy. "All right. I'm— down."

THE DABROOS STROLLED TO A square near the harbor, in a part of the city they'd never known was there. The night passed in authentic splendor: for entertainment they had the moon, the vast glittering swath of the Sky River, flights of dark bats and pale moths, the softly tottering lights of ships at anchor. And shortly before dawn, there was a cold, hard, refreshing wind. The sky began to fill with clouds and the square began to fill with people. A few raindrops fell, but the people ignored them.

It looked like a holiday crowd, but somehow it was vibrating with a mood none of the Dabroos had ever felt before, a mood that chilled them in a way the wind had not, the morning somehow darkening instead of dawning, something oppressive that wasn't the air.

"Pappy?" squeaked Ella. "Do you know what's going on?"

"No," Buddy was forced to admit.

Suddenly Coastwall, his own Coastwall, capital of the country his family had ruled time out of mind, seemed alien. The crowd grew a purpose. People started climbing up onto carts and barrows for a look at something. Ugly words and cruel laughter crawled forth. A carpenter's mallet began ringing. From near the harbor a sneering hurrah swept through the crowd.

Ro-Ro was tallest, so she was the first to see what they were building.

A gallows.

CHAPTER 50

EVEN THOUGH FRED AND PETIR EACH wanted to show the other one a brave face, the crossbow incident had thrown them into a state of undeniable paranoia; they'd been holed up in the suite ever since. Of course Fred still planned to meet Doktor Kwaga on Petir's behalf. That was never in question. That would be like going up on a high wire: so far out of the ordinary that its very audacity would make it possible. It was mundane acts like eating, talking, and venturing out the door of the suite that were hard to carry out, now that someone had tried to kill— well, one of them, anyhow.

"Let's not keep assuming there's some sort of assassin on the loose," said Petir as he rolled a barely-touched breakfast cart back out into the corridor. "It might have been a genuine mistake— the number of young dolts here who play with weapons would surprise you. They're experimenting, I suppose. Mind-healing Doktors say we all have a feminine side."

Fred pushed a piece of smoked eel around his plate, then got up and added the plate to the cart, looking both ways up and down the corridor before he shut the door.

A deep gray sense of premonition continued to hang over Fred. In the scholarly atmosphere of the suite, surrounded by philosophical books, he came up with some impressively baroque reasons for it; but finally he decided it was not premonition, but mere common self-reproach. He had an option unavailable to Petir, and to avoid using it was emphatically *not* the virtuous thing.

In the guest room, Fred folded the too-big MKU tunic and knit pantaloons he'd been wearing and arranged them neatly in a drawer; if he didn't come back, at least no one could say he'd been a slob. Once again he slipped into his Prophessor's robe. He put a few things into his sleeve pocket.

"I'm going to go out for a bit, all right? Don't worry." The last part was as much for himself as for Petir.

Once he reached the square with the greasy cobbles, it didn't take long for Granny's wenches to find him.

They were dressed as common, brass-helmeted, maidenroot-chewing town guards, and came slouching toward Fred in postures of tedious duty, thoroughly disguised but for their expressionless faces. The scant handful of dodgy-looking people carrying on their business in the square thought nothing of them: two municipal functionaries, walking the square in the presence of a stray Prophessor who seemed to enjoy talking to himself.

"Well, this trip's been a deep-damned disaster!"

The Prophessor was clearly agitated. His skin looked clammy and there were sleepless smudges under his eyes. As he walked, he seemed to gain a nervous energy; his ranting grew more intense.

"My research was progressing exactly according to the plan— let me repeat, *exactly according to the plan!* In fact, I'd uncovered a truly productive and unexpected avenue toward the desired information! In other words, I wasn't larking around! But then..." and here the Prophessor rummaged furiously in his sleeve pocket. "Then some local yob tried to— to— shoot down my reputation!"

Onto the cobbles he hurled a few bits of assorted trash: a scallop shell, some dried-up old norrange peels, and the tail of a kite, attached to something that clanked when it hit the stones, one end stained a rusty brown. He kicked at the kite tail, separating it from the other rubbish, until it began to unwind.

"Imagine, someone taking a, a potshot at my research! Did they think it would go in one of my ears and out the other? Or perhaps it was someone else's credibility they were trying to poke holes in. In other words, was I the target of ridicule, or simply caught in a crossfire? To paraphrase: *what the seven-sided gutterpumping pock?*"

The Prophessor tore at his hair with shaking hands. The guards traded looks with one another, looks of mild alarm. The gentleman seemed on the verge of a fit.

"This helps no one, do you understand, no one! If I'm... if I'm... afraid I can't hold my head up among my peers... then my scholarship will suffer! I won't be able to do the job, is that clear? To sum up: *This can't happen again!*"

Fred hadn't experienced stage fright in as long as he could remember, but as he turned on his heel to stride away, he felt wave after wave of— no, it was just ordinary fright. He fully expected to feel a razor-sharp thud in the back. But no such feeling came. He took a few steps. Still he remained alive.

Through the corner of his eye he saw one of the guards retrieve the kite tail and quickly wind it back up. As she tucked it into her waist pouch, her movements were perfectly casual; then the second guard strode past Fred, so close that her truncheon ruffled his robe. Despite the heat, a shiver shook him. His message had been received. Now to get the scab flaps out of there.

———

THAT EVENING HE AND PETIR dined on some cheese-topped flatloaves and opened the balcony doors for the first time since the incident.

"Let's stop worrying about it," said Petir, nonetheless staying well away from the patch of sunset. "I won't ask where you went or what you did today, Brother Malfred. But I do have news. Remember how I wrote to a certain someone, asking whether he's available to meet regarding the item? While you were out the answer came. It's yes."

Handing Fred a slip of paper with a note on it, he flung himself down on one of the divans arranged around a low table. "And I paid the Bass Tubehorn player's healer bill. I really wish to give the worthy fellow a cottage and nine acres, but if I ask Da to authorize it he'll wonder why. I'll have to give him cash. I'm going to sell that painting above your divan, there, to the College of Art anyway, to raise funds for when you buy the... the item from that wight who isn't my friend anymore."

Fred could tell Petir didn't want anyone to see him wiping the corner of his eye. So instead he turned his attention to the note:

My esteemed colleague. I respect your judgment and will be pleased to meet the person you deem appropriate for my project. But I must fly— time is on the wing. Regards, K

"He means that for the details, he'll send me a dove," said Petir gloomily, indicating an empty cage in the corner of the room.

"Ah."

"Mm."

The two of them munched flatloaf in silence, Fred eating his completely and Petir leaving chunks of the crust.

Sometime after sunset, a flash of gray flew in through the still-open balcony doors. Fred floated awake from a dream in which Dok was tracing one fingertip through the intricacies of his scar and saying "ooh" in the saddest voice— a voice which, alas, resolved into the burbling coo of a dove.

The bird pecked at the flatloaf crusts, holding out a leg with a sea-green enameled capsule on it.

"Petey," whispered Fred, shaking Petir's shoulder. "Wake up. The message is here."

Petir yawned, stretched, rubbed his eyes with his big puppy-paw hands. In the moonlight from the open balcony, he picked up the dove and opened its capsule and Fred was paying so much attention to this that it took him three looks straight at the thing lying on the table beside the paper flatloaf trays to realize that it was a shabby, old stirrup-winched crossbow. Its wooden tiller had been violently split, the trigger was torn out and the whole thing was wrapped in the bloody kite's tail.

Wait: not just wrapped. Tied. Neatly, in— what else?— a bow.

CHAPTER 51

FOR ALL CORVINALIAS KNEW, THE BREATHLESS Heights might have been a boundary between the realms of life and death. Maybe he *had* died with the vulture. Maybe he was a ghost.

But soon he found that he grew hungry, became tired; that bodily functions continued on as before; that his memories had not been rewritten but only added to; and thus he was forced to conclude that he was indeed alive.

His senses all told him he was in a world much like the one he'd left behind. Some of the trees were different, but they were still trees; the bugs and frogs and mice he found to eat tasted different, but they were wholesome food; in fact, Corvinalias found the new land to be reassuringly mundane.

So he flew east.

His reasoning was: *The Peaceful Ocean is east.* It's hard to miss. And if I can find a place I've already been, then that would prove this is a new part of the same world. Knowing that might help someone! And so, with a future ahead, his memory of the cranes began to heal. Not dull, not diminish, just... heal. He began to suspect that they knew something he hadn't, and had welcomed their violent end as the quickest way to a final peace. The wisdom fish would probably say so.

Eastward he journeyed, or slightly south of east, flying not up high in the rapid air current but lower and slower, at map height, learning. There was much to observe and besides, now Corvinalias felt invincible. He began to get heroic: he swooped down to look straight into the face of an orange-striped broadcat. He chased a venomous snake up a tree. He eluded the wrath of a pack of vicious monkeys. He leaped from the head of one monster lizard to the next, all the way across a huge silvery river.

He began seeing Uman settlements again.

They started small. Little knots of houses, little gardens. But soon it was undeniable: he was back in Uman country, where fields and paddocks took their places in the landscape. He'd almost forgotten what they looked like.

He saw a city.

And beside the city a canyon, with something in it that made him freeze in midair with a yelp of pain.

Corvinalias had often boasted— and it's not boasting if it's true— that magpies could see at least seven times better than Uman-beings could. The Uman he had most often boasted it to was his old pet Fred, who had been with him at their first sighting of the Heart of Stone, Dame Elsebet's rotating, power-generating mountain back in the Whellen Country.

This thing in the canyon was something like that— but nothing like that.

The thing down below, set apart in its gorge as though the neighboring city were afraid of it, was no vast benevolent slowly turning Heart of Stone. It was small. From map height, it was only a pinpoint, so that meant up close it was... the size of a hand? A Uman hand? It was spinning so fast it was almost invisible— but just the same it was very, very visible. Painful to look at. The sight of this thing hurt like staring broad-eyed into the sun— worse.

Corvinalias turned back to circle it, mustered up his new heroism and looked down again.

Searing bright chaos shook his eyes, tore his perception.

In that impossible handsbreadth, the fragile unsung boundaries dividing reality into moments and substances had broken down. Everything there was, ever had been, ever would be, all were there at once: infinity, shredding and forging itself in a catastrophic violet heat.

Corvinalias cried out again, stalled in flight, caught himself. He dipped a wing to swerve away from the sight of the thing. It was evil.

What?

Why had he called it evil? Nothing had happened because of it. The vulture had been evil; this thing, whatever it might be, had only hurt to look at. A rose bush hurt if you landed on it: that didn't make it evil.

Corvinalias angled his wings, flared his tail and swooped to a halt at the top of a blueneedle tree which resembled a small, unkempt version of Cloudyblue. Grasping a twig between his right main finger and thumb, he swung himself around as he perched so that he was facing in the direction of that thing, although he really didn't want to be. It was hidden behind the rim of the canyon, but Corvinalias felt as though he shouldn't turn his back on it.

Blue needles rustled. He turned hastily to the traveler who'd landed beside him.

"Hoy, excuse me, good lady..."

"Me man," grumped the traveler.

"Oh, I beg your pardon." Well, how should he have known? The fellow was a nearly unmarked brown. "Good gentleman, can you tell me anything about that— that— object in the canyon, that—"

"No understand."

"I saw a place over there by the city, with, well…"

"Sorry. No speak you."

"Thing?" Corvinalias sounded a bit desperate. "Bad thing?"

The traveler glared. "*You* bad thing." And he flew away.

For a long time, Corvinalias clung to the twig, swaying with the thin scented air and thinking, frantically thinking. He couldn't ignore that… thing. It was there. Active. Working. Shattering, emitting, generating, annihilating…

His thoughts kept falling apart. He kept having to shake his head, hard, and start all over, because words had edges where their meanings ended, and they simply burned away if he tried touching them to this… thing. Figuring out what it could be, describing it— those might have been good intellectual puzzles for the Scientific Institute or the Poetry Fanciers, if not for the terrible urgency he felt, a sensation of time running perilously short.

Something must be done about it, and soon. Must be done soon.

Must be done *now*.

Corvinalias launched himself from the blueneedle tree. That… thing had turned his adventure into a mission.

CHAPTER 52

THE DAY FOR THE LADIES' COMBATIVE art examination came, and it was held in a perfectly peaceful garden, just as the Queen had promised. The time was set to coincide with little Prince Nedward's nap and wonder of wonders, he fell asleep right on schedule. The nursemaid hardly had to rock his cradle.

A picnic pavilion was set up for the event in the midst of Whellengood's front lawn, near the wildflower garden and the rock garden; inside it stood a sideboard set with cool drinks and a pair of wicker chairs. Now and then a groom rode across the lawn, exercising three or four young horses, each one with its halter roped to the next in a long string; but the colorful scene was meant as training for the animals, not as a show for the grooms, and they refrained respectfully from watching. In fact, if it weren't for the horses' distinctive grassy smell the Queen wouldn't have noticed them at all. There were no archers, no attendants, no other onlookers: the event was entirely private and special.

The King, in his strongly visible black and white overcloak, was in fine spirits.

"I can do it Margadet I feel ready I think I can watch you because I know you are not really in danger you are only showing what you have learned this will be interesting."

"Precisely, Your Majesty!" exclaimed Lady Verocita. "There's the right attitude. Now here is your seat. You may observe the test, or withdraw behind the curtain, just as you wish."

The Queen said: "Elsebet, please. You go first. I insist. I'll sit with Enrick and we'll watch. That way, sweetheart—" this to the King— "you can get used to it. I won't leave you alone."

The examination consisted of Dame Elsebet and Lady Verocita bowing to one another, and then partaking in an escalating series of mock attacks. Again and again Dame Elsebet demonstrated her ability to escape from Lady Verocita, even as the situations the knight presented her with grew more dire: in the end, she freed herself from a nasty-looking hold about the neck. Throughout the performance, the King remained completely still, facing forward in his chair. The Queen heard the wicker creak only once.

"Are you all right, dear?"

"It's all right Margadet I'm not frightened any more it was only for a moment she is all right now oh how did that happen!" and he made the whooping noises she had come to know as his laughter. "That was a surprise oh yes I was surprised I think I just learned something Margadet did you know sometimes things look worse than they are."

"That's true! Sometimes they do!" The Queen had not expected this much; she was elated.

"Nedward's nursemaid tells him a story sometimes Margadet she tells him an old story maybe you know this story about the brave little smallcat I remember it from when I was very young sometimes later when we were older Fred would make fun of it and tell it in a stupid way but what I mean is that in the story the brave little smallcat sees the big-maned broadcat having an adventure and he decides it is time for him to have an adventure too this is like that Margadet I used to hear the story and not think about it but now I think oh do you ever feel like I mean do you ever feel like—"

The breeze in the front of the pavilion was blocked. Dame Elsebet and Lady Verocita were there.

"I'll come back and hear you finish telling me later, dear. Now I'm going to try passing this test. Let me give you a lucky kiss. Here I go!"

The Queen heard ruffling steps on the grass before her. She heard the swish of a robe, bending downward as its wearer bowed. Then there was a powerful grip around one of her wrists and, without even thinking about it, she turned her hand and moved her arm and, just as she'd learned to do, stepped sideways into a warmish silent place where the breeze didn't blow quite so much; her wrist popped free and the warmish silent place said "well done, Your Majesty". But before she could reply, a hot meaty arm snaked about her neck, closing rapidly inward upon her throat; as if by reflex the Queen brought her hands up to grab the arm and tilted her head forward. As the crushing arm bridged across her chin she felt a small burst of triumph, for now she knew she was safe and had plenty of time for the rest of the story to play out: the part where she dropped to her knees, hunching as though she were hoisting a pack; where for a moment the weight of her attacker spread across her shoulder, then peeled off and flew; a silky whistling noise as the attacker's legs whipped through the air, a sudden lightness, the crush of the grass before her and a breath from down by her feet that, somehow, sounded congratulatory. And then—

A thunder of hoofs passed not far away, a few horse squeals and a frustrated human growl. From the pavilion the Queen heard Dame Elsebet shout, "Oh, *pocks!* My new filly just got loose from the string somehow. I'll have to go help catch her— oh, blisterboils, she's jumped the hedge— please, don't stop the examination. Nobody pay any attention to me. I'll be back in a moment."

A flicker of understanding passed between the Queen and Lady Verocita: together they waited for just the same heartbeat, and then continued the test without interruption.

Move led to move. Each was a puzzle more complex than the last, a greater challenge, begun with the Queen at more of a disadvantage, until finally she was sprawled flat on her back, straddled by a crushing weight and staring up into a hazy silhouette.

Blind little Margadet de Vonn had never been allowed to truly fight with her sister, the way equally matched children will fight. All she knew about the nameless art was what she'd learned at Whellengood. She had no reservoir of youthful impulses to draw from, no instincts; and that was good, for it meant she had no bad habits to overcome. In a swift calculation she understood her attacker's position upon her, felt the lightening which signified an upraised arm about to strike, and like a machine built for this purpose the Queen pulled up her opposite knee and brought it squarely into the attacker's back, to send her tumbling, offering something to seize and that was an arm and the arm was a lever that moved the shoulder that moved the body whose foot was trapped and suddenly here was an idea and now *she* was the attacker and then came two taps against her side.

"Congratulations, Margadet! Beautifully done! I don't know if you realize it, but you improvised that last move completely on your own. I didn't teach it to you— you had an insight, and the skill to see where it led. That is the mark of an artist! And we do call these the combative *arts*, so I endorse you wholeheartedly. You pass!"

"Do you hear that?" the Queen cried joyfully to her husband in the pavilion. "Verocita said I pass! She complimented my— my artistry! Did you see it?"

Silence.

"Enrick? Were you watching me?"

Nothing.

When Dame Elsebet returned from catching the filly, she found the pavilion empty.

CHAPTER 53

Nᴏ ᴏɴᴇ sᴛɪʟʟ ʟɪᴠɪɴɢ ɪɴ Wᴀʜᴀʏᴇᴇ had ever been to the Feud Islands. Owa Lulu came the closest: she remembered once having interviewed an old, old gentleman who'd visited them, but who refused to talk about the carnage he had seen there, calling it "an affront to all propriety". But now Ata Maroo, Ata Steera, and Owa Lulu herself prepared for a voyage to the fateful place.

It would be difficult to approach the islands themselves owing to some very sharp and dangerous rocks ringing the whole country; but after much consultation of charts— Re Ata Pako was delighted to hear that his wife and daughter were taking an interest in charts and even joined them one day at the Archive, from which he had to be removed physically after a twelve-hour frenzy of dust-blowing, fold opening and walking of compasses— after much preparation the party had decided on the best way. They would make the long, weary journey in Ata Maroo's well-provisioned catamaran, leave the craft well outside the rocks in the care of the adult Cloud Whales, and come in on individual rafts hitched to the four calves: one each for the three women and one for Alvert, who would not be dissuaded.

And so it had been done.

Ata Maroo put away her whale-pipe and climbed from the platform of the ship down onto one of its big, hollow outriggers. Here she opened a locker and began throwing single harnesses down into the sea.

"All right now, *ipo*. Please, *please* again promise you do not shake hand with islander, ah? Also do not look in eye, make no noise— *ai!* I wish you would stay here aboard ship."

Alvert crossed his long muscular arms and dug in the way only a man raised in the cleft of a mountain can. "I wouldn't feel right, a-stayin' out here while you're in there wi' them barbaricans, Maroo."

It was useless to argue. Alvert was mild but persistent and he would swim in on the tide if he had to. Ata Maroo growled and sighed and prepared his raft.

"All right, but I will take number Four. He feisty last few weeks— learned lot of bad trick from Papa's calf Eight-four-seven. Maybe even hanging around with bad crowd from open sea." Sure enough, as she said this the young whale before her paused with his tusks only half in the harness and uttered a rude-sounding giggle.

But at last they made it in safely, flying what they hoped the Feud Islanders would understand were flags of truce, and they were not attacked.

The party of islanders who met them in a shallow, crystal-blue circular bay had thick, gruff-sounding local accents. At first even Owa Lulu had trouble understanding them. Of course it didn't help that their terrifying carved helmets covered their mouths: in fact the Feud Islanders were plated like lobsters in elaborately decorated armor, and led Ata Maroo's party along a teak boardwalk all the way to the edge of town before showing their faces.

Ata Maroo shuddered at the sight of them. It was true that four of her teeth were filed sharp, as had been the fashion when she was a child, but these people had many more filed teeth than she did, and frightening geometric scars all over their cheeks and foreheads as well. They wore perpetual scowls, spoke roughly, brandished barbaric-looking weapons such as axes adorned with sharks' teeth, and moved in a militant, stylized fashion. Their leader was a man, but a very fierce-looking one, wide and brawny enough to give Ata Maroo a fight if it came to that.

"Like ah said to ya back thar. Whas yer reason yous here now?"

Owa Lulu stepped bravely forward and bowed. "Greetings, good gentleman. We are from Wahayee, here to ask for your cooperation in settling a pressing matter that concerns the Headmother of the Hundred Clans."

"Hunderd Clans! Wahayee! Hwell! Thas some fancy long ways yous come. Tell what, yous folla me to the Palace. The *real* Palace. Not that other chicken shack." The man spat and his companions growled "Thas right" and "uh yap" and nodded their heads till their long, pale, wavy hair rippled.

Between two equally splendid red-brick palaces lay a plaza of brick-red clay, divided by a chalk line that looked as though it had been erased and redrawn at least a hundred times. From out of the palaces came two equally ruthless-looking delegations; neither side would let the other be first to welcome what one called "the Wahayee Crew" and the other called "Them Headmothers", so a handsome pair of sennit pavilions was quickly erected in front of the palaces. After that came an argument over whose pavilion would be first, and two sennit mats were hurriedly spread; then the same argument erupted over the mats so Ata Maroo, Ata Steera, Owa Lulu and Alvert stood between them.

"Wanna offer yous a drink," said the leader of one faction.

"Drink! Ha! *We* offerin yous some food," said the other.

"You like some flowers?" asked the first leader.

"How bout some joolery?" asked the second.

The leader of the first faction's hand began stealing toward the hilt of a sword that looked as though it could slice up a whale. "Well now, you back off. My people found em," he hissed.

The second leader made a move for her war club. "Then *you* stop hoggin em!"

Again Owa Lulu pushed herself into the thick of danger.

"Good leaders of a noble people. Please sit. Yes, yes, like that— you on your mat and you on yours— that's perfect. We have come to propose two solutions to your situation. After hearing them, please deliberate, and choose the one which is satisfactory to all."

And thus it began.

From Ata Maroo poured the most beautiful, well-reasoned speech she felt she'd ever given. She knew she had the tone just right, knew she was being charismatic and persuasive.

"I've studied your history, good people, and I've found it filled with great heights of valor— and great depths of sorrow. There's a lot that must be faced up to, understood, forgiven. But nothing worthwhile is easy, and peace, at long last, will give you the freedom to prosper as never before. Here is my proposal..."

And then she outlined a series of peace talks, lasting up to a year if necessary. She explained how she would give these her utmost priority, being prepared to stay in the Feud Islands until the origins of the violence had all been discovered, the grievances all aired, the ramifications all considered. She would do this for them, promised Ata Maroo, because personal inclination as well as duty bound her to complete whatever she began; and at the end of this effort, promised Ata Maroo, there would no longer be any feud between the factions. There would, in fact, be no more factions at all, but a wholly new people, moving toward a whole new future.

There were murmurs all around when she took her seat on the packed red clay. The leaders of the factions, armor rattling, turned to give one another a long look— and it didn't take a career diplomat to see a spark of agreement pass between them. Ata Maroo exulted inside, especially when she heard what her mother said next.

Ata Steera stood up, dusted her sarong, straightened her sash and her apron.

"Leaders," she said, in a voice that held no conciliatory tone whatever. "I see here before me a clearly prosperous and healthful country, full of proud and fit people, that is divided equally in two. It seems to have been so divided since time began, and shows no sign of changing. Indeed none of you have ever asked for it to be changed— and it won't be. I propose that my daughter, my mentor, my son-in-law and I take our leave of you. Thank you for your hospitality."

If Ata Maroo had been sitting on a chair, or even a cushion, she'd have fallen off it.

But that would have left her with nowhere else to fall, when the leaders of the Feud Islands' two factions looked at one another again, then at Owa Lulu, and said almost exactly the same thing at almost the same time:

"We like the second one."

"Yap, that last lady. What she said."

Ata Maroo was aghast. "But— but— but—" she stammered. "What about the war? What about all the destruction?"

The leaders misunderstood her.

"You wanta see some battle, dontcha."

"Yap, time for a battle. Gone be a bloodbath for sure! Streets gonna run red! Ever one aim straight fer the heart!"

And before she could say any more, the leaders slapped their helmets back on, whooped out some blood-curdling screams, and the streets flooded with armored warriors, swinging spears and knives, flinging

them with terrifying accuracy at a huge heart-shaped target chalked on
a faraway red brick wall.

Drums boomed out. Bells and whistles sounded. Wave after wave of
islanders poured into the plaza, whooping and whirling not to the
hawkish roar of war drums, but the infectious beat of music.

Armor shook like feathers. Weapons wagged like conductors' batons.
Again and again, the armies of dancers met in clashes of rhythmic
motion. One side would push the other one out of the way, but then
the situation would reverse, and reverse again; the energies of the
dance swept back and forth like oars and intricate formations broke and
re-formed and interleaved.

Ata Maroo would have enjoyed it if she hadn't felt completely numb.
She might even have been amused by the way some of the dancers
failed to get into position— they looked so hangdog about it, as though
they'd done something very wrong— oh dear, maybe they had.

"Aw naw, yer man got lost in battle," snorted the leader of the first
faction, pointing at one of the unfortunates who couldn't find his place.
"His warrior life is done— put him on a boat! He gone spend the night
after life in the Place of Shame!"

"Oh? Well look *thar*," countered the second leader, pointing at a woman
who had stumbled and was rubbing a skinned knee. "She fallen on
the battle field! Haw haw! Get her a blood bath!" And as the shamed
man brought a bucket and helped the shamed woman wash her knee,
soapy water spilled onto the clay of the plaza and was trampled into
crimson mud.

Ata Maroo felt like she would faint. She couldn't even look at Ata Steera
or at Owa Lulu. She had no idea she'd wanted to be Headmother quite
so much. Or maybe all she wanted was to get away from the corrosive
sting of failure. Immediately.

"*Ipo!*" she shouted through the music at the grinning, shimmying Alvert. "I leaving. I getting raft and going to ship and follow those people to wherever this Place of Shame. I feel— *Ai!* I feel I need it."

CHAPTER 54

CORVINALIAS WAS IN A DESPERATE RUSH to warn the Umans in the city beside the canyon that they were in danger. Surely it was madness, absolute madness, to live within ten leagues of that... thing.

He planned to enter some authoritative-looking place in the city, find out what language they spoke there, and if necessary learn the correct words to say: *Everyone get out of here immediately!*

Most Uman-beings were impressed by his ability to imitate their speech— they were vain that way. But the truth was, Uman languages were laughably easy to pick up. They were hatchling peeps compared to most civilized bird languages, or to something like Bat, with its extreme high pitch and burdensome system of parallel vocabularies, or to his particular favorite, Cloud Whale, which could carry up to six different messages at once on its buzzing, crackling framework, even offering operations between them such that message 1 could refer to message 2 ... but no. Corvinalias was in much too big a hurry to indulge himself in thinking about hobbies.

He quickly found a ridiculously simple way into the city's largest building: fly through a door when no one was looking. The people inside were all too extremely busy to notice a bird.

I hope you're all working on that problem of yours! he wanted to shout. I hope you're busy figuring out how to move your city away from that... thing! And if not, I hope you don't swat me with a broom or shove me out some window before I can explain the trouble you're in!

The people were armed, like guards or soldiers, but somehow they had the demeanor of Prophessors, too, as they hurried among rooms full of paper-laden desks, where big drawings of ships were pinned up on the walls. Corvinalias found that strange— they were nowhere near any ocean.

He hopped onto the bottom of a cart in which people were transporting books. On this cart he traveled along, peeking into rooms whenever it stopped, listening for connections between these Umans' language and others he'd known. He was already starting to understand some of what he overheard.

The deeper Corvinalias got into the building, the more elaborate the soldier-scholars' uniforms became— and although they didn't look anything like those he'd seen around the Uman king's palace back home, he assumed all their complications corresponded to rank. If so, he was soon among very high-ranking people indeed. All the better. They could command everyone to evacuate the city.

And then the book cart stopped in front of a huge handsome room, where a great sheet of canvas hung on one wall, painted with a map Corvinalias knew as well as his own wingtip. It was his native Isle of Gold.

The people clustered around the map were the highest-ranking yet, pointing and gesturing, and he'd have bet a flight feather that one of them had just said "far less important" and another one had said "get the notes, close the door".

Hands reached out to take a book; the cart began trundling away. Corvinalias sprang from it and raced back to the huge handsome room. Its door was already closing, but he darted inside before it shut. Clinging unobtrusively in a corner, watching everything with vision seven times sharper than that of a Uman, and listening with an understanding that grew clearer by the minute, he witnessed a scene that began with the people lowering another map from a roll near the ceiling. A map of the Whellen Country, with emphasis on the Heart of Stone.

CHAPTER 55

THE TICKING OF CAULKERS' MALLETS, THE rasping of saws, the chanting of workers— it took ten thousand and ten operations to build ships, good stiff weatherly Midland Sea ships, the way they built them in the yards around Coastwall. And many a seafarer would have found it strange to hear the sounds of a Coastwall yard, here where the sun rose not from behind the white eminence of Brewel Hall across the harbor but out of the melancholy pure blue vastness of the Peaceful Ocean.

But Wilem Honestmansson did not consider himself a seafarer at all. In fact, he didn't even consider himself Wilem Honestmansson. Not anymore. Not for a very long time.

That was the name he'd had in a little wool-lined cradle, in a village surrounded by white birch trees and the cold forbidding mountains; it was the name he'd had at Vonn University— one of only two Yondy names in the whole student body; it was the name he'd had when he went to work at the Heart of Stone, building more of the equipment that freed Dame Elsebet de Whellen's people from cruel backbreaking toil; and it was the name that heralded his undoing.

Because if his father had hadn't pretended to be an honest man, then perhaps Wilem would have had no trouble. After all, a fellow named Wilem Thiefsson would hardly have lived in fear that someone might learn how his family had become, at least by Yondstone standards, so wealthy. Such an honestly-named fellow wouldn't have given any thought to the proposals of certain foreign-sounding gentlemen who met him outside the Engineers' Guild lodge and suggested a bargain, by which his skills and knowledge would be exchanged for the promise that no one in Yondstone ever become angry with his family. So he had left the Heart of Stone, left the Whellen Country, left the Kingdom altogether; and he'd left his name, too. Now everyone called him

Zo-Ba, which he knew meant spy, but there was much to be said for an honest name.

For the first ten years he'd lived and worked in the Skylands. That was the name he privately gave to the high plateau country where he was taken. It did bear a mild resemblance to that part of the Whellen Country where the Heart of Stone offered its gentle constant help to humanity, but here the people had no such help; here wights and wenches alike were preternaturally strong, working like ants, completely unbothered by the thinness of the air at their country's dizzying altitude. They brought forth fields of barley and herds of shaggy cattle that would have earned good silver at any fair in Yondstone, and would not have seemed unhappy but for two things which gave their country the uncanny feeling of being somehow held prisoner.

First of these was the way the land rose upward, upward, as one went west until the very world terminated in a fearsome wedge of impassable airless mountains, death even to approach. The second problem was a certain mound of stones that was obviously cursed.

This mound was set in the bottom of a canyon. It was roughly as big as the Whellen Country town known as Good Market, and during the course of a day it tumbled such that every dawn would find the stones arranged in some slightly new configuration.

The centuries had taught the people of the Skylands that this mound moved in a roughly circular fashion, but in recent years it had begun accumulating nearby stones at a rate which made it seem likely that, given a few more centuries, the mound would pull the surrounding landscape into the canyon and then, given a few eras— for the Skylands was old and had experienced a number of eras— it would pull in the entire country and after that, perhaps it would really buckle down to business.

Zo-Ba was therefore assigned the task of removing it.

And with his combination of an excellent VU education, dogged Yondy persistence, and an army of local workers— not to mention the fuel provided by his constant worry that, should he fail, people back home might visit his family's big, prosperous, thatch-roofed estate one evening with their candles carelessly unshielded— he did it.

The difficulty of moving the stones was, at first, merely physical. True, the workers complained that the stones felt strange, and were hard to dispose of, and that some workers went missing. These difficulties increased as the size of the pile diminished; parts of the missing workers were soon discovered with disheartening regularity; and when these parts began to appear wearing clothing and jewelry which the workers in question had most certainly not last been wearing, many tried to quit, including Zo-Ba himself. His overlords would have none of it. They were building a city beside the canyon, and putting their own version of Vonn University in it; the campus had the definite air of a military installation, including armed persons who made sure that no one, including Zo-Ba, lost faith in the project.

Soon the pile of stones was small and it was not only still moving— in fact it had accelerated greatly, its rotatory habit plainly visible to anyone, anywhere— no, the trouble now was that the stones were starting to turn into other things. Workers who approached it, wearing the protective gear and using the machines that Zo-Ba devised, often discovered that the things they were to move frightened them, or saddened them, or made them so frantic that it could be difficult to stop them from rash acts such as hurling themselves into the pile. The protective fences erected around it never lasted long. They either turned into other things or were pulled in and destroyed. Until one day, with the unwinding of the final object— a long, unrecognizable strip of something bearing signs of life, which had to be burned for a month in a limestone pit to get rid of it— the Skylands looked upon the pile's naked core.

They looked for only a moment, those who dared, through purple glass goggles an inch thick; then they backed away and left the canyon through a gate which they locked up tight and posted guards in front of, guards who never lasted very long. The brightest minds from the Skylands' martial new University went into a certain huge building and bent themselves strongly to the plans they'd been making ever since Zo-Ba had explained how unsafe this thing he was being asked to dig out really was.

Indeed, the minds in the huge building had been very busy with these plans. They insisted that their original idea had been for the thing in the canyon, which they now termed the Generator, to be harnessed for power much like the Whellen Country's Heart of Stone. But as that plan was obviously off the table, they pivoted with surprising alacrity to a plan which was simplicity itself: they would seize control of the Heart of Stone. All that would be required was a way for the Generator to provide a weapon portable enough that it might be used to bargain with the Domina de Whellen.

Quickly the minds in the huge building revised their plan. Quite reasonably, they pointed out that, even if the Domina agreed to such a bargain, in order to take away any output from the Heart of Stone, it would be necessary to seize control of the rest of the Whellen Country. And then, the minds in the huge building further pointed out, there was a King who would certainly frown upon seeing one of his vassals' countries get a new ruler. Since he or the other countries would certainly offer resistance, said the minds in the huge building, the best plan would be to conquer the Kingdom entirely.

Everyone in the huge building heartily approved of this plan.

At this point, the number of people employed at the martial University swelled enormously; the entire city isolated itself from the rest of the Skylands and Zo-Ba was joined by more foreign engineers, all of whom had worries similar to his own. Such people disappeared into the depths of the huge building, rarely to be seen on the campus outside, and the second phase of Zo-Ba's work—developing the means to carry the weapon— began.

It would be difficult for the Skylands to project any meaningful power without some access to the Midland Sea; their only connections to the rest of the world were a river full of waterfalls and a few roads snaking down out of the high plateau into a rich green coastal country that wanted little to do with its barley-growing, shaggy-cattle-herding neighbor. Fortunately a few of the stones from the Generator had turned into substances at least superficially resembling silver and gold, so the problem of access was resolved by means of bribing shipyards on the coast. Bribery, the minds in the huge building insisted, was best. A straightforward purchase of the yards would have raised questions.

This, then, was where Zo-Ba found himself: in a secret shipyard in the coastal country, listening to bought-and-paid-for wrights as they crafted vessels which could sail into any harbor in the Midland Sea without looking out of place. It hadn't been easy to reach this stage. For his part, he had never been a seafaring man, and as for the local shipwrights, besides being forced into various bargains they were forced to learn completely new construction methods.

To this end Zo-Ba's overlords had allowed him to make a few journeys back to the Midland Sea with their other spies, in order to learn how ships might be built to incorporate a hidden place for the weapon.

His engineer's mind had observed Midlandis as directed. But his Yondy heart had seen the Lantern shining over Coastwall harbor, had followed its light on the Denna away northward, and had imagined that broad brown river narrowing to become the Whellen and the Little Good and the Troutwalk and finally a thin icy spring in the side of a mountain called Snow Flowers, where he had washed his hands as a boy after handling a particularly stinky goat. His heart yearned to know whether the spring at Snow Flowers was still flowing, and whether his family had mourned upon being told of his death in a mill accident. Zo-Ba was a smart man. He found a way to learn these things without his overlords hearing of it.

And because now he knew that his parents had passed away and his cousins had sold the estate and the Honestmansson name was no longer of any concern to him, now Zo-Ba looked past the shipyard on the melancholy pure blue vastness of the Peaceful Ocean. He decided he'd had enough of this weapon. He decided he was going to tell someone.

CHAPTER 56

DAME ELSEBET, QUEEN MARGADET, NICOLO THE major-domo and
every knight, maidservant, and functionary at Whellengood
searched the estate for hours, but failed to turn up any sign of the King.
The Queen was dazed with worry, as she had never before managed to
completely lose a husband; and Dame Elsebet was in a frightful state
precisely because she had.

Fifty-one years had passed since the gruesome event that had nearly
destroyed her mind. It had been her fault, entirely her fault; that's what
gave it such destructive power. And she couldn't help but think *this* was
her fault, too— if she hadn't gone off chasing that filly, if she hadn't let
the Royals come to see her lands... but no, she forced herself to think.
No. There is no way to decline hosting one's sovereigns, and no way
to tell what untaken paths might have led to. The Great God Almighty
gives us a universe of infinite possibilities; only madness can come of
trying to see them all.

These thoughts, combined with her breathing exercises, quelled the
threat of a relapse into insanity, but just barely. Dame Elsebet found
herself standing at the closed, guarded front gates, cracking her
knuckles, shredding her bare fingertips with her teeth. She felt dizzy,
she felt ill; she needed air and needed to lie down; she wanted to leap
upon a horse and flee; she wanted to shrink until she disappeared.
Gravel crunched behind her.

It was the Queen, guided between two lines of Castramars household
knights and carrying an ominously silent Nedward. "They're starting to
look in the... the... dangerous places," she said. "Places like... the wells..."
and her eyes flooded with tears.

As though she were listening to someone else, far away, Dame Elsebet
heard herself speaking.

"Dear Margadet. This isn't advice, because who am I to be giving advice? But it's something I think you should hear.

Today we did some exercises and we passed some tests about danger, facing danger, as though there's only one kind— the kind that comes at you attacking, the kind you can fight against. But my dear child, if I might be allowed to call you that, I'm sorry to say there's a worse kind of danger. It's the kind that comes when tragedy has already happened, when you find yourself in the aftermath, when you never even got a chance to fight— the danger of letting all that destroy you. It nearly happened to me. I don't know why it happens or how to stop it, only that the danger is there, and you should know of it. So if they... *find anything*, Margadet... I hope you're stronger than I was..."

Suddenly the guards posted at the gate were unable to contain themselves any longer. They rushed toward Dame Elsebet and the Queen; the Castramars knights' swords flashed forth; but the guards were not making any kind of treacherous attack. Rather, they threw themselves face down upon the drive. One of them even pulled the back of her tunic away from her neck as she did so, and wailed:

"We've committed a wrong upon you, Your High Honor, by not telling you something, and now we're committing maybe an even bigger one on someone else, *by* telling something. But we can't keep our mouths shut anymore—"

The other one began wailing, too. "No matter who we promised what to—"

"We will humbly take the consequences—"

"You can chop us in four pieces, Medame—"

"But we *have* to tell Her Majesty—"

Dame Elsebet rarely shouted. Her last shout had been about fourteen months previous. But her emotions were ramped up to explosive force and her patience was utterly lost.

"What in the seven-layered stinking scabflaps are you jabbering about? And get up, Nicksie, Liolla, you know I'm not chopping you into any pieces! Gods afar, your mothers were born at Whellengood. Now tell Margadet this secret immediately!"

"It's about His Majesty the King—"

"He had us promise not to tell anyone he left—"

"But we figure since they're married, that makes them legally something like the same person, so it might not really be telling any—"

"Out with it! Where did he go?" shouted Dame Elsebet, now that she had warmed up her shouting apparatus.

"He left the Hall, Medame, Majesty. He went out the gate. He asked Ferranica to drive him in the power carriage."

"Drive him where?"

"We don't know. But he was waving his arms like *this*." The guards waved their arms in an off-balance, angular fashion and baby Nedward's distraught little face brightened. He burst out laughing, and the Queen released a long, grateful sigh.

"Elsebet," she said. "I can't tell you how happy that makes me. I'm told Enrick waves his arms when something amuses him. Neddie. Did those goodwives wave their arms the way your father does when he's happy?"

Nedward began nodding so hard his mother could feel the bounce of it but then, catching himself, he changed his answer to: "Uh-huh, uh-huh! Listen, Ama, yes!"

Dame Elsebet was already halfway up the drive. She shouted back over her shoulder as she ran. "I'm going to get a pack of hounds, and hitch up something fast for us to ride in! We'll find him. My country is only so big. It's not exactly the center of the world."

CHAPTER 57

I N AN ANCIENT LITTLE DINGHY WITH faded paint, broken seats and a big crack somewhere that leaked steadily, Zo-Ba lay on what he thought of as the floor, getting drenched with spray and clinging to any fingerhold he could grab. The craft was moving with terrific speed and seemed to be accelerating; the way it bumped over the waves, Zo-Ba was certain he would fall out and drown before he could tell anyone anything.

He'd stolen the little dinghy and had managed to propel it a respectable distance from the shipyard by wiggling a single oar stuck out over its flat rear wall. He'd long ago learned this wall was called a transom, but he still thought in Yondy.

After some time he discovered that if he twisted the oar a bit as he wiggled it, the dinghy went faster. Or maybe it was only the tide carrying him out to sea. It didn't matter. He was just glad to be heading toward the islands he knew were east of him somewhere, a vast number of islands, full of people well known to travel far and wide. Some of these people would surely notice a stranger in a small boat and take him in; he would thank them, and observe them carefully, and then decide how to explain about the weapon. This was as much as he'd been able to plan before the local rum wore off and he lost his nerve.

But about an hour out, the little dinghy had begun filling with ocean, and the tide had become far too strong to fight, and Zo-Ba started to worry that his canteen of drinking water— the largest one an important engineer could unobtrusively carry to a shabby dock full of decrepit little boats— would turn out to be inadequate: he might actually die before he met some islanders. All of this was bad enough, and then the dinghy took off flying.

It did this because instead of islanders, a group of three black-and-white whales had found him. They'd surrounded the little dinghy, pushed it about and gnawed at it with their sharp teeth, and snickered at him in eerie echo of the kind of laughter he'd heard from vicious boys back in Yondstone. One of the whales had pointed out the short rope dangling from a part of the craft Zo-Ba knew was called the bow, and the others had snickered harder, clearly in agreement that this floating thing must be used as a toy. Shouting at the whales only made them snicker more, and then they'd erupted into a noise so loud it was like a hundred dozen cicadas all at once. Somewhere in the very depths of that noise Zo-Ba could have sworn he heard the language of the shipwrights' country saying *Hoy, you stupid little animal, get ready to fly!*

Now he was flying, and soon might be dying, and the whales clearly thought it was hilarious.

With one of them pulling on the rope, the dinghy went fast enough to frighten Zo-Ba.

With two of them pulling, it went fast enough to terrify him.

And when all of them bunched together, leaned on one another and put their backs into it like a scrum of ball-players at a village fair, he threw himself down on the wet floor, clinging and bracing and even praying.

Had he treated his own personal god well, when it had come into his life in human form disguised as someone or other? It was too late to wonder now. Soon he'd be judged, he was sure of it.

The dinghy struck a wave so hard it might as well have been a stone wall, flew high into the air, hit the end of its rope and flipped. Zo-Ba was thrown into the ocean. He choked on a great gasp of salt water and began to sink.

But a cushion of darkness rose up at him from the depths. It touched him, lifted him. A warm ovoid hole opened under the fingertips of

Zo-Ba's right hand and instinctively he caught the meaty rim of it. A slow, hot wind blew in and out of this hole as the waters parted and the late sun of the waning day shone down upon him. He was lying upon a vast, coolish, slippery hill that burst into a thunderclap of roaring and squeaking and crackling that was half to be heard and half— no, more than half— to be felt.

The mother whale had never been so angry in her life. Her words of wrath paralyzed her son and the nasty companions he'd picked up somewhere. The young whales dropped the rope. Two of them fled for the horizon, leaving behind just one who suddenly seemed very small compared with the giant whose nostril Zo-Ba was clinging to.

Noise, noise and more noise. The mother whale tried to rebuke her son in the quietest possible voice, lest she deafen the Uman hanging from her nose— yes, she knew she had a Uman hanging from her nose and would thank her sorry child not to change the subject.

Of course Zo-Ba had no idea what was being said. All he could do was cough out inhaled water, try to cover his left ear with his left hand, jam his right ear into his right shoulder, and wait. Soon, he thought, some friend or relative or stranger he'd met during his life would come striding over the horizon to take his hand and lead him off afar to the courtroom of Ye Gods.

That did not happen. Instead, the rest of the now-meek young whale's family arrived, towing a handsome boat of the kind Zo-Ba knew was called a catamaran.

Someone blew a note on a whale-pipe. The creature whose nostril he clung to tipped him carefully onto the deck of the catamaran and Zo-Ba groaned, "Oh, mercy on a miser-ble wight who only ever done what he did for his people back at Snow Flowers."

"What's that 'bout Snow Flowers?"

Two faces looked down upon him through the glare of sunset. One of them was a beautiful native woman and one of them was... a gigantic Yondstone man, with a definite north-of-the-Ebenzells drawl.

Zo-Ba squinted up at him. "Am I dead? Are you my god?"

"Seems like I'm one o' the most popular gods goin'. I'm everywhere. It's enough to swell a wight's head, like. So— you're from down the green side o' them Ebbies. What's a meadowlander Yondy a-doin' all the way out here?"

Alvert had meant to be funny. He thought he'd get a reply like "what am I doin' here? How 'bout you?". He never expected the fellow on the deck to say:

"Been helpin' some Skylanders get set up to rip a split in the world 'n threaten Elsebet de Whellen wi' whatever comes boilin' out."

CHAPTER 58

THE WHELLEN COUNTRY WAS A PLACE that welcomed innovation. In any of the Kingdom's other countries, eyes might have widened at the sight of a mother and her baby, strapped into a harness-racing sulky with the mother's sash and bolstered into place by copious piles of pillows, the sulky being drawn by a gray gelding with a lean, sun-beaten white-haired woman riding postilion. Jaws might have dropped to see this rig racing along in hot pursuit of a pack of hounds, noses pressed into the clay of the Trade Road, while a formation of knights in the Castramars and de Whellen colors cantered behind. Last of all came Nicolo the major-domo, clinging to the mane of a smooth-pacing sorrel mule with one hand and holding his geometrically perfect black wig tight to his head with the other.

Every so often one of the hounds would pause mid-sniff, point its muzzle toward the sky and utter a lusty howl. These howls multiplied as the pack entered the town of Good Market. There the whole pack went into full cry, their exclamations growing shorter and louder and more emphatic the closer they drew to the town center. An evening market was set up in the main square, so Dame Elsebet and the knights were forced to slow to a walk, but the hounds saw no such obstacle and, yelping and singing gleefully, they rushed straight for the courtyard of the Coachmaid's Rest in a mass of long wagging tails and huge flapping ears— though one of them did stop in the square long enough to eat several cogwheel-shaped cookies from a vendor's barrow.

Up above them, something caught everyone's eye: hounds, horses, Dame Elsebet and the Queen, baby Nedward and all the knights— even many of the vendors at the market— turned to look at a black and white geometrical something, making a series of vigorous angular postures from the inn's largest upper balcony.

"It's Enrick!" cried the Queen. "I can see that cloak I invented for him!"

"Wait, wait till we're stopped— the grooms will take the animals— I'll help unwind this sash— step right down here, Margadet, that's the way. I'll lead you up the stairs— well, at least *to* the stairs— oh. I see you've got the handrail. I'm right behind you!"

The Queen found the King in Fred's room. She sat with him on the edge of the featherbed and at first neither of them spoke. They only held hands, until at last the King said:

"I was hoping to summon you later it was going to be a surprise I wanted to summon you later to come see my adventure."

Nedward crawled into the center of the featherbed. "Looky, Da-da! Listen, Ama! Watch this!"

"Bounce quietly, Neddie. I want to hear your father."

"I think watching you fight must have made me very brave Margadet because remember how I was telling you that now I understand how some things look worse than they are well all of a sudden I realized something Margadet I realized that all this time we've been at Whellengood we've been inside the glass building that bothered me so much and nothing bad happened to us at all so I thought maybe the glass building just looked worse than it is and that made me think about all the machines—"

He paused to take a deep breath and then went on, as relentlessly as the hounds. "I found a very odd machine that was much too complicated to look at and I realized it was a carriage Margadet even though it is a machine like the ones that go back forth up down and the ones that spin around and around it is a carriage and it can go places and best of all no horses.

"And then all of a sudden I really did feel like the brave little smallcat and I wanted to have an adventure so I thought I would ride in the machine carriage to Fred's town and see his palace of course I forgot that he isn't here he got sent away oh my that does keep happening to him there's something about Fred that makes people want to send him away well that's not my concern Margadet what I'm concerned with is having an adventure and so I came here and I did it Margadet I did better than not be confused by machines or not be afraid of horses I tamed a whole lot of monsters Margadet do you want to see them?"

The Queen's eyes did widen. Her jaw did drop. "Monsters?"

"Yes I have a whole lot of monsters I tamed them do you want to go see them? You and Elsebet and Nedward?"

Nedward leaped from a mound of pillows. "Yes, Da-da! Let's see mmmonsterrrs!"

THE BARMAID OF THE COACHMAID'S Rest led the party out a rear gate, through a paddock and into the barn where she ran a side business boarding festival vendors' draft animals by the night. She bowed to the Royal Family, said "I'll be right outside in the yard if you need me, Your Majesties," and left them in the presence of...

"This one is the scariest Margadet it is the very biggest though of course it doesn't have as many horns as the others but come feel how big it is it is a giant." The King stepped fearlessly into one of the stalls and began patting a huge brown ox. The creature turned its ponderous gentle-eyed head toward him and pressed its broad slippery nose into his cheek; instead of flinching away from it or yelping in fright he gave a surprisingly mild burst of laughter, explaining, "Pat it here Margadet yes just like that but be careful not to be loud or sudden the giant cow monster doesn't like anything too loud or sudden. But now this one here this one has four horns Margadet I can count them by looking but you will have to come over here and count them by touch do you feel them? One, two, three, four, and its coat is very curly I can see how deep your hand sinks in oh Margadet isn't this monster fun to pat? It looks like a sheep but I have never seen a sheep with two horns going up and two going down it must be a monster sheep well that's all right I tamed this one too."

"Da-da! Ama! It's soft!"

"This is a Vonn Country breed, sweetheart. They're trained to pull small carts and it's normal for them to have—" the Queen paused, then went on: "—only two horns. You're right, this one *is* a monster. I'm so proud of you."

"Oh Margadet that makes me very happy and wait I have saved the best one for last. Come over here into this cage across the way now this monster has so many horns almost more than I can count so it must be the very wildest monster there is."

The Queen had a far harder time identifying this creature. Before the King took her hand and guided it to the beast's forehead, she quickly ran her fingers across a horse-like face, short furry ears, and a ragged stub of something that felt like torn leather around the base of... antlers. Her hand browsed up and up a vast sculptural pair of bony trees, moving about as the creature shook its head. Something clicked into her mind; she recalled hearing about this beast, the dray-deer, a creature used by people who lived in cold faraway lands. "You're right again, sweetheart. This one is the wildest of all."

"*Was* the wildest Margadet because now it's tame. Even Nedward can pat it, that's how tame it is. Oh Margadet oh! Do you want to think about something funny?" and here the King began to laugh again. He laughed for some time, but not very loudly, so as not to disturb the animals, and finally he explained his amusement.

"Think how funny it will be when Fred gets back, and he finds out his palace was all filled up with monsters, and he would have had to deal with them except I fixed it. That's not how things ever went with us before. He was supposed to fix what was wrong with *me*. But really we shouldn't be surprised things have changed. After all, this is an upside-down town."

CHAPTER 59

O F THE THOUSANDS OF CRAFT ON the broad brown Denna— Old Mama river, Carrier of the World— and of the hundred or so which were at that moment rowing northward, one was a moderately-sized rowing barge at whose oars sat a family of three.

Felip, Irona and Kestrella sat right amongst the oarmaids, learning what it took to pull correctly in a heavy team. They pulled mostly in silence. There was much to learn, as the craft slipped through the lands that belonged to their family, lands they had never really seen before. Sloughs and bluffs, cropland and waste land, spruce villages and poor ones all showed themselves by turns as the leagues passed by; and there was much to think about.

Each of the three had their own turn of mind. Perhaps Felip read the world passing around them as pages from a book; Irona as motions on a stage; Kestrella as light and shade on forms. But it was certain that, for each of them, the subject in mind was justice.

On that day in the square by the harbor there had been justice, of a sort. Or so they heard. They heard about this wench who was coming in the wagon, who soon would mount up on the scaffold, who'd swing for how she'd killed that wight called Shuggy or Joogy or what did they call him, this wench who hadn't said nothing whatever to defend herself and nobody had said no word for her. Her kind deserves it, they heard it said again and again. If nobody says no word for you that means you done it. That's justice. And anyway the Esquire of that quarter had his own word to say: such people were to swing. And so she had.

Afterward, when the crowd took lucky pieces— torn-off pieces of the rags she wore and the fingers she had and the hair the hangman's skimpy hood barely covered— they heard this was justice, too. The moment a killer stopped kicking, all the bad luck turned to good. But if bits of a body were lucky, then was it just for only the cruelest fighters in the crowd to get them?

The hanging itself was still more justice. Or so they were told. But if hanging really brought finality to such a matter— brought instruction to the public, and vengeance to the wronged— then was it just that no one bothered to learn exactly *why* the wench had killed the wight, or indeed if it was really her, and not someone else, who done it?

Felip had thought not. He had grabbed the collar of a scribe selling souvenir poems, and told him to write a bulletin from the Seigneur of the Brewel Country then and there, booth and customers be damned: a bulletin stating that new laws were coming with the very next sunrise, laws that every Esquire and every Burgess and every magistrate and constable were to hear and know. And then without another word the family had returned to their home across the Denna, which now seemed a place grotesquely out of proportion to any notion of justice, and Felip sat all night long in a garden representing their country.

The next morning dozens of messengers ran forth. A hundred doves flew from their cotes. Thousands of signal flags flashed from ships. All of the Brewel Country— from Coastwall to Oldmarsh, Spireburgh, Mummers' Bluff, further— received a legal decree.

These were the wishes, effective immediately, of His High Honor Felip de Brewel, Seigneur of the country and all its fiefs and holdings:

That the College of Justice at Mitsa-Konig University would receive the largest grant in the Kingdom's history, and put it toward the study of such questions as were now in the mind of their Seigneur.

That capital punishment would now be decided upon by judges hearing evidence, and not simply by counting up the words spoken for or against the accused.

That the mere order of the local official— whether Esquire or Burgess or Domina or Seigneur— would no longer be all that was required to save or condemn.

That the body of the condemned would no longer be torn by the crowd: the hood was to become a full, protective covering, applied before the fatal moment.

And lastly, that the sight and sound of that fatal moment— which Felip, and Irona, and Kestrella, had for the first and last time in their lives the horror to see— would henceforth be screened from the crowd: and here the decree suggested a set of upraised canvas sails, and the roaring of drums; at any rate by *something*. For while the current law might insist, said the decree, that life pay for life, and that this be done out in the light of day rather than in some secret chamber— to scar a blameless observer's mind with such memories was not justice.

"Felip. Take these, dear. Your hands are turning raw." Irona stopped rowing and began to peel off one of her silk gloves. It was already shredded, but better than nothing.

"Or take my sash, Da," said Kestrella, making to unwind the traditional broad sash she had wrapped about her sober linen robe and tunic.

Felip shook his head. The trip to Whellengood would be long and he knew full well that he wouldn't be rowing most of it. The barge had a comfortable cabin, in which he and his family would rest and dine: they were still de Brewels. But for now he wanted to hurt, at least a little. The books all said it hurt to change. He wanted to show up at Cousin Elsie's ready to make obeisance to the King— and ready to learn what made her world, and her hospitality, and the love she shared with her people, so refreshingly authentic.

CHAPTER 60

PROPHESSOR DOKTOR MAGISTRE FREDNICK CASMARR'S APPOINTMENT to buy the Tacular Specs was set.

Doktor Kwaga was to be in disguise as a masked healer, and he was to meet Fred on the chosen day, at sunrise, at the base of the Gerasonde Tower— one of five towers, each at the corner of a pentagonal red brick plaza. Doubtless he'd picked that spot because every morning, the plaza hosted a bustling market: just the place to camouflage the sale of almost anything. Meanwhile Petir, who was proud of his perfect eyesight— a real rarity among philology students— planned to watch Fred from a sedan chair not far across the plaza.

As the two of them stepped into the chair by the light of a porter's lantern, Petir murmured: "I have my pad and pen. The moment the sunrise bell rings, I'll turn this glass, here. Then I'll note the exact time when you..." and he mimed unhooking something from around his neck.

Fred nodded. Under his robe was slung a messenger's canvas bag with an ingot of gold in it so heavy as to evoke his awe— and he'd lived for twenty years on an island riddled with gold mines, close by the side of a king.

But now it was his turn to mime to Petir. He raised his eyebrows to indicate a question and scribbled in the air, referring to the Documentary Artist who was supposed to watch the proceedings from halfway up the tower opposite, after flickering a mirror to indicate his position. In reply Petir nodded; then in unison they both took deep breaths and made a mudra which, in the language of the Spiral-Striding Fakirs of Pharendolia, meant *my wish comes true*. The bearers raised the chair. Off they went.

In the silvery light before sunrise, the market seemed frozen. Buying and selling were forbidden until the bell should ring, and town guards kept order, prowling among the waiting barrows and carts. Fred didn't spot his particular friends among them.

Against the pinkish-gray sky the rest of Spireburgh's towers reared up in silhouette, looking for all the world like the masts of Coastwall Harbor. But these were on quite another scale, and instead of swaying gently with wind and water, they were as rigid as laws, the sky changing around them. Most of the towers were square; a few were round, and one was triangular, but in the dimness their silhouettes were all the same: sharp-edged, dark and flat, a history inked on the ever-unrolling scroll of the city.

At the cool stone foot of one of these pen-strokes, Prophessor Frednick Casmarr leaned against the Gerasonde tower and waited. Petir's sedan chair squatted at the base of the neighboring tower. No mirrors flickered from anywhere. A distant giggling and shouting meant that students who'd passed the night in the cheaper taverns far from the University were making their sottish ways home.

All at once the sky over the Eastern wall of the city grew pale and golden. A pompous glowing sliver slid up into view and the bell in the Esanella tower, the one where the Documentary Artist was supposed to be, began its peal. Everything surged into motion. The plaza filled with the cries of vendors, the protestations of buyers, the noise of trundling produce carts and bakers' barrows, cranking coffee grinders, flashy commercial gimmicks gauged to draw attention. But none of the flash was from a mirror, and Fred caught no sight of anyone who might be the perfidious Doktor Kwaga.

"Figs, Mesir?" asked a fruit vendor, setting up his cart in exactly the wrong place. Its colorful display— figs and currants, jars of jam, the last of the year's peaches and the first of its pears— blocked Fred's view of Petir and thus vice versa.

"Blisters, man! Can't you put that somewhere else? I'm— I'm bothered by the exhalations of fruit. They emit a vapor. They make me itch." The fellow just stood gaping at Fred, who finally leaped unexpectedly high and shouted: "Move that damned thing before I kick your beans!"

The vendor lifted the handles of his cart. "I don't even sell beans. That would be a vegetable barrow. Oh, look— here comes a—"

"Get out!"

The fruit man rolled away just in time for Fred to see a sharp light twinkling from a small window halfway up the Esanella tower. His heart slowed down a notch. The Documentary Artist was there. All right, so Doktor Kwaga was just a bit late. Nothing else was wrong.

And then with a horrid clamor of youthful snorts, belches, jocular noises and idle gab, a flock of students joined him against the tower wall. And oh, for the love of every god, did they really need to be first-year boys from the College of Healing?

Obviously enamored of the fact that they were studying the compassionate art, each boy displayed some piece of his clinical gear: green glass goggles and broad-brimmed hats, canes to twirl, cloaks to flare, looking for all the world like shabby black or brown birds with blank, stupid faces— and then, of course, there were those of them who wore masks.

Now Fred began to panic. Everywhere he looked were the long leather snouts of the healers' protective equipment, so many of them that he could smell the antiseptic herbs stuffed inside.

A masked student at his left shoulder burst out with a guffaw that straddled the line between childish squeak and mannish boom: "Hoy, got any more brandy?"

Another one, at his right, stank to the heavens. There was clearly something other than herbs inside the snout of his mask as he groaned: "Do not. Say. That. Word."

The left boy repeated "brandy" and the right one fell upon him. Not in the sense that he attacked; no, the right one collapsed toward his fellow, glancing off of Fred in the process, spinning him around so that he saw neither Petir, nor the Esanella tower, nor which one of these masked morons could possibly be the Doktor he sought. Then a cane slipped under Fred's black-robed arm, expertly pulled and pinned it, and he was being walked toward quite another one of the five towers: the Lembertana, which rose from a broad building with a big arched portico. Underneath this portico all was shadow, and with a lurch of the innards as sickening as that of the drunken student Fred realized that neither Petir nor the Documentary Artist could possibly see him anymore— if they'd even been able to follow where he went.

The masked healer who had led him was tall, broad-shouldered and moved purposefully: in no hurry, but wasting no time. They came to a halt in a busy section of the portico, near the booth of a harried scribe.

"Got the— the thing?" asked Fred.

The mask pulled aside. "Yes," said the healer, who was Dok.

CHAPTER 61

THE PLACE OF SHAME HAD TURNED out to be a perfectly pleasant island, no more than a few hours' canoe paddle to westward, almost no distance at all by whale. There, Ata Maroo sat with Alvert sat in a longhouse and listened to failed Feud dancers pouring out their woes.

At first these woes sounded ridiculous to Ata Maroo. They grieved over such minuscule errors. Some momentary confusion, some tiny hesitation, some harmless stumble, and the dancers cursed their lot as though they had committed some unpardonable wrong: it almost made her want to laugh. But then she considered her own woes. Who was to say they were bigger?

She recalled the things she'd said to the One Who Listens during the thunderstorm and then, slowly and shyly, Ata Maroo repeated them, in the Westlander language, to her human husband and was surprised— or was she, really?— when he kissed her and said: "I know all o' this, Maroo. You told me the first time."

After that it seemed so easy to talk about these things. They strolled together in the flower-scented sun of the Place of Shame, asking each other questions and trying to come up with answers. But evening came, and although the failed dancers were doomed to stay in the Place of Shame overnight, Ata Maroo and Alvert left. They planned to take the catamaran back to the Feud Islands, pick up Owa Lulu and Ata Steera, and go home to Wahayee.

But on the way they rescued Wilem Zoba, and that changed everything— a bigger change than if Mount Grumble had overflowed with white-hot molten stone.

Now, on the softly swaying moonlit deck of the catamaran, Alvert and Wilem Zoba were talking softly and urgently with one another. Owa

Lulu was packing two very small bags. And Ata Maroo was hugging her *ebee*, because this was a goodbye moment. She and Alvert were going home not to Wahayee but to Midlandis.

Home, through the devilish maze of the Herb Islands, around the hidden shoals and frightening deep basins in the Warm Straits, to the brandy-black Midland Sea— but this time, they would travel in no sort of craft. They would go in the ancient way, riding on the backs of whales. They would fly at a breakneck pace, by the shortest route they could find, eating raw fish by day and pausing by night to sip water from whatever seep they might find in the earth of an island; if no island were near, they would quench their thirst from the water found in fishes' eyes. They would do this, because there was not a moment to lose.

The whales they planned to ride were having a goodbye moment, too. Their calves, including the wayward number Four, would be forced to grow up: they had important jobs now, and the first one was pulling the catamaran back to Wilem Zoba's shipyard.

Wilem planned to tell his superiors he'd got drunk, been swept out to sea, and was rescued by these two nice old Wahayee ladies— see them?— who couldn't understand a word he said. He'd keep working on the weapon, but as slowly as possible, and wait for someone to get in touch with him. He now considered himself a zo-ba loyal not to his Skylander captors, but to Snow Flowers, the Whellen Country and the Kingdom. He would serve as their window into the mind of the enemy.

After that, the whale calves' second job would be taking Ata Steera and Owa Lulu back to Wahayee.

Ata Maroo gave in to one final embrace of her mother. "Congratulations, *ebee*," she said. "There can be no better Headmother than you."

Only a few hours before, the very thought of uttering those words would have driven a nail of misery into Ata Maroo's heart. They would have meant a future without purpose, a long unrolling of meaningless years, the shrinking and vanishing of the Ox-Train Queen. But now, after hearing and believing Wilem Zoba: now there was a threat on the horizon, a quest to undertake, a calling much greater than the green feather crown.

When at last the two women propped themselves away from one another, their arms wavered and seemed to want to draw them in again. But time was precious and all things must end.

"Give Papa all, all, all of my love. I don't know if we'll see each other again or not— but then, that's true of everyone, every day, isn't it? Goodbye, *ebee*. At least for now."

Ata Maroo went to Owa Lulu and took her small bag. She kissed the old lady's cheek. She lowered herself to the outrigger, beside which Alvert was already seated upon whale Two. Ata Maroo climbed onto number One's waiting back— and paused.

"Ah! I almost forgot. It wouldn't be proper, would it, without this."

And then she breathed out the breath the previous Headmother had given her, the one she'd carried in her for forty-one years, halfway across the world and back. It really belonged only here, in the Peaceful Ocean, and never should leave again.

Ata Steera took it up.

At-last-yes. That was proper.

CHAPTER 62

WITH ONE GLOVED HAND, DOK HELD her mask pulled down; with the other, she gripped the brim of her hat; and between the two was her face, that lovely face with its halfway smile, that smile like no one else's. She laughed. That laugh. Fred couldn't speak.

"Frednick Casmarr. Look at you! You're a way bigger operator than you let on! All right, I'll admit it. You had me... fooled." She winked. "You're alone, right? Didn't bring any thugs to bump me off?"

Fred found his voice. "What! How could you even *think* of such a horrible—"

"Easy, easy. It's just a joke. Although it does happen. Buyers do it so they can keep the money and still get the goods. You might be a big operator, Fred, but this life hasn't turned you bad... that might be what I love most about you. Now. How about that shiny yellow brick?"

Fred felt as if he were in a trance. Love *most?*

"Get your mind back here, me mally. I'm asking for the money. Got the money?"

"I do. I do. I surely do."

"Well? Hocka bocka, Mesir. Show me."

Fred realized he was having that feeling, damn it— something here was fake. What? The gold brick was genuine. Dok was no hallucination. Maybe it was the Specs themselves: counterfeits?

"Uh— not yet. First *you* show me yours. Your thing. The thing."

Dok pointed to her hat. "This?"

Up on its brim, sitting as unobtrusively as you please, was a pair of old-fashioned whalebone sun goggles, the kind whose eyepieces are slits rather than lenses. So those were the Tacular Specs. So those, through their narrow gates, would admit a fleeting glimpse of the future.

"No deal unless they work. I'm going to try them."

"Easy, now! Hands to yourself. They're up on my hat so the wight I'm representing can see 'em, but they're pinned tight and my hat's tied on. I'll unship them."

While Dok worked at this— and it couldn't have taken more than a few seconds— an infinity of feelings passed through Fred. Whoever she was, whatever she was, good or bad, fraudster or friend, all of it was jumbled together so tightly he couldn't tell one feeling from another. It was as if everything that existed were happening all at once.

"Here they are. You'll see the next five seconds or so, but after that the view waits for life to catch up with it." Dok pushed the Tacular Specs over Fred's eyes.

They hurt. Like the pain of light after days of darkness, but deeper, a pain not only in the eyes but somehow in the faculty of vision itself. And all other senses were obliterated. No sound, no touch, no scent; just a void in which moments yet to come played out like scenes in a Whellen Country picturebox show.

In that show Fred saw Dok before him, subtly different, somehow new. Something was missing from her, some barrier that up till then had been separating them; now she was letting him in. She was closing her eyes, parting her lips, falling into his arms...

The view went blank. For a horrific moment Fred didn't know what had happened. But when he realized it was only the end of the preview, a wave of joy swept him. The Specs showed the future. The things he'd seen were about to actually happen!

With hands he couldn't feel, he pushed the goggles up his forehead and stretched out his arms just in time for Dok to fall into them.

But she fell hard, and fast, and with a terrible cry. Her open mouth struck his and split his lip. Fred's whole world tasted of blood.

A ripple in the crowd around them: someone darting away. Fred couldn't tell what had happened except that Dok lay heavy in his arms, her struggling already far too feeble for one so graceful and strong, already waning and fading as he staggered backward. He caught himself and used all the strength in his shaking legs to kneel slowly, to take care, to ease her collapse to the hard red bricks. She was so still.

And then there was nothing around him anymore but a tunnel, and nothing in that tunnel but Dok. Brilliant Dok, whose lips were turning purple. His treasured Dok, in whose back stuck a knife, a knife, the very knife from the pen-case Fred had stolen on his first night with her, the pen-case that was gone from his sleeve.

CHAPTER 63

BACK IN GOOD MARKET, WHERE DAME Elsebet and the Royals had decided to spend a few days at the formerly monster-infested estate of the town's absent Esquire, two flights of guests arrived.

First came the de Brewels— in an ordinary hired carriage, wearing subtle, simple clothing and rolling a single trunk.

This unassuming behavior was like nothing Dame Elsebet had seen from her cousins before. True, they'd never been cruel or ill-meaning people. But in all the years she had known them, since those of Donn Felip's grandfather Sisco de Brewel, neither had they ever been quiet, or deferential, or introspective. At first Dame Elsebet was afraid young Petey might have died: he was not with them. But she soon learned that Petey was simply away at school, and Malfred off on some sort of retreat in a grotto; that the family's new outlook had been occasioned by other, most unexpected causes. The three of them even offered to perform the Greeting of Deepest Supplication toward King Enrick and Queen Margadet, who declined it completely and welcomed them, if not with open arms, at least with genuine willingness to put away the past.

And so for a time, a warm-hearted holiday mood prevailed among the party gathered at the Coachmaid's Rest, abounding in optimism, looking forward to the future.

But then came Count Corvinalias— feathers shredded, tongue lolling, nearly dead of exhaustion.

When he hit Dame Elsebet he was barely in control of his own flight; he would have skimmed over her and crashed straight into the limestone pavers of the courtyard if he hadn't somehow caught the thick golden embroidery on her shoulder and clung to it, leaning on her neck.

"You weren't at Whellengood," he panted. "Gate guards said you were—ah, let me catch my—"

"Why, Your Excellency! Has something happened to you? You sound as though you'd been and back to every hell... oh!" Corvinalias toppled into Dame Elsebet's waiting hands.

To his great dismay, all the hours he'd spent preparing an explanation somehow went by the wayside and he began panting out words faster than he could organize them. "Medame. You're all of you— at least I think all of you— in terrible danger. From— something I can't explain. I don't know how I did it, but I got to where that thing is— and I went to a city that— and into a building where— and then I rushed back here— because now I can— " Tears of frustration began to ooze through the tiny feathers around his eyes. Anyone could see that he was afraid she would think him insane, ignore him.

But of all people, Elsebet de Whellen would never do such a thing.

"I'm going to carry you upstairs, Your Excellency. Will you drink some water? Will you take a... a bit of ham? You may need some sustenance as you gather your wits. I wish to hear every word of this, my poor little friend."

Up in Fred's room, Dame Elsebet made Corvinalias a nest of quilts and set him in it. She held up a saucer of water for him to sip from, pulled a chair to the bedside and waited. Waited, until her patience was rewarded.

He told her about the Breathless Heights and the Uman city hidden behind them; he told about that evil... thing; and he swore he'd stake his life on it, that those people he'd heard— the people with their uniforms and maps and secret ships— had long been spying on the Kingdom, and now were poised to make a move. But he didn't tell about the cranes or their egg. For right now they were fine where they were, deep inside him, and their story could wait till the Kingdom was saved. *Or destroyed,* he couldn't help but think, remembering the cranes one last time before he shut the vault of his soul around them.

In her turn, Dame Elsebet told the other Uman-beings.

She was persuasive.

They understood.

The Umans readied themselves to face danger, and readiest of all were their King and Queen.

A crew of workmaids kneeled in a semicircle before their rulers, some with their eyes respectfully upon the ground but others frankly unable to keep themselves from looking at them— a striking family, with gentle exotic faces, strange indeed but then that was to be expected: they were royalty, a breed apart.

The Queen's voice rang through the courtyard of the Coachmaid's Rest. "We will take no needless risks by moving from this spot— this inn is now the seat of our Kingdom, and the property upon which it stands is to become a fortress. I appoint you, goodwives, to cause the building of palisades and the positioning and arming of defenders. And now we need our court. The following persons will be summoned to us..."

As the Queen listed the people she wanted brought to Good Market, Nicolo was busy noting them down with a slate and pencil. When she concluded with "His Majesty, His Excellency, Her High Honor and I will retire to the inn. We will not be disturbed," he bustled through the crowd of workmaids and kneeled before the Queen.

He coughed a little. Finding it made no difference, he harrumphed a bit. Finally he decided to do the unthinkable and simply address her— but the King beat him to it.

"Margadet there is a gentleman here. His mouth is open. I think he wants to talk to you. This gentleman here wants to say something to you no Margadet he is over here."

"Looky, Da-da! Listen, Ama!" squeaked Prince Nedward, leaning out from his mother's grasp and grabbing just enough of Nicolo's geometrically perfect black wig to whip it away, exposing a stubble of dull ginger hair. Behind his spectacles the major-domo's eyes went wide as he watched the Prince twirl his wig around and around until it was a frazzled mess. But what could he do, except gulp down a lump of embarrassment and say:

"Your Majesty. I volunteer to bring back the persons you have listed. I require no escort. I know the way, and have resources upon whom I can call for whatever I might need. May I, then...? A thousand thanks, Your Majesty, for this mark of trust. I won't fail you."

"He won't," Dame Elsebet assured the Queen. "Mesir Moktabelli is an extremely reliable gentleman. I sometimes think he's the one really running my country." She peeled his wig from little Nedward's grasp, smoothed it the best she could and helped him set it back on his head before giving him a farewell embrace. "May your god speed you well, Nicolo. Oh, now, don't be shy. I've known you for thirty years."

CHAPTER 64

THE ONLY ONE WHO CAME TO see Fred in jail was Petir, and the news he brought was bad.

"Mesir Doak has looked over your case and, well, Brother Malfred, I'm not going to lie to you. He doesn't find any hope. As his, well, overlord's son— for whatever that's worth— I've ordered him to strive his utmost. But it's impossible, isn't it, to know whether he really is doing so. And here in Spireburgh he isn't their Grand Constable, just another citizen."

Petir dropped onto the hard bench outside Fred's cell with rote despair. "Kwaga is gone. And my family, too— I have no idea where they went. Not even Rhonso knows. They've never done anything like this before. I wonder if it has something to do with their project— but never mind. That was never anything affecting you." Petir's hands shook a little as he formed a shape that, in the language of the Fakirs, meant *we cannot know*. And although his voice was admirably steady, tears wet his cheeks and he really did look very young.

"Even Cousin Elsie, and the King, they're all gone somewhere... I'm so sorry, Brother. I'm so sorry I lost you. I ran all over that plaza— how could I be so oblivious— I had you in my sight. It's all my fault."

"No. It's not your fault, Petey. Someone else did it."

"But who? Please, Brother Malfred, please put your hands down. I realize we cannot know. It's just that I can't stop asking the question. *You* aren't a murderer. I know you're not! Because— do you want to hear something, well, maybe crazy?"

At Fred's nod Petir continued. "All my life I've had a kind of a knack for something. I know when people are lying. My mind just... tells me." Then he looked into Fred's face, the face of someone who had much the same talent, and admitted: "I know you're not a mystic, Brother Malfred. And not even really a monk. I knew it from the moment Da introduced us, when you botched the Supreme Greeting of the Gem In the Lily. But I don't care. I never did. You have the— the heart— of a— scholar— oh, Gods, I'm sorry."

EVEN IF HIS HIGH HONOR, Seigneur Felip de Brewel, could have been found and brought to Spireburgh in time for Fred's trial, it wouldn't have mattered. Under the new laws, words from authority no longer overrode other considerations of justice. And though at first it seemed hopeful that such vouching no longer bore any real weight with the law— for there were precious few Brewel Country citizens ready to say anything good on Fred's behalf, and maddeningly many who could testify that he was an unlicensed Fool, a flimflam operator, even a litterbug— the fact was that, since judgment now hinged upon evidence, there too Fred was in deep trouble. What scant evidence there was pointed to him, or was interpreted as pointing to him, by officials who wanted murder punished quickly— the more so if it were committed by a con man from Coastwall, during the commission of a staggeringly brazen crime in which one of the University's most precious possessions was somehow inexplicably lost.

So Fred was not really surprised when the judge pronounced him Dok's killer, and sentenced him to hang.

The waiting was, as the saying goes, the hardest part.

He'd been on the point of death before, in the way Dame Elsebet had been toe to toe with monsters: That kind of imminent death—blood pounding, breath catching, everything slowing down— provoked easy and natural reactions. But this was a different kind of imminent death: one that only sat, like a burdensome guest who everyone knew would, in the end, force the host from his own home. It was hard coming to grips with such a thing, and didn't seem worth the trouble. So he let it sit.

As to his feelings about Dok, he kept them both to himself, and from himself. In place of feeling, inside him now lay an impenetrable dark mass, too heavy to move, too cold to touch, that offered an uneasy promise: don't disturb me, and in return—

No. Just don't disturb me.

Fred's cell had a window, through which he could watch them building his instrument of execution. Nice touch, that, he thought: as an entertainer, he appreciated details. Thanks to the window, he knew he would pass from this life on a device conforming to what were known as the Brewel Country Humane Reforms Regarding Capital Justice. To discourage a zealous public from trying to climb the scaffold, it had a base solidly covered with vertical boards. To promote a clean break, as it were, there was a stout and well-calculated gallows. To prevent an anticlimax, a reliable, thoroughly greased and tested trapdoor. Most innovative of all were a series of posts around the front of the stage— for Fred thought of it as a stage— up which would rise a magnificent canvas curtain.

In due time Fred had undergone the pre-show rituals: the last meal, the very short cart ride. And when he finally mounted the stage and turned to the audience— for he thought of them as an audience— he considered his last words.

What would he leave them with? He had some ideas: "I'm busy just now, but I'll swing by later", "Does this tie make my neck look broken?", and "Ladies and Gentlemen... watch as I cause this whole, wide world to disappear".

But when the moment came, nothing seemed right. In fact, what seemed right was...nothing. Well, maybe not nothing. A back flip. A handspring. A sixfold entrechat. A bow. And then the main event.

The front row of the crowd crept slowly forward, shy of the new procedure, strangely docile. Fred didn't find it hard to meet their eyes: none of it seemed real. Faces stared as their owners reached out for the drawcords that raised the canvas screen— hand over hand, hoisting its sections up like sails, for this was after all the Brewel country; and as the screen blotted the crowd from Fred's view the hooded executioner slipped a bag over him— a full-body bag, descending like another curtain from crown to sole.

In this canvas cocoon Fred felt himself take a breath, his final breath. He wanted to leave this life in serenity. But his brain had other ideas, like thinking: *hoy, aren't you forgetting the*

As the boards disappeared from under his feet and he was falling.

CHAPTER 65

SOMEWHERE IN A SUPREMELY DISCREET BUILDING, behind a padded door, upon a marble-topped desk, lay a document, freed from its significant yellow cover. A Director of something known as The Bureau pushed this document strongly forward with two fingertips, and brought a meeting to order.

"Gentlemen. I have some written notes here for your perusal, should you wish to consult them after we conclude. They outline the situation more fully, but if I may summarize: we have just received intelligence—" and here the Director nodded at a sharp-nosed gentleman with a mildly disheveled black wig— "intelligence which confirms that the situation has reached a crisis. The Adversary is no longer merely observing us, but has assumed a posture of definite threat. Our operation is now priority number one. Understand that after we leave this room, the notes will be destroyed and the operation— upon which the survival of this Kingdom may well turn— will begin. May Ye Gods bless King Enrick."

A murmur of agreement; the Director poured a small glass of brandy, turned over a sandglass and, sinking into a tall chair behind the desk, began.

"Agent Number Nine reports that, following extensive observation, the subject was successfully recruited." The Director held the paper at arm's length and squinted at it before opening a drawer and bringing out a lens. "More than one attempt was necessary. This is far from a bad thing: it speaks well for the subject's presence of mind. In the end it was a false charge of murdering Number Nine herself, and the attendant false trial and execution, which won the day. The preternatural initiator, these so-called Specs, are safe. We have them on indefinite loan, so that we may..."

From the group before him, a voice— quiet, but strangely penetrating, interrupted: "If you please, Your Worthiness. Go back. False execution? I thought those were phased out years ago."

"True, and it most likely cannot ever be attempted again. But we seized this opportunity because conditions were perfect for it— the humane measures that are now the law in the Brewel Country call for a, a... dignified privacy at the crucial moment. So when the crowd at the subject's hanging helped to raise the screen around him, they were conveniently blocking their own view of the event. And any city with a College of Healing has no shortage of corpses with which to fill a canvas bag." The Director chuckled, choked a bit and took a sip of the brandy.

The murmurs that followed were approving ones, but there was more on the agenda, and the sandglass was running.

"Going forward, Number Nine will continue to serve as the subject's controller: she has developed a subtle but effective rapport with him. And as for the subject himself— he, gentlemen, is The Bureau's masterstroke. The identification and cultivation of this subject was, if I may say so, an extra-large bell on our hat. Look at these qualifications—" and the Director handed papers around the room. *Ohs* and *ahs* and upraised spectacles followed them.

"Yes. Remarkable physical skills, readily adaptable, literate, and most important: having been nearly inseparable from His Majesty for over twenty years, the subject is intimately familiar with the mannerisms of royalty. It is therefore our goal to position him in the extreme upper echelons of the Adversary's society, in the new persona of a discontented exile. From there, he will pass us intelligence by means of a network so startlingly innovative that discussion of it, alas, will have to wait till our next meeting. Here is a copy of one of the documents supporting the subject's new persona. Gather round my desk, here, and look upon it. It is the only extant copy and after we leave here tonight it, too, will be destroyed. Number Nine is very proud of the original. She calls it her finest work."

The thick, cream-colored vellum page had margins encrusted with carefully drawn ornamentation: scenes of battle, burning palaces, banners flying in glorious victory or rent in tragic defeat. At the very top glowed the golden emblem of a moon half in shadow. And in the center of the page, in calligraphy like coiling, thorny vines, were the words:

> *Down with the Castramars usurpers,*
> *glory to the only, imperishable Royal House,*
> *and long live the true heir to the throne of Midlandis,*
> *with your help soon to return and claim his birthright:*
> *His Most Illustrious and Serene Majesty*
> *Malfred I*
> *of the House of Hwardelocq*

THE GENTLEMEN SOON WENT THEIR ways; as the padded door closed, the sandglass dropped its final grains and the Director, left alone, now consulted a schedule, sighed, and slid down from chair to floor.

It was a tolerably long slide: the Director suffered from a condition whose chief manifestations were an extremely short stature and a persistent slowness to age. But perhaps 'suffered' was the wrong word, for it was precisely these characteristics that had, decades before, attracted The Bureau's attention; the Director was not a mere desk-bound agent but an active one, possessed of a cover persona that was supremely natural once the two disguise elements were in place.

Out from a lower drawer of the desk they came. First the wig of matted curls, which really was quite comfortable and perfectly hid the Director's short black hair, peppered with gray. Next the false teeth. The Director sighed again, for these were less comfortable, but once they were in— grimy, gappy, childishly small— the illusion was complete. The brat strode with great dignity through the padded door, through the discreet building that housed The Bureau and then, squealing and snickering, skipped out onto the streets of Coastwall, ready to play.

The Heart of Stone Adventures will continue with

DOOM'S DAZE

coming in 2022

Sign up for my newsletter
and get updates at

evasandor.com

Made in the USA
Monee, IL
03 November 2021